I0675032

FOREIGN LAND

This Foreign Universe – Book 1

A Novel by
J.S. SHERWOOD

FOREIGN LAND
This Foreign Universe – Book 1
Copyright © 2021 J.S. Sherwood

All rights reserved. No part of this book may be used or reproduced in any manner whatsoever, without written permission, except in the case of brief quotations embedded in articles and reviews. For more information, please contact publisher at Publisher@EvolvedPub.com.

FIRST EDITION SOFTCOVER
ISBN: 1622537432
ISBN-13: 978-1-62253-743-3

Editor: Becky Stephens
Cover Artist: Sam Keiser
Interior Designer: Lane Diamond

EVOLVED PUBLISHING™

www.EvolvedPub.com
Evolved Publishing LLC
Butler, Wisconsin, USA

Foreign Land is a work of fiction. All names, characters, places, and incidents are the product of the author's imagination, or are used fictitiously. Any resemblance to actual events or persons, living or dead, is entirely coincidental.

Printed in Book Antiqua font.

BOOKS BY J.S. SHERWOOD

DEDICATION

For Meaghan,
Forever my person.

PART ONE

Chapter 1

Smith stood on a small mound of gray dirt, leaning on his shovel. His eyes were bloodshot with exhaustion and despair. His son sat a few yards away, knees bent, bald head hung down. Abe was nearly sixteen, but in that moment, Smith saw him as the young boy who had been afraid of the dark.

A cool wind blew Smith's long, gray hair into his sweat-soaked face as he drew deep breaths. The helmet of his survival suit lay on its side at his feet, the clear glass cracked. Thankfully, the air was breathable, so now he only wore his issued suit—crimson red with black side stripes— to keep him warm. Something in the air of this new world irritated his skin, and he kept scratching at the speckled scruff that covered his face.

This new planet. Aethera.

His new hell.

He looked around at what had been accomplished in the last few hours. Fifteen shiny colony domes sat in a perfect row, fresh from their vacuum-sealed packaging. The purified white of the structures shone even brighter against the bland landscape. Fourteen of them were exactly fifteen feet across. The last was twice that size and had been meant for the captain and her family. Now it was being used as triage for the injured. Smith watched as two men carried a woman through its doors. Even from that distance, he could tell she'd lost a leg.

To the east of the domes, in the distance, a range of mountains stretched north and south as far as he could see. The base of the mountains were ashen just like the dirt he dug in. It slowly changed to a dusty red as the elevation increased, and the top of each was white with snow. They pierced into a gray-orange sky that Smith would have found beautiful under different circumstances. But that night it felt ominous, as if it would simply cave in at any moment. And if it had, he wasn't sure he'd mind all that much.

They had planned to land on the other side of the mountains, where the treetops reached to the sky and the roots weaved strongly into moist, healthy soil. But they had ended up in the dark, dusty emptiness that surrounded him. With no rover or ground transports in working order, they had decided to set up where they were.

South of where he stood, the desert went on and on. To the north, past the horizon, was a vast ocean that covered over half of the planet. Based on the pictures the drones had sent back, the largest animals on the planet lived in those waters. Cascading, clear green water estimated to reach depths of over ten thousand feet. Shadows appeared just below the surface. Long, oval-shaped creatures that sped through the waters at blistering speeds. Smith had been most excited to see the ocean; he'd never had the chance to see it on Earth. But now he wondered whether he would survive long enough to see it. Whether any of them would. Across the ocean, two continents. One covered in sand and natural stone pillars, the other a massive tangle of overgrown plants.

A few hundred yards past the domes to the west lay the bent, smoldering husks of their ship. Something had gone wrong when they entered the atmosphere. All Smith knew was that he had seen flames, heard explosions, and awoke covered in burns, cuts and dirt. He helped the others salvage who and what they could: 121 survivors, fifteen colony domes, some clothing, enough foodstuffs to last 121 people about two months, two crates of tools, and one crate of weapons. Between Smith and the mangled metal were at least twenty other survivors, all digging for the same reason Smith was.

All burying their loved ones.

Smith, burying his wife.

Evalee. Gone.

Sylvia, Evalee's sister, silently walked up and sat by Abe.

With a gut-wrenching cough, Smith turned back to his mound and shovel. The gravity here was much stronger than what he was used to. Double what it had been back on the Ship of Nations. Half a G more than on Earth. Slowly, painstakingly, he scooped up some dirt. Let it drop into the hole that held her body. Each time the dirt landed in the hole with a soft thud, Abe flinched. Smith's wife had always been the one to comfort the boy. Smith loved his son, loved his wife, but how was he to comfort him? It seemed impossible to do when it felt as though his very soul had burned away, left his body in a trail of smoke that he was sure would never return.

She was somehow still intact when he had found her. Dead, but intact. Yet, as Smith looked at the body of the woman he knew and loved, it was both her and not her. It was still her sleek brown hair and olive skin. It even still smelled like her, despite the burns that covered her body. But something had changed, and Smith would have to consider what that meant.

He continued to fill the hole, scoop after agonizing scoop. All he could think of were the dreams he had of what that day was supposed to be. He had imagined it so clearly the night before.

They would land amid towering trees that rose dozens of feet above them, the fresh breeze weaving through the branches. The day would be spent planting row after row of seeds with his son. When afternoon came, he would spend it with Evalee, filling their small dome with what little they had. They were supposed to be making a home together. Eating a meal in open air. Talking together on what the future would bring. Living a beautiful life. He had even planned on asking her if she was ready for another child. He knew he was. Or had been the night before as he fell asleep next to his wife.

Was it worse to ponder on happy memories that would never be, or to burden one's thoughts with the sorrows that might yet come?

***

Twenty years ago, Smith never would have left Earth. Sure, it had turned bad, but it was his home.

A home ravaged by wars that set energy advancements back decades, leaving many nations scrambling to find what fossil fuels they could. This only led to more violence, more fighting over territory and political control.

The new generation ship and colonization plan was funded by a non-profit organization known as Humans for Humanity. They were determined to send "the best of humanity" out to colonize the universe. Multiple fresh starts in the hope that at least one planet would get it right.

Smith had seen humanity and was never completely convinced.

The ship was leaving to colonize other planets, but also to leave the deteriorating Earth behind. The divides between various groups continued to grow so vast that many believed those gaps would never be closed. Many wanted to leave on the Ship of Nations, but not all who wanted to were accepted aboard.

For Smith, he had an easy in with his occupation as a biotech farmer. They needed someone like him. Someone who could maintain healthy crops for years in the vastness of space, using recycled water and cutting-edge biotech to do so. Smith had won multiple accolades for his advancements in the field and was well-known in the industry. And, at the time, he had no personal ties to keep him on Earth.

He, as with everyone else, went through exhaustive academic, physical, psychological, emotional and even spiritual testing. Academic and physical were his strongest areas, while spiritual was his worst. This was due to his lack of faith in anything of a religious or spiritual nature, and H for H believed faith was an integral part of a "full human experience." It wasn't that he was supposed to believe wholeheartedly what Humans for Humanity taught. If that were the case, only a handful of zealots would have been allowed aboard. H for H did not believe traditional family units were the best way to raise a family, nor the way families would be in the afterlife. According to H for H:

"Humans are most productive and happy when in a workplace family. Multiple adults and children living and working together, each with a designated role to play. As post-humans in the afterlife, this is how our lives will be. We will each be assigned a role in the After that correlates directly to how we worked, played and treated one another."

Smith and many others would never adhere to this lifestyle. On top of that, everyone who adhered strictly by H for H standards rarely showed emotion. It was a common joke that the zealots had had their human brains replaced by computer chips. So, H for H compromised, and chose people of various ideologies. They decided, after days of debate, that what a person believes was not as important as how a person treats and cares for others. And the hope they had that humanity could be better than what they'd become on Earth.

What they wanted, the people they thought should spread humanity across the cosmos, were those who would accept and embrace all humans, whether they agreed or not. After all, it was the lack of such people that had continued to widen the chasms between the various groups.

Smith had been seeing H for H ads for months before he finally went into their massive complex. Every time he sent a message, he would be told it was sent "Thanks to the help of Humans for Humanity." When he walked past their looming complex, his watch would shout, "Humans for Humanity needs *you*, Smith, to help spread the best of humanity across the universe." For a long time, he had no intention of leaving Earth. Sure, things were bad, but Earth was his home. Until it wasn't.

Chapter 2

After the living were done burying their dead in the new soil of Aethera, the survivors gathered outside the small circle of domes. The pale red sun hung in the sky straight above them, the rays sending off less warmth than Smith would have liked. There was a light, cold breeze. Winter had been Evalee's favorite season on Earth. The cold air felt fresher, she would say. The crispness of it made her feel more alive. When they were selected to be part of Colony Six, the first thing she did was research the weather on Aethera. With an annual average of sixty-five degrees Fahrenheit, she couldn't wait to get off the ship and breathe in the brisk, chilled air unsullied by human creation.

Morbidly ironic, then, that her first breath on that planet had also been her last.

Just knowing, even believing, a part of her still existed somewhere, anywhere, would have lightened Smith's load. He opened his eyes and, for a moment, imagined his wife's beautiful, smiling face floating in the sky. Then it disappeared as he remembered the look of her lifeless face in the ground.

The children that had survived played inside a dome while a group of adults gathered outside to discuss what had happened. *Although,* Smith thought, *it wasn't really a discussion at all. At least not in the way Evalee would have held a discussion.*

One man yelled at the two remaining engineers, his sharp blue eyes wet with grief. "How the hell do we still not know what went wrong?"

It was Jonstin, a small, stubborn man Smith had known for many years. It was nearly impossible to convince him he was ever wrong, even if spit right in his face. He had been piloting the vessel when it went down.

"You checked everything," he continued, "and told us we were clear for entry! I trusted you and led over three hundred of our people to their deaths."

Jonstin stepped back, and many shouted similar questions at the engineers.

Evalee's sister, Sylvia, the lead engineer, stepped into the middle of the group. She was tall, sturdy and sharp. Her hair was so short it barely poked out of the gray hat she always wore.

"Shut. The hell. Up. All of you," she said.

They followed her request.

"Look, I'm sorry for everyone's loss," she continued. "I truly am. But you seem to be forgetting that I, too, lost someone. I found my sister's corpse this morning. Do *not* talk to me as though this was my fault, or that I am unaffected by this tragedy simply because you think I could have stopped it from happening."

She looked around, daring anyone to question her again. No one did.

Her voice calmer, she said, "As far as we can tell, it was a malfunction with one of the computers. We're not sure, but it seems that the heat shields meant to protect the hull on entry went active only on certain sections of the ship. The other sections were exposed to the full heat and force of entry."

The colony ship they had flown to Aethera was made using raw materials excavated from various asteroids the Ship of Nations had passed since leaving Earth. The hull ended up not being as impervious to heat as they had hoped. To counteract this, the computer engineers created energy shields to protect the ship's integrity. Yet these, too, proved to be less effective than hoped.

Sylvia narrowed her eyes. "But let's really think here. Would our energy be better spent figuring out what went wrong, or figuring out how we're going to survive?"

There were some grumblings at that, but no one raised their voices again. Smith folded his arms and looked down, the pain of his loss threatening to break to the surface, the gravity of the planet nearly as heavy as his heart. He imagined himself laying in that gray dirt, slowly sinking into it until he melted in with the planet's core.

"Have we gotten a message to the Ship of Nations yet?" someone asked.

Sylvia shook her head. "Our comms are down."

"All the other colonies got messages to the ship within twenty-four hours," a woman noted.

"So, if they don't get a message, they might come back for us," another said with a hint of hope.

Smith took a step forward. "We shouldn't count on that. I mean, I hope they do. But we shouldn't focus on that. We keep moving forward, figuring out how to survive. If help comes, I'll welcome it. But if not, at least we're doing everything we can to survive in the meantime."

He took a deep breath, closed his eyes and opened them. When he did, he saw something on the ground inches away from his foot that he could have sworn wasn't there before: a handprint. Smith could tell immediately it wasn't the imprint of a human hand. It had the same basic structure, but the fingers were larger, thinner, and there was no thumb. It was a soft handprint, barely denting the ground. Whatever this thing was, it weighed far less than its hand—foot?—size would suggest. That, or it was extremely graceful.

He looked around and found three more prints close by, all leading away from the new camp. He looked at them more closely, trying to determine what the creature looked like. The prints followed a distinct, evenly spaced pattern. Two by two, he realized. Whatever it was, it walked on four legs.

"We have just a few months' worth of food and water," Sylvia said. "We need to get some crops planted now and find a water source."

She turned to Smith, who was still staring intently at the ground.

"Uh, yeah," Smith stumbled. "I, as far as I can tell the soil here is good...."

He paused and tried to slow his breathing, wondering if the prints were real or imagined. He was always calmer and more confident when Evalee was with him. Would he ever regain that confidence, that sense of peace?

"I've got some tests to run yet, but I did get kind of deep into the ground while... I was, uh, digging...."

A brief silence. Nearly everyone softly nodded, having spent a large part of the day doing the same. Smith looked at the ground again. More footprints. Six, eight, twelve that he could see.

Sylvia nodded at Smith. "Let's get those tests going now."

Smith cut her off. "Wait, wait. Shouldn't we get a perimeter up first? You know, for protection? We... we don't know what's out there."

Sylvia smiled. "Our preliminary studies of the planet showed no lifeforms large enough to pose a threat, but it's not a bad idea."

"I know, but just look at th—"

He was cut off by the door of a dome being thrown open. Two teen boys fell onto the ground. One lay on his back. The other straddled him, hands gripped tightly around the other's throat, knuckles white.

The one on top yelled, saliva dripping from his mouth. "There is!"

Smith and Sylvia jumped at them, pulling them to their feet and away from each other.

"No there isn't! It's all stories! Lies!" the one in Smith's grip yelled.

"You shut up," the other one screamed.

"Both of you, shut up," Sylvia said in her firm but quiet tone.

They did.

Smith turned the boy around. "What's this about?"

"That one," he said, pointing to the other boy, "is tellin' all the little kids in there that it'll all work out. That they'll see their dead mommies and daddies and sisters again. That they're just waiting in Heaven. Watching over all of us. It's. Bullshit."

He spat toward the other boy, who was now quiet, head hung forward, tears dripping down his face. Sylvia let him go. He sat down in the dirt, the gravity seeming to speed his drop. Slowly, he dropped to his side, pulled his knees to his chest, and let the tears fall. Abe came out of the dome and squatted next to the boy, placing a hand on his shoulder.

"Stop," Sylvia controlled her voice as much as she could. "What's bullshit is that the two of you are fighting about something like that at a time like this. Right now, it doesn't matter what our beliefs are. I couldn't care less. Believe in an afterlife. Don't believe in one. Believe in reincarnation. Doesn't matter. My goal—our goal—is for each of us to survive. Regardless of belief or opinions. We're human, and no matter what happens, we better not stop acting like it."

She looked around at everyone, and Smith realized she had just become the new captain. Perfect fit, in his opinion. Not that it mattered to her.

"Smith, soil. The rest of you, stay busy putting up whatever defense systems we didn't lose in the crash."

Smith smiled. "Of course, captain."

Others echoed the response.

As the two walked away, Smith looked for the handprints he had seen. They were gone.

***

One night back on Earth, Smith walked back to his small apartment as the sun set in front of him, the constant smog in the sky working as its own type of sunglasses. Another five businesses had closed along his daily route, including the last place in the neighborhood to offer sandwiches with actual meat instead of "lab enhanced" imitations. He never cared much for politics, but the law instituting a 30 percent tax on real meat had, in his opinion, been one of the worst in recent years. Not only did it put great men and women out of business, it also meant his daily meatball sub became his weekly meat meal, and he had to walk an extra five miles to get it.

As he turned onto the street of his apartment, he heard shouting. A group of people had gathered outside the building. Across the street, in front of an old church, another group. Two officers stood in the middle of the street, as if they could stop the dozens around them if things escalated to violence.

One side was shouting that the country needed a government-sanctioned religion, like England used to have, because the people had grown too far from God. The other side screamed that all organized religion should be banned because it only led to bigotry and "sin shaming."

Smith shook his head and sat on a bench. It was exactly what he hated about politics—two extreme sides of one issue, yelling slurs at one another as if their beliefs made them less than human. So many people convinced entirely that they are right, that the law should make everyone live in only one specific way. Unwilling to compromise, to discuss, to accept that laws can encompass and protect everyone. Smith himself was not religious, and had known many bigoted people in all groups, religious or not. And he had also known many people who sincerely cared about their fellow men and women, regardless of race, group or religious affiliation. But those type of people seemed to be a dying breed, replaced by people blindly fighting imagined battles against entire groups based solely on ideology.

The screaming intensified. Smith looked back at the protesters just as a gunshot echoed off the buildings. A woman in front of the church fell into the street, clutching her hand over her throat. Blood pooled out between her fingers. One of the officers ran to help her up. Just as he grabbed her outstretched hand, another shot rang out. The officer's head snapped to the side and he collapsed.

The street erupted in screams and gunfire from both sides. Body after body fell to the ground. Blood splattered in the air and pooled in the streets, slowly running toward the drain in front of the bench Smith sat on. Something flew across the street in a large arc, heading straight for Smith's apartment building. A bomb. Homemade, from what Smith could tell. It barely missed the heads of the few surviving rioters and dropped into an open first-story window.

An entire section of wall blew out into the street. The building wavered back and forth, and slowly collapsed. Everyone inside died. Mothers. Fathers. Grandparents. Children. The single mom and her toddler twins who had lived next to Smith. Once a month she gave Smith a free meal from the diner where she worked in exchange for free fruits and vegetables from the biotech farm Smith ran. The cost of fresh, healthy produce had skyrocketed in recent years, but she wanted to keep her children as healthy as possible.

And now Smith would never be able to help her or her little ones again.

Chapter 3

Smith crouched over a small plot of soil with Sylvia and Abe. The young man listened to his dad intently. He periodically rubbed his hairless head. He'd been born hairless, as had many born on the Ship of Nations in recent years.

"Test results, Smith." Sylvia stated the request firm and calm.

"Well, I'll let Abe explain it to you."

Smith handed a small tablet to his son, and gave him a minute to look over it.

"Make sense, son?"

Abe grinned. "Like pure O_2. Sylv—captain, it's crisp. Clean. Not as good as the ship, but it'll take seeds. And... no. Yeah. No."

Abe turned the tablet toward his dad and pointed to it, asked if he was reading it right.

Smith nodded.

"Pure O_2." Abe tried to catch his breath. "Lots of microorganisms. Organic material."

"Good," Sylvia said.

"Very good," Smith agreed. "It means we won't need to use as many bionanites as we thought. Especially since we lost some in the crash. This will help us spread out what we have left."

"And," Abe said, scratching his head, "there're larger organisms. Small feces. Little shits, but too big to have come from anything as small as a microorganism."

"The probes didn't bring any soil back to suggest that," Sylvia said.

"The probes also got through the atmosphere safely," Smith shrugged.

Sylvia glared at him. "Stop saying shit like that. If there's something living in the soil, how come no one saw anything when they were digging the graves?"

"Maybe they were too distracted putting someone they love in the ground," Abe whispered and looked away, as if he had just remembered the death of his mom.

"That," Smith said, clearing his throat as he squeezed Abe's shoulder, "or they only live in certain sections of the ground. Or they heard the digging and moved away. Or something else."

He pulled out a small vial, scooped some dirt into it and placed it in his shirt pocket. A cold wind blew in and clouds darkened the sky.

"The sun will set soon." Sylvia stretched. "Get everyone together. Have a small meal. Set up watches for the night."

"I'll volunteer to be on watch first." Smith patted his son's shoulder. "Abe too."

Abe nodded silently.

They stood and walked back to the others, shivering against the cold. The setting sun cast a soft red glow on everything, making it look like red water was rising from the soil.

"This place is off, Dad," Abe said. "Like someone messed with the O_2."

"Everything's screwed up in one way or another, son."

"No. They're not. At least not on the ship. Not like this."

"Okay, yeah," Smith agreed. "Much less controlled here."

"It was supposed to be more natural here," Abe said. "More life. Fresh, crisp, pure."

Smith smiled. Abe talked just like Evalee did, with a love of the universe's beauty.

"Well, it is purer on the other side of the mountains." Smith pointed to the red peaks. "Where we were supposed to land. Besides, we found some signs of life. More than we expected."

"Yeah." Abe shrugged. "And a lot of signs of death."

Smith grabbed the boy's shoulder and squeezed. He left it there for a moment until Abe pulled away.

If Smith had died and Evalee survived, what would she say to Abe? How would she comfort him? Smith tried to play the scene out in his mind, but all he could conjure was an image of Evalee and Abe sitting silently together. *Perhaps there were no words that could bring the kind of comfort they were both searching for*, Smith thought.

***

The morning after his apartment building collapsed, Smith gave up on Earth and went to meet with Humans for Humanity.

When he first entered the H for H complex, he half expected a group of zealots to surround him, drug him, and pull him into a back room until he had been well and fully brainwashed.

But when he walked into the large circular building at the center of the complex, he was greeted by a lone girl seated in the middle of a round desk in the middle of a large, empty room. The floor was a checkerboard of dozens of colors and shades. On a pillar to his left, a large sign provided a key for what each color represented. The light green represented the African Muslim population of the world. Brown, those who followed the political left. Yellow, those who refused to accept the additional six states that had been added to the United States when they took over sections of Mexico in order to save the economically crippled country, though it noted that H for H did not condone their violent acts against the new states. And dozens more, representing all races, ethnicities, ideologies and anything else H for H could think of.

At the bottom of the sign an elegant inscription read, "We accept all. We are all human."

Smith appreciated what they were trying to do, but he also felt that there were times when one had to take a stand. And wasn't H for H taking a stand against the vast segregation of the world by sending a generation ship to the stars in an attempt to escape the pollution and corruption that had overtaken Earth? Smith sighed and walked to the desk. He didn't like thinking too deeply on politics and religion because he always saw the flaws and contradictions.

So, like many others, Smith went to H for H not to join them, but in the hope that he would get away from the confusion that covered his planet.

The woman at the desk looked up at him and smiled.

"Good evening, Brother Smith," she said in a calm monotone. "Are you here for information on joining us? Or applying to be on our grand ship to the stars?"

"Applying," he said with a nod.

She smiled. "I thought so," she said to Smith. "Brother Hughes!"

A door at the far end opened immediately and a tall, round man bumbled out with an exaggerated smile on his face.

"Brother Smith, Brother Smith!" he bellowed. "We have been hoping the esteemed farmer would come to join us in the journey to spread the *true* humanity across the universe."

The man embraced Smith and pulled away.

"Just Smith, please."

"Oh right, right. Of course." Hughes shrugged. "Force of habit around here. Walk with me, Smith."

Hughes walked quickly, and spoke even faster.

"So excited you came to us, Smith. We've been discussing the need for a biotech farmer on the Ship of Nations, as we've named it now. Our engineers have created a brilliant farm that will last for generations to come."

"I've heard. Your personally targeted ads got me."

Hughes nodded and paused for a sliding door to open.

"Let's start the application process right away. You want to start with physical, spiritual, psychological or emotional? We can skip academic. We know you're in biotech farming."

Each test was one of endurance. They had him running and lifting for nearly three hours without a break. Subjected him to dozens of simulated situations ranging from embarrassing to terrifying. He handled each with results far above average.

At the end of those, he sat with a sister from H for H in a soft recliner for his spiritual evaluation.

"What is it you believe, that you live your life by, brother?" She paused. "Smith, I mean. Just Smith."

He peered at her and slightly tilted his head to the side. He had expected the question, knew that H for H held a person's belief in high regard. Some zealots, against H for H teachings, even regarded one's strength of belief a direct link to their value as a human.

Smith knew this, but hoped the woman did not follow that extremist view. He decided to tell her the truth.

"I believe in being good to people."

"And?"

Smith shrugged. "Trying to enjoy life. To learn while I'm here."

The woman took a few notes. "Any set of principles you adhere to or connect with? New Judaism, perhaps? Or the morals of Latter Day Saints? Or something a little less strict, like Neo Catholicism?"

Smith shook his head. "No."

"Why is that?"

"They all have good guidelines of how to live a good, kind life. But they each come with their own beliefs of life outside of this one. Of a loving god, or an afterlife, of a heaven and a hell. I... I just can't believe that. But"—he took a breath—"I can't say it's not real, either. It's just all so... so improbable."

"Smith, you know one day you'll most likely need to get off the fence?"

"Maybe," he said quietly. "Maybe."

An hour later, he received news that he'd been accepted to be a part of the Ship of Nations.

Chapter 4

The sun had set over the new planet. Smith wasn't sure he could ever call it home. Without Evalee, would anywhere ever feel like home? A jerry-rigged electrical fence surrounded the new colony in a hexagon, dim lights at each corner. Smith, Abe and a few other men sat in a circle. Each one of them had lost a wife or a mother or a child... or all three.

One of the men, bald and thin with dark skin, pulled a harmonica out of his pocket.

"This," he said, choking back tears, "been in my family since the late nineteen hundreds. I was going to give it to my son, but he...."

The man trailed off and looked toward the dirt where the bodies were buried. No one spoke, but it was obvious they all felt his pain, each with red eyes from grief and tears. Smith had so many things he had planned to do with Evalee—for Evalee—but now none of those would happen.

A slow, mournful melody swam from the harmonica. A folk tune from the New American Folk Revival in the early twenty-second century. Smith had heard it many times when he first apprenticed as a biotech farmer. He closed his eyes and listened as two shaky voices joined the bleeding harmonica.

> *My child left me far too soon,*
> *He'd barely left his momma's womb.*
> *But Death came quiet, yeah*
> *Death came fast.*
> *He said "Your child's life,*
> *It will not last."*

A bittersweet tear fell down Smith's cheek. The loss of Evalee left him empty, crushed, but at least he had not lost his son along with his wife.

"Your child's life
Is not yours to keep.
I've closed his eyes,
Put him to sleep."

And I told Death,
"But he's so young,
Take me instead.
C'mon now,
Take off my head."

At that, Death laughed,
A piercing sound.
Then he called forth
His Hellish Hounds.

Overcome with a heaviness that pushed his shoulders to the ground, Smith joined the mournful wailing with his own raspy off-pitch singing.

I watched in fear as Death, his wolves,
Ran through my yard, broke in my home.
They dragged my wife out in the snow,
And bled her dry, 'til her skin turned cold.

The voices went silent. The harmonica continued its mournful humming as one by one, the men wandered off to their domes. Abe went off to check on a friend who'd lost her brother. The harmonica stopped. The man who had been playing it stood and told Smith to wait. He soon came back with two warm bottles of beer, sat down, and handed one to Smith.

"Where the hell did you find these?"

"I found a small case tucked inside a crate of blankets."

"Thanks for sharing your stash." Smith tilted the bottle to him. "You're Fritz, right?"

"Yessir, Smith."

Smith clicked his tongue and looked to the sky. *Was a part of Evalee up there, somewhere?*

Fritz nodded and pressed the bottle to his lips, slowly tilting it back.

"I used to listen to that stuff all the time," Smith said.

"Me too." Fritz inhaled deeply. "But it's different now. When I used to play these songs they were just, I don't know, stories."

"And now they're too damn real."

Fritz nodded.

"Right."

"Who sang that one, anyway?"

Fritz smiled. "The Almost Homeless. My dad always tried to get me to play, but I never wanted to 'til I heard those guys."

"Yeah, yeah." Smith took a swig. "Most of their stuff was pretty heavy, though."

"Downright depressing." Fritz laughed. "But those were the times."

Smith nodded in agreement. The early twenty-second century was marked by worldwide record unemployment highs, nearly 50 percent in the United States. A few wars ended while dozens began. In the States, the middle class was officially declared "dead" by many economists. Theft and assault rates had increased exponentially. Smith's own mom had ended up in the hospital after a thirteen-year-old girl mugged her with a stiletto.

And it had only grown worse from there, until Smith and Evalee made it onto the Ship of Nations. It was meant to be their ticket out of hell.

Smith motioned to the chunks of ship in the distance and the dozens of graves nearby. "You think all this is better than being on Earth?"

"No idea. For all we know, they could've nuked every piece of land to dust."

"Or they all figured out their shit and new treaties were signed this morning."

They looked at the ground in silence, then broke into a laughing fit.

"No way in hell." Fritz continued to laugh.

"This shouldn't be funny." Smith tried to control himself but failed.

"No," Fritz said.

Abe walked back over and sat down.

"Who put the extra helium in your O_2?" he asked.

"Ah, Earth's gone to hell, young friend," Fritz said and waved his hand dismissively and stood up.

"Yeah, that's why we left," Abe said and sat down.

Fritz chuckled. "True," he said. "I'll come take over for ya in a few hours, Smith."

"Thanks, Fritz." Smith glanced over at Abe. The boy sat, head hung down, eyes half open. Most likely feeling the same heaviness Smith felt. That weight pulled Abe's head forward, threatening to drag the boy into the dirt face first. Smith stood, pulled his chair until it touched Abe's and sat down. He pulled Abe's head onto his shoulder. Wanted to speak but knew if he opened his mouth the wailing of a broken man would be the only sounds to escape him. Instead, he put an arm around Abe's shoulders and hummed the tunes of The Almost Homeless. Soon, Abe was asleep.

Smith leaned back in his chair, shifting his gaze from the flat landscape to the new stars above him, thinking about what shapes people might make out of them. Not him, of course. People who had an eye for that sort of thing. Smith preferred the natural, disorderly beauty of the stars, and did not enjoy trying to add human-interpreted beauty to the sky. It was beautiful as it was.

Where was the Ship of Nations among all those stars? How was Tashon, his apprentice, doing as the ship's new chief farmer? *We should've just stayed on the ship*, he thought over and over. He knew thinking that would do him no good, but in the silence and dark of the night he could not help himself.

Abe shivered in his sleep. Smith got up, unfolded a small survival blanket and draped it over his son. Sat back down. Every time his son inhaled, his nose made a high-pitched squeal. It used to keep Smith awake on the ship, but Evalee had loved it. One of his quirks, she had said with a grin. Nearly everything she said had been with a grin and a light in her eyes.

Sighing, Smith stood up and rotated his chair forty-five degrees. Sat back down. Scratched his arm and face. He hadn't stopped itching since his wife died, although he barely realized the excessive scratching. Something next to his son caught his eye. He jumped to his feet, his heart pounded. The same footprints he had seen earlier walked right in front of him, into the distance. Then, almost instantly, sound was surrounding him.

It sounded like...wind? He felt no breeze on his face. It reminded him of when he was little, back on Earth. He was visiting his grandma, who lived on one of the last traditional farms around. She had let him sleep on the patio, and he remembered being lulled to sleep by the calm chirping of crickets.

Crickets? Here? But they wouldn't be exactly like the ones on Earth. He listened again. Closed his eyes. Yes, similar to crickets. But there was also a soft grinding mixed in. And it was only coming from one side of the settlement. Where they had gotten the soil sample. Making sure Abe was still asleep, Smith walked toward the sound as quickly as his new weight would allow.

It was at the opposite side of the perimeter, the same way the footprints had gone. Smith walked at a steady pace, curiosity fueling him more than fear. Reaching the fence, he peered into the darkness. The sound grew, and the ground itself seemed to hum. The speed of the "chirping" increased. It was joined by an intermittent high-pitched pulse, and each time it reached a crescendo, Smith winced as the tone drove into his eardrums. A gust of wind blew past his right side. He jumped, then looked down. The same handprints had appeared, on his side of the fence. Smith looked back into the darkness and saw...something.

Something he didn't quite understand. A figure, made of something like dark smoke. It was low to the ground. It looked like a dog, but skinnier and longer with a "nose" that came to a fine point. And it moved — no, rushed — toward the sound. Smith lost sight of the figure as it disappeared into the dark.

The chirping, grinding, high-pitched beat grew faster and louder. It flew as sound waves into his ears, freezing him in that spot. More gusts of wind blew past him, faster than the first one. He couldn't look down but knew if he did there would be more handprints. The sound reached a pitch that Smith was certain would blow his brains out. He felt something in his right ear burst. A warm stream of blood trickled out and down his jaw line. He forced his eyes shut, tried to scream but had no idea whether he made any noise. Then it stopped. Silence. Smith's legs buckled underneath him, and he hit the ground so hard he sent up a plume of dust.

***

The first day at colonization prep, Smith found himself in a small conference room with a couple of engineers, a few soldiers, a woman and her apprentice. The chairs were metal, a thin layer of padding failing to make them more comfortable. A small desk was nestled into the corner, the window behind it showing the dense fog pollution that refracted the rays of the setting sun. Smith and his jittery apprentice were the last to arrive, two of the only biotech farming experts left on Earth. He kept eyeing the olive-skinned woman to his left, unsure of what to think of her.

She sat, cross-legged on her chair, her hands resting on her knees. Her hair was pulled back, and she whispered calmly with her apprentice. Smith kept catching words like "energy" and "communication" and "serenity." Something about her just made him feel at once peaceful and confused.

"You need something, Smith?" she asked.

Damn, he'd been staring.

It was no surprise she knew his name. Everyone in the encampment did. He was one of the last remaining Smiths of the human race.

"No, sorry," he said quickly.

"Then why are you looking at me like a man, once blind, now blessed with vision, seeing the sky for the first time?" She smiled and tilted her head to one side.

Smith looked away in embarrassed confusion, then looked back at her. "And," he said, "why are you looking at me like a lost and needy dog?"

She laughed as if she had never heard anything more hysterical.

"I'm Evalee," she said.

He took her to dinner that night.

What he loved and hated about it were the never-ending questions she had for him. It was a new experience for him to have someone so interested in his life. He didn't know what to make of it. He rarely talked about himself. But it felt good to have someone so invested in finding out who he was.

They sat side by side on a bench outside Smith's favorite restaurant. It was one of those rare nights when the stars were visible through the smog of pollution that hung over everything those days. And the only reason the smog had thinned was because of a government mandate to shut down half of the nation's factories for a month. They would all be running again within the week.

"How is your apprentice, the up-and-coming biotech farmer?" she asked over a plate of tofu. "Has he taken to genetically rearranging organic material into something more pristine?"

Smith took a swig of a warm bottle of beer.

"Tashon's incredible," Smith said. "Just the other day he brought life back to an orangeberry bush I had given up on."

She looked at him, her lips curled slightly upward. A smile that he would soon associate with peace. Comfort.

"How's your apprentice?" he asked.

"Sylvia. She's wonderful. Hard worker. She soaks up the lessons like desert dirt when the clouds finally drop their life-giving water. She's actually my sister."

Smith's eyes opened wide in surprise. "They allowed that?"

"Special circumstances," she said. "Our beloved parents died working on the majestic Orbital Observatory when it went down."

"Damn," Smith said and shook his head.

He remembered the day well. Terrorists had taken down the OO, along with NASA headquarters. They proclaimed that man was not meant to leave the Earth. That all of them had to live out their consequences on a dying planet. He had just become a farming apprentice when he saw it on the screen. The massive OO in flames, slowly and silently falling into Earth's gravitational field. The terrorists had calculated it perfectly so that when it hit ground it crushed the NASA station and all its equipment.

"I'm sorry," he whispered.

"Thank you." she smiled. "I've made peace with it."

"How?"

"There's a life after this one. One more grand than this one, if you can fathom the idea." Smith looked away. He'd never been much of a believer in an afterlife. He believed in being good to people. Doing his best to just be good, and if there was an afterlife, he hoped that would be enough to land him in heaven or paradise or wherever it might be.

"You think this life is all there is?"

"I don't know."

She moved closer to him. "At least you admit it. Most people commit themselves to an absolute 'no' when the truth is that they simply do not know. But admitting you don't know something? That leaves all the doors open. It doesn't blind you to truths that might contradict what you've made the determination to believe."

They continued to talk late into the night, and Smith was continually amazed by the way she looked at the world. Committed to her beliefs, yet open and understanding of his vast lack of belief.

He spent nearly every night after that with her.

Chapter 5

The Ship of Nations was essentially what the name would suggest, carrying thousands of people from hundreds of nations selected by Humans for Humanity.

It looked like a large bullet, cut in half lengthwise, slowly spinning through the darkness. A large rod ran along its flat side. Sticking out of the rod, opposite the half-bullet, were smaller rods, spaced every ten meters. The half-bullet, which consisted of all the ship's useable space, spun slowly around the main rod. The small rods, each ending in a sphere, spun at the same rate. This created a gravitational pull of roughly half of a g, which varied slightly from level to level.

The ship consisted of thirty stories. Each story was split into two or more sectors. Entertainment, education, food, farming, recreation, living spaces. Nearly half a million souls aboard. At the bottom level were the colony ships, which periodically broke off as a group left to settle a habitable planet.

Smith and Evalee had been selected as two of the chiefs on the Ship of Nations. Smith specialized in biotech farming. The science of getting bio-engineered seeds to grow in virtually any type of ground. It took finesse, experience and trials to tweak the essence of each type of seed based on the type of ground.

Evalee was Chief of Communication, although critics of the skill referred to it as manipulation. Her job was to keep her mind and emotions calm and cool under any condition and, in turn, help others do the same. She could talk nearly anyone off almost any ledge. A woman wants to kill her cheating husband? Evalee could talk her out of it, while also calming the woman's mind and giving her a sense of security to do what she needed to. A week after meeting her, Smith saw Evalee stop a young teen from slitting a teacher's throat in the Education District by looking into his eyes and knowing how to connect to him. The words that would make him feel heard and understood without spilling a single drop of blood. The first time Smith saw her skill in action, the only word he could think of to describe it was *magic*.

About six months before the Ship of Nations was scheduled to depart, Smith was teaching a young man the art of using nanotech to add and remove components in the biotech seeds and the food they grew into. As usual, the boy needed little guidance from his teacher. They worked in the massive farming sector that covered three and a half square miles. It was inside a large, glass greenhouse. Outside, the air was thick with smog and pollution. One of those days that required a breathing mask just to take the trash out. Inside the glass, though, was some of the freshest air to be found on Earth.

Row upon row of manufactured soil made up the farm. They had nearly every fruit and vegetable native to Earth, and then some. Green trees, bushes and vines filled the large room. Benches were scattered around, and many spent breaks and evenings enjoying smells and colors that could be found nowhere else.

The two farmers were using the nanites to correct a problem that made their plum/apple hybrid grow thick brown fuzz on one side. Smith laughed in amazement as the nanites made the fuzz fall off, one strand at a time, from each fruit in an entire bush.

A door to their left creaked open. Evalee walked in and stood quietly by the door, waiting for them to finish. Her eyes and cheeks were wet.

"Keep going. I'll be back."

As Smith walked toward Evalee, she walked to a bench under a blooming peach tree and sat down. He sat down and gave her a slight nod to let her know he was listening.

"Sylvia quit. She quit her apprenticeship with me."

"Huh." Smith had learned in the last few months that it was best to let Evalee talk everything out before fully responding.

"It's just so.... Damn." She paused and shook her hands in the air. "You know, I've been trying to breathe and center my mind. Like I'm trained to do, like I've done hundreds of times with so many. But I can't. I can't because...."

"Because...."

She turned and looked straight into Smith's eyes.

"She quit to work as a dancer downtown. Smith, she's too damn young for that. Too damn young. Too smart."

"Damn right she is."

"I don't get it. Choosing to stay on Earth instead of leaving on the ship is bad enough. But staying on Earth and changing to that kind of... career?"

Smith shook his head in disbelief. Evalee's sister turning to that kind of life? And weeks before leaving on the Ship of Nations. Before starting a completely new life full of endless possibilities.

Evalee sighed, dropped her face into her hands and screamed. A young couple on a bench the next row over glared at her. Smith smiled and waved.

Evalee picked her head up again. "I tried so hard to talk her out of it. To talk her off this ledge. But she knew at least half of the techniques I used. And she's just so damn stubborn."

"She got that from you, you know."

That earned one short laugh, and another sigh.

"Ev, what's the first lesson you learn when you start studying communication?"

Another sigh. This time Smith could tell she was beginning to calm down.

"The first lesson is that it doesn't always work. People can still choose their own way. What we do is not mind control. We simply bring those on an edge to a calmer, rational mindset."

Smith sat quietly as he let Evalee think that first lesson over for what was probably the hundredth time. After a few minutes, he stretched his arm and pulled her close to him. He hugged her tight and found that he didn't want to let go. And he realized that if she didn't have an apprentice trained when it was time to leave Earth, she might have to remain on the planet.

That night, Smith made his way to the downtown area. Normally, he would only go to that area if the Hubble Foundation was presenting new findings at one of the venues. It was barely a year ago that they had announced the completion of the Ship of Nations and taken him on a virtual tour of its massive interior.

But there were no reports for him to attend. Blinded by glowing lights of nearly every color, Smith consulted a map that was projected on the black, metal floor. The ceiling above him was high and covered with projections of a night sky to make it seem like the real stars weren't being blotted out by decades of human waste.

He had never been to the Live Entertainment sector before and had never wanted to. He wasn't sure he wanted to now. But he had to find Sylvia. The decision she had made was destroying Evalee, and he hated seeing Evalee in so much pain. Locating the quickest route, he stuck his hands in his pockets and went to find Sylvia.

As Smith walked, he tried to keep his mind clear. To not focus on the worst that could happen, as he usually did. But what if it was worse than Evalee thought? What if, stars forbid, she was a drug addict and he found her dead outside a Fry Burger with needle holes in her arms? Smith's gut told him something like that was bound to happen—but his gut was rarely right. So, he tried to focus on outcomes that were positive, yet logical.

Perhaps Sylvia started working as a dancer to make more money. Apprentices, after all, earned a meager stipend. But then Smith would walk in just as some sleaze was about to cross the line with her. He would swing the jerk around, pop him one in the nose. Sylvia would be grateful and realize that 500 creds a night was not worth putting up with those pervs. The two would walk back together, Evalee would have her sister back, and they would all leave on the ship together.

Who was he kidding? He'd never been inside a dance club before. The only time he'd ever hit someone was when he was ten, and that was his younger brother. He'd knocked the poor kid's tooth out and been forced to clean the air filter for a month. His mind drifted back to more pessimistic thoughts. But he kept walking.

The storefronts to either side told him he had entered the clothing district with 3D ads telling him he needed these briefs or that jacket to improve his quality of life. A particularly ostentatious one followed him as he attempted to walk away. It was an animated shirtless man, biceps larger than Smith's head. Washboard abs, pecks like nothing Smith had seen.

"You want to look like me? Of course you do! And you can. Just follow me to Rick's Gym and Steroid Center, and we'll have you busting out of your shirts in weeks."

Smith moved on. The ad followed him, repeating its pitch until Smith got out of range. He couldn't help but laugh at how ridiculous the ad was and wondered how many people it brought into that gym.

Another few minutes of walking, and Smith was in Club Alley. One long stretch with clubs on either side. He'd never been there before, and the ads were more perverse and pervasive than anywhere he'd been. Holograms of near-naked men and women danced seductively, spoke sensually. Smith did his best to ignore them. Something about this type of entertainment had bothered him and, in some ways, intrigued him. Which bothered him even more.

The entrance to the closest club was guarded by two men wearing all black. Both had large barrel chests, long hair and protruding guts. One wore sunglasses. They looked like twins. Smith walked toward them.

"Twenty creds to get through the door," one said in a deep voice.

"Nah, let's cut this one a deal. Fifteen creds," said Sunglasses with a grin.

"Actually, I... uh...." Smith stumbled.

"Drunk already? My kind of man!"

"No, no. I'm, uh, looking for someone. Specific."

"Oh, yeah, I catch your drift. What's this request look like?"

"No, dumbass," Smith said, his nervousness portrayed as aggression. "An actual person. Name's Sylvia."

The two looked at each other. Sunglasses whispered something in the other's ear.

"Okay. Here's the thing. We know who she is. Just started working down the street, around the corner."

"Another club?" Smith asked.

"Yeah, kinda. But not like ours."

Smith shrugged. "Huh?"

"See, man, she works at a full-blown brothel."

In seconds, Smith's aggression turned to rage. In two steps, his nose was an inch away from Sunglasses' mouth. It smelled of mint and alcohol.

"How the hell you know that? You go see her? I swear, if you went to see her, I'll—"

"Hey, man!"

He pushed Smith away from him, but soft enough he stayed upright.

"I never seen Sylvia like that. Or anyone. I don't have to pay for sex." He laughed and puffed out his chest.

"For shit's sake!" Smith yelled.

"Watch your language," the deep voice said gruffly.

"Where the hell is she?"

"Say sorry first." Sunglasses sneered.

Smith fought the urge to take a swing. He needed to find Sylvia, not end up unconscious outside a dance club.

"I'm sorry. Today's just been a sh—" He paused. "Crap-storm. I just... I'm sorry, guys." Smith curled up his lips in the most genuine smile he could manage.

"She's at Pixies, man. Take a right at the next intersection, away from the main stretch."

Smith punched the wall to the left of Sunglasses' head and walked off.

"Take a left just after the dancing panda," Sunglasses yelled. "And cool the hell off or the owner'll throw you out!"

The only thank you he received from Smith was an old-fashioned flip off.

He would have found Pixies without the directions. Ads for the place followed him as soon as he turned past the Panda. The closer he got to Sylvia, the more perverse and provocative the dancing holograms became. Smith hated them. The way they swooned, danced and enticed. Mocking and trying to replace something honest, something real. Something they weren't, something they would never be. Something that Smith hadn't felt in a long time. He didn't want Sylvia becoming part of that lie.

Then, she was there—Sylvia's hologram. She called to him, sang to him, danced.

"I'll do anything," she sang and smiled. "Anything at all."

He got an erection and averted his gaze. It sounded like Sylvia. But Smith had spent so much time talking with her that it was obvious the hologram's voice was computer-generated. They probably hadn't been able to get the real Sylvia to sound enticing enough. Smith shook his head. A pit grew in his stomach. He let the pit grow. Let it give him direction. Purpose. Anger.

It was like he had taken a drug. He was barely aware of what he was doing. Blacklight spilled out of a doorway. He walked in, demanded to see Sylvia. The man behind the desk pointed to a glass wall to his right. A row of women in lingerie sat on chairs, posing for him. Sylvia sat three chairs from the end. He met her eyes. As soon as she realized it was him, she turned away and covered herself with her arms.

Smith stepped in front of her, put his hand on the glass.

"Sylvia! Come on! Come out!" His voice crackled.

She didn't respond. Her eyes remained focused on the floor.

Smith pounded the glass. It vibrated under his fist.

"Sylvia!" he screamed. "Sylvia! Come on!"

He slammed his fist on the glass again, shaking the entire panel.

The man came out from behind the desk and tried to shove Smith out the door. Smith pushed back. Threw a punch. Landed it. The other man collapsed.

An alarm blared. He was surrounded by men holding batons. Swung his fist again, dropped another body. The back of his head cracked. He groaned and dropped to the floor. The men kicked him in the back and stomach until the patrol arrived.

Chapter 6

Smith's mind was aware he was no longer sleeping, but he didn't want to open his eyes.

"Ev," he mumbled. "Ev... Sylvia, she... oh, Ev...."

"What are you talkin' about now, farmer?"

Smith opened his eyes and squinted at the white lights. He lay in a small cot inside one of the colony domes. Evalee was not there, of course. He sighed and looked for the source of the voice. It was Gretch. An older woman with long, white hair and large glasses. She wasn't a doctor. Then Smith remembered their medical team had all died in the crash.

"Good thing Jonstin found you when he did. You would have frozen out there without your coat."

Smith struggled to hear her.

"Why are you" — he cleared his throat — "talking so quiet?"

She walked closer to him and crouched down to eye level. He turned to meet her gaze.

"Your right ear drum, Smith. It was ruptured. You might not ever hear from that side again."

Smith nodded and then he sighed. "Abe? He was with me."

"He's fine, just fine."

Smith nodded again, relieved.

"Smith?"

"Yeah?"

"What the hell happened?"

He laughed at that, but she didn't seem amused. "You mean you didn't hear that?"

"Hear what?"

"The... the crickets. That high-pitched, pierce-your-ears chirping?"

"I don't think anyone did, Smith."

"What...?"

Smith closed his eyes, trying to recall his last memory. He had heard something, and it had been loud. It should have woken everyone up. Then he remembered —

"Abe was outside too. Did he...?"

"No. He hasn't said anything. I can ask him."

"No, no. I will."

"Okay."

"He had a cap on. A hood too."

"What?"

"Abe's ears were covered."

"Oh, yes, I see."

"And everyone else was inside."

"Yes, they were."

"And the footprints?"

"What?"

"The... the foot— Ugh, maybe I'm just crazy."

"Maybe. But maybe not. Something made that ear blow out. And crazy can't do that."

"Yeah."

Smith slowly shook his head back and forth. *How could he be the only one who saw the footprints? Or heard the crickets, or whatever the hell it was? He knew that he had heard it. Wouldn't be convinced otherwise. But couldn't that be one definition of insanity? Being so convinced of one's own reality, despite what everyone around you is experiencing as their own reality?* Smith sighed.

"You rest a bit. I'll go get Abe."

"Thanks, Gretch."

"Call me doctor, farmer," she said and smiled.

Smith tried to smile back. His eyes weren't in it.

***

When Smith opened his eyes again, Abe was sitting to his left, staring at a small tablet, engrossed in whatever was on the screen.

"Hey, Abe."

"Dad!"

"How you doing?"

"I'm crisp." Abe put a smile on. "You ready to get off your ass and back to work?"

"Ha. I think so, son. I think so."

"Crisp, Dad. Pure O_2." Abe nodded and looked at his screen. "I took soil samples. There's only small shits east of us."

Smith smiled, happy to see his son happy. "Good. That gives us plenty of area to get some food growing. What should we plant first?"

"I already planted two rows of the orange corn and three of the potatoes."

"Ha! That's my boy." Smith patted his son's knee.

"I hope they grow. Soil's not like on the ship."

"Ah, we'll figure it out, son."

Abe smiled at his dad, then turned away as his smile faded.

Smith sighed. "Look, Abe, I... uh...." He closed his eyes.

"Yeah, I wish Mom were here too."

"Right, right."

Smith pulled the boy's head against his chest. It felt so small, fragile. Like if he squeezed too hard, it might shatter. His son quickly pulled away. He'd never been big on hugs and physical contact.

"Oh, Dad?"

"Yeah?"

"I'm glad you didn't die like Mom."

For some reason Smith laughed at that. He stood up, his body wobbling back and forth. Apparently, ears really did affect balance. Putting a hand on his son's shoulder, they walked toward the door. As they did, he asked Abe to stay on his right side and be his ear for him.

There were no windows in the colony domes, and as they walked out Smith was surprised to see it was nighttime. He instinctively pulled Abe close and scanned their surroundings. Apparently, they had all been scared by what happened to Smith. There were now six men on watch duty, one at each corner of the perimeter.

It was also busier than Smith had ever seen it. Someone had found an old ball, and the older kids were kicking it around. The younger ones ran in circles, screaming and laughing. He tried to convince Abe to go play with them, but the boy would not.

Nearly everyone else was bustling around, doing what they could to improve their little colony. One group was setting up cots and filling each dome with as many as would fit. Smith realized that with the few homes they still had, nearly twenty people would have to sleep in each one. Another group sorted through crates, organizing clothing into piles based on size and use. And the rest seemed to be comforting each other, talking in hushed voices or not talking at all.

Smith saw all this as he scanned the area looking for the new captain. He found Sylvia off to the side talking with Jonstin, the pilot, and two young men wearing engineer's hats. Smith recognized them but could not remember their names.

Waving, he caught her eye. She quickly said something to the three men and broke off to greet Smith.

"Hey, good to see you up and walking." She shook his hand and patted his back.

"Thanks. What's going on with those guys?"

She glanced back at the three, who seemed to be having a heated discussion. "Jonstin is still fuming that the ship he was piloting burned up. Understandable, really."

"Very understandable, but I'm still keeping my eye on him. I've never liked him."

"Very understandable," she said. "But you should know he's the one who found you on the ground the other night."

"Huh."

"So what the hell happened?" Sylvia asked. "A lot of people are freaked out by it."

Smith sighed and shook his head, still shocked that no one else had heard the noise. After a moment, he began to speak, telling the new captain what had happened. As best as he could remember. She listened intently without interrupting. Once he finished, there was a brief silence. He looked down and Abe and saw that the boy was scared. *Damn, I shouldn't have talked about that in front of him,* he thought.

"I think I know what happened," Sylvia said.

Smith stared at her. Abe stared at the ground.

"You still have that vial you filled with dirt?" she asked.

"Yeah." He pulled it out of his shirt pocket and handed it to her. As he did, he realized that it was empty. He put his fingers back into his shirt pocket and felt a small pile of dirt.

"Sylvia, what the hell...?"

"Take a look." She handed it back to him. "On the side, the glass is cracked."

Smith took it, squinted at it and then turned it in his fingers. On one of the sides was a crack—no, more of a shatter. It was a jagged circle, about the size of his pinky nail.

"I filled a vial, too, that same day. I had it on a table, and I watched it crack before my eyes. Something came out of it."

"The living organisms?"

"One living organism. Let's go to the captain's dome. I'll show you."

"Did you kill it?"

"No."

"Okay. Abe, you good?"

"Crisp, Dad."

They quickly walked to the larger colony dome that served as the captain's quarters. Smith was surprised at how empty it was. A cot, a table and a chair. A large bullet-proof glass box sat on the table.

"Is it in there?"

"Go take a look."

He walked steadily to the box. Whatever was inside appeared to be asleep. Its shape was a bit like the beetles he had seen back on Earth. But it was almost double that size, and the scales that ran across the creature's body alternated colors. Silver, green, silver, green. Smith could tell by looking at it that it was part mechanical, part organic. And its mandibles looked like large, shining scimitars.

Smith opened his mouth to speak but closed it. He wasn't sure what to say. Seeing a living creature, let alone one that had been joined with tech, on this new planet, seemed impossible. None of their tests or reads reported anything that would suggest such a creature.

"That guy's not one hundred percent organic," he said finally.

"I know."

"So that means that... that—"

"It could mean lots of things, Smith. But I need to check your ear. Sit down."

He did, trying to calm his body as his mind raced. How had something that big been in his vial? Did he scoop up an egg, and it hatched in the vial?

Sylvia stepped closer and pulled out a small pair of pliers.

As she moved them toward his ear, Smith pushed her hand away.

"What the hell, Sylvia?"

"I'm just checking your ear. Please, I think...." She looked at the hybrid insect in its cage.

"Think what?"

She sighed but didn't respond.

"C'mon, Syl. Just tell me what's going on."

Silence for a few more seconds.

"Okay. Okay. Look, see, I was sitting at my table looking over the prelim research to figure out what the hell we're going to do here. My vial was sitting on the table. At some point I fell asleep. I woke up 'cause that thing was crawling up my neck. I swear if I hadn't woken up, it would have crawled right into my ear."

Smith was quiet. For a few seconds, at least. He tried to hold in a laugh but couldn't help it. The noise burst out of him, and before he knew it the laughing brought tears to his eyes.

"So your theory is that one of these guys crawled into my ear? C'mon, Syl."

She pulled a small jar out of her pocket and motioned for Smith to look inside. At first Smith just thought it was another one of the same creatures, but smaller. No, he realized, not smaller. Broken. In the jar was what looked like the head of the beetle and part of its torso. No longer than a quarter of an inch. Dried yellow fluid caked the severed end.

"You found a dead one?"

"No, Gretch did."

Smith was about to ask where, but the answer hit him before he could. He instinctively put a finger in his broken ear. Nothing there, but he felt sick.

"She's not a trained doctor," Sylvia said. "But only half of the thing was there when she pulled it out. No idea about the other half."

"You remember," Smith said. "That you, the engineers and the biologists all said there was nothing living on this planet?"

"Yeah. It's turning out we were wrong about a lot." Sylvia sighed and sat down.

"You think the other half of that thing is in my head?"

Sylvia sighed and shook her head. "I don't know."

Smith nodded. "It doesn't feel any different in there."

They both went silent. Smith held his fingers up to his ear and snapped. Nothing. He did it again, next to his other ear, and the snap was clear. It was odd, being broken on one side and whole on the other. Then he felt something move under his skin, just above his right ear. Reflexively, he pushed against it with his fingers, but nothing was there. He let his hand fall to his lap and told himself it must have been psychological. But if it was psychological, where was the other half of the beetle? Again, he felt something move behind his broken ear. Bile rose in his throat, but he swallowed it back down. Told himself there wasn't an alien beetle crawling around in his head, and believed it, even if only temporarily.

"You remember when I left the brothel?"

"Yeah. I was still in intensive care." Smith sighed and closed his eyes. "Kinda remember you comin' to see me."

"I came every day."

Smith smiled and nodded.

"I don't think Evalee ever told you what happened after I left," Sylvia said.

"About how you decided to transfer to engineering?"

"No. I was at Pixies to pay off my ex's debts. He... he forced me into it. Hundreds of thousands of credits. Threatened to kill Ev if I didn't."

Smith shook his head. "Damn, I didn't know."

"And when I left, he was furious. Drunk. High. He came after me."

Smith looked into her eyes for a moment, trying to imagine how that must have felt. There was no way he could really understand what she had gone through. But he could try. That's what his wife had always done. What she had tried to teach him to do.

"I was with Evalee. We were at that bench in the far corner of the Farm District. Then he was just there. Right in front of me, towering over me. His eyes were wild. I could tell the debt collectors had been to see him. His clothes were torn, both eyes black. Looked like his jaw was broken. He had a knife in each hand.

"But before he could do anything, Evalee stood up, got between him and me. And she just started talking. I have no idea what she said, or if he even said anything back. But he left. I never saw him again."

Smith closed his eyes and rubbed his face. Evalee had rarely kept secrets from him, but he knew why she'd kept this one. If he had known, he probably would have found Sylvia's ex and beat him to death.

"Evalee saved my life, Smith." She paused. "I miss her like hell."

Smith coughed, caught his breath. "I need to go check on Abe."

He stood up and walked out, unable to hear Sylvia call after him.

Chapter 7

Jonstin was one of the best pilots the Ship of Nations had ever seen. So much so that it took hours of convincing, and some bribery, to get him the Lead Pilot spot for the colonization. The higher-ups wanted to keep him on to run the small ships that collected materials from nearby meteors and dwarf planets. But Jonstin was adamant that his time on the ship was done, that his little brother was ready to step up.

Smith was upset that Jonstin was given the position, but for different reasons. He simply didn't like the guy.

"So, Smith," Jonstin said the first time they met. "What kind of a name is that?"

They walked side by side down a narrow maintenance hallway. All members of a colonizing party were required to study basic mechanics and repair. Pipes, wires and grates surrounded them. It looked like most of them had been welded, taped or glued at some point.

"Used to be one of the most common names of the human race."

"Ha! Funny what used to be considered cool."

"Had nothing to do with cool. Some people honor the names they're given."

"Huh. If you say so. Anyway, aren't you like the last Smith or something?"

Smith stopped at a pipe that had a small steam leak and pulled out a wrench. "Yeah. Smiths are survivors, though. Hand me a soldering gun."

"Again, if you say so. Here you go." Jonstin handed the tool to Smith.

"Didn't you change your name to something stupid?" Smith lit up the soldering gun.

"You got that half right. I did change it. Jonstin Flyingman."

Smith kept fixing the leak, the light from the soldering gun casting a blue glow in the dark hall.

"You know, 'cause I'm a pilot? I fly?"

"Yeah, I get it. What was your given name?"

"Jonstin Thorsten."

"Yeah. Much better than Flyingman. All fixed." He stood up and walked off, Jonstin jogging to catch up.

"You don't really like me, huh, Smith?"

"Haven't decided yet."

"But you think you're better than me."

"I'm no better than any other person. Definitely worse than some. But, no, I don't think I'm better than you. I put value on things that you don't. Look at the world differently. That doesn't mean I'm better."

"Man, you're just sayin' that so you don't make yourself look bad."

"If you say so," Smith said calmly. But part of him wondered if the pilot was right.

To prove to himself Jonstin wasn't right, Smith invited the pilot to join him, Evalee and Sylvia for dinner that night.

They met at Jenza's, a small and unpopular restaurant in the ship's entertainment sector. Smith and Evalee shared a plate of a "Hearty Fruit Salad, fresh from the farming sector!" Sylvia ate a traditional vegetable salad, while Jonstin had an enormous plate of deep-fried imitation steak. He cut and shoveled it into his mouth like a trencher working with a child's toy tools.

The conversation started out as the awkward small talk of new acquaintances and continued that way until Jonstin was on his third beer.

"You know," he said louder than necessary. "I'm glad H for H commissioned this ship. It got me out of that hellhole formerly known as Earth."

He took a large gulp from his bottle.

"My dad was a bastard." He held his bottle high in the air. "I don't think H for H had most of their other shit right. Earth didn't go to hell because we weren't getting along enough. No, that's bull. We started accepting everyone's shit, no questions asked."

He slapped the table, then waved at the waitress for another drink.

"I think you've had en—" Evalee started, but Jonstin shushed her.

"Damn, did my dad beat me." He belched loudly. "'Scuse me. Yeah, we started getting along too well, know?"

The waitress put another bottle on the table.

"Thank, thank, thank you." Jonstin's lips curved into a crooked smile. "See, think here, everyone was born where they s'pposed to be. Wealth. Health. Color. We shouldn'ta started minglin' everyone together, know?"

"Jonstin." Smith pulled the bottle away from him. "Let's go."

"He'd hit my mom too. Yeah, yeah." He lazily tried to grab the bottle from Smith. "Is fine. We really want to fix human problems? We need worldwide caste system. Yeah we do. Those deservin' gettin' everything we deservin'. Those not deservin' gettin' not."

Smith stood up. "You deserve a charged WireSnake up your—"

"Smith!" Evalee jumped to her feet and placed a hand on his shoulder. "Enough. Let's get him to his quarters. I don't think he means what he's saying."

"Then why're you saying that shit, Jonstin?"

But Jonstin had passed out, head dropped on the table.

They had been the only ones in the restaurant, and the waitress had promised not to say anything about what she heard. Ev convinced Smith and Sylvia to keep it quiet too. The outrage that would ensue on the ship if anyone heard a Chief Pilot talking like that? Unimaginable. Smith would just have to watch the man much more closely. He never spoke like that again, but Smith never stopped believing those were Jonstin's true, inner thoughts.

Perhaps, Smith told himself, he was better than just a handful of people.

***

A few days had gone by, and Smith still couldn't hear with his right ear. People kept approaching to ask how he was, only to startle him. He'd almost punched a few people who'd inadvertently snuck up on him.

He'd barely slept. Every time he tried, his mind would run rampant. One minute he would be wishing Evalee were there to tell him it would all work out. The next he would become convinced that something was in his head, crawling around his brain. Was the bump on the back of his head new? Was it in the same spot five minutes ago or was it moving?

Down time was impossible, so he was constantly doing something. Usually it was with Abe, focusing on getting the crops growing. It was harder here than it had been on the Ship of Nations. The soil there had been perfect and healthy in every spot. Here, though, the quality of the soil seemed to change every square foot.

They were outside the fenced perimeter, looking for some good ground. Smith had refused to go to where he'd heard that screeching noise.

"Got a crisp idea, Dad," Abe was saying. "You think there's a way to control our nanotech to alter the makeup of the soil?"

"Ha. I hadn't thought of that." Smith thought for a moment. "But I don't think so. See, the biotech seeds and the food that grow from them are made with biotech that is engineered to react to the nanotech. But this soil is just... soil. It's a clever idea though."

The boy stuck his hand into the soil and scooped some up, slowly letting it fall back to the ground. "It's not terrible soil, though. Half-pure," Abe said.

"Yeah, half-pure," Smith agreed.

"And half is better than none, right, Dad?"

"Ha. Yeah, just like your mom would say."

"Yeah."

And with that, they got to work. Smith, using a small tube to pull out dirt to form perfect, quarter-inch holes. Abe following behind, dropping a seed into each and filling the hole again. They'd done this countless times on the ship and it didn't take long for them get into a familiar rhythm.

As the sun moved across the sky, Smith watched the shadows stretch out from the bent skeleton of their colony ship. Looking at it, he wondered how any of them had survived. Fate? Luck? Why had he been among the survivors? The boy would have been fine without his father, right? But Abe without his mother, him without his wife, the universe without Evalee? That was a life, a universe that Smith could not make sense of.

Pain pulsed through his skull, stretching out from above his right ear. Sweat formed on his hairline. His skin swelled out, then back in. Or did it? He closed his eyes. Slowed his breaths. *There's nothing living in your head.* The pain faded, and he went back to farming. He turned his attention back to the task at hand and let himself get lost in the comfort of repetition.

After what felt like forever but also no time at all, something grabbed Smith's shoulder. He turned around and pulled back his fist. It was one of the engineers, the young man. Leonard. He was tall and lanky, with a deep voice that didn't go with his thin frame.

"Hey, whoa, Smith." He jumped back. "Didn't mean to sneak up on you."

"Yeah, yeah. It's okay. Sorry, I got lost in the work."

"And your ear's screwed up," Abe chimed in.

"Yeah, thanks, Abe." Smith chuckled at the jab.

"Yeah, anyway," Leonard said. "Sylvia wants everyone gathered to eat some food and discuss how everything is going."

"You mean Captain Sylvia," Smith said.

"Actually, she doesn't want to be called captain."

"Huh. That doesn't surprise me. C'mon, Abe. Let's go."

It was a long walk back to the colony. Smith hadn't realized how far they'd wandered looking for soil.

"So she doesn't want to be captain?" Smith asked.

Leonard shrugged. "Never said that."

"So she does?"

"Some people don't like that she just assumed that role."

"But she's Lead Engineer. She's got more leadership than anyone who survived."

"I agree. But not everyone does. They're saying it takes more than just telling people what to do to grow a colony into a city, a nation and a world."

"True. But we can't grow anything yet. We're basically in survival mode. Don't have the supplies to grow right now."

"And that's Sylvia's standpoint."

"And what are the others saying?"

"If we're not moving forward, we're moving backward."

"Huh."

"I mean, it does make some sort of sense."

"But what do they want us to do? We are moving forward. We've started growing crops. We've assigned homes. We've taken security measures."

"Yes, but some people are saying it's not enough. That Sylvia's just creating the illusion of moving forward. And they're blaming Sylvia for the crash landings. But, you ask me, I think the guy just wants to grab a power spot while he can."

"Oh, damn. It's Jonstin, isn't it?"

"Oh, you know him?"

"Unfortunately."

They both chuckled, and Abe gave his father a quizzical look, but didn't say anything.

When they got back to the colony, it looked like all 121 survivors were out. Small groups were scattered around talking. Some standing or leaning against the colony domes, others sitting in the gray dirt. Nearly all of them wore the standard issue blue coveralls. Smith loved wearing them. They were comfortable, and the fabric increased and decreased its temperature using the same tech Smith used to fix his biotech crops. Unfortunately, his had been lost in the crash. And all the ones that had belonged to the recently deceased were far too small for him.

Instinctively, Smith looked for Sylvia. She was in the shade of one of the homes, whispering with one of the engineers. The one with shoulder length hair and a big nose. Smith couldn't recall his name. The two seemed deep in discussion, so Smith decided to let her be. He looked around, trying to figure out what was going on.

He spotted Jonstin. The pilot was walking around, shaking hands and laughing with anyone he could. Smith wouldn't have been surprised if the budding politician were to hold up a baby and kiss it. If any babies had survived.

Jonstin saw the farmer and made his way toward him.

"Hey, Abe, go join the kids over there. I'll get you in a minute."

Abe jogged off, kicking gray dust up behind him. The boy had never seemed to like Jonstin, either.

"Chief Farmer Smith." Jonstin stuck out his hand.

Smith grabbed his hand and shook it. "Jonstin."

"Look, I don't know what you've heard, but—"

"I hear you're causin' problems. Nothin' new."

"Good to see you're healed up."

"Thanks."

"Look, I know Sylvia is basically your sister or whatever, but I'm just trying to make sure us few survivors endure for decades to come. I'm planning for the future."

"If you say so."

"Farmer, just listen to what I have to say when I get in front of everyone. I have some good ideas, you know. And a lot of people respect you. They might make up their minds based on your opinion."

"Yeah. They probably will."

"Ha! This guy!" He slapped Smith's shoulder. "You're a good guy."

Smith just nodded in response as the budding politician walked off, shaking more hands and smiling bigger than seemed humanly possible. Shaking his head, Smith went to join Abe and Tom. He suddenly realized he hadn't seen any of those handprints since that first day. Had he imagined them? No, he was sure he had seen them. Besides, if he had imagined the handprints then that would mean he'd imagined everything that led to his busted ear. And he knew without a doubt what had happened. Hadn't it?

If he really thought about it, he wasn't sure. He knew something bizarre happened. Something that left him half deaf. But part of him wondered if it had just been something in his mind that made him see those things. And then made his ear blow out. Really, there was only one thing he knew for sure: this new home felt nothing like home. He wished he could lay facedown in the dirt and let the gray earth pull him down until his body and soul melted and joined with the core. Or sit down, let whatever might be in his head eat its way to his brain stem until he collapsed. He rubbed his hand all over his head, feeling for a bump. He found a small scab. How long had that been there? For a moment he imagined the scab bursting open, a bloody beetle creature crawling out of his skull. But the scab remained still.

"Dad? Daad?"

Damn, he'd made it to his son and had been standing there staring into space. Abe and the other kids had stopped playing to look at him.

"Yeah, Abe, sorry. How you doing?"

"Fine."

"You sure?"

The boy just shrugged.

"Yeah, me too."

"Is... is there an alien bug in your brain?"

"Hope to hell there's not."

"But if...." Abe's voice trailed off.

"If there is," Smith said, "that'd be the shits."

He pictured Abe finding him on the ground, a hole in the side of his head, a trail of blood and brain matter leading to an enlarged biotech cricket.

"The real shits," Smith whispered.

"The biggest, runniest shits ever."

"You're disgusting, son." He slugged Abe's arm and looked over to see a young man and an older woman walking toward him. It looked like something was bothering them.

"Chief Farmer Smith," the woman said with raspy voice.

"Please, ma'am, just Smith will do."

"Okay, then. Smith. We're worried."

"About what?"

"What's happened already, what might happen. Are we going to make it?"

"You know, I think we will. No reason to think otherwise."

Smith noticed Abe was paying close attention to the conversation, but pretending to not care.

"But why are you asking a farmer about that? I think Captain Sylvia would be the best one to ask."

"Yeah, she's great. But something she did or didn't do caused our problems."

"We don't know that. And placing blame isn't going to help."

"Okay. There's also only two chiefs left. You and Chief Pilot Jonstin."

"What is it you're saying, ma'am?"

"A chief should lead us. And we all know Jonstin is only looking out for himself."

"Ma'am, I appreciate the thought. But I'm a farmer. Not a leader. Not a politician."

"C'mon, man," the young man jumped in. "Chiefs are trained in multiple aspects of science, mechanics and human relations. We also know that you learned a lot from your wife in Communication. You could actually be good for us."

"And" — the old woman stepped closer — "you care about people more than most."

"I'm not sure about that."

"You care about 'em more than Jonstin does."

"Can't argue there."

"Look, just consider it. Jonstin's talking about callin' for a vote. He does, a lot of us are tossin' your name in."

"Ma'am, that's kind. But please don't."

"Why not, Dad?"

Smith sighed and shook his head. Abe looked intently at his father, and Smith wondered what his teen was thinking. What his boy was feeling. Would he be okay? Would any of them?

Smith turned back to the woman. "Look, I've never led anyone. Never been great with people."

"But you're kind, Chief Farmer."

"And so are you, ma'am. Can I vote you to be our fearless leader?"

"And you're funny." She smiled. "And I am far from fearless."

"As am I," Smith said.

"I think we all are, Dad."

"Please," Smith said. "After everything, I just want to farm. Make sure we get enough food growing for everyone. That's what I do."

"But you could do more."

"I really don't think so, ma'am."

"Listen, just think about it. We need someone with a level head."

Smith nodded and looked away, wondering if he did have a level head. He was partially convinced that he was lying nearly dead in the gray dirt, hidden by large chunks of shrapnel. Dreaming up all this insanity. His dreams had always been vivid, intense.

But real or not, Jonstin had gotten a loudspeaker and climbed on top of a small stack of crates. People gradually went quiet as they turned to look at the waving captain candidate.

"Hey, hi, hello," he said. "Before I start, I want to thank Sylvia for all that she has done for us so far. She really has done great. I'm not trying to undermine her in any way."

"Yeah, right," someone yelled. "Liar!"

A few more heckles and some laughs.

Jonstin calmly waited for everyone to get quiet. "Look, I'm fine with it if you disagree with me. I just want to talk about what I think we can do better than has been done, and how I think I can move us more effectively into a secure and productive future."

More shouts, some cheering and some booing.

Smith was quiet, waiting for Jonstin to say something more than political puffery.

"But before I get caught up talking about my ideas, I want Sylvia to come up here too."

Smith scanned the crowd for her, knowing that she would hate being called up there. But when he did find her, she was already halfway to the crates, smiling at the others as she passed them. When she got to the crates, Jonstin held out his hand to her. She ignored it and climbed up herself.

"Sylvia, again, thank you for helping all of us through these difficult few days."

"No thanks needed."

"Ah! She's humble. I like that!"

He looked at her expectantly, but she didn't respond.

"Okay, then," Jonstin said. He looked around at the crowd. "We've all talked among ourselves about what's going on with the leadership after the tragic death of our former captain. Sylvia took the reins and has done a tremendous job getting us started. But I think its time we put the power of captain to a vote, seeing as how there are conflicting opinions on how we should move forward."

Some of the crowd shouted in agreement, others shouted that he was power hungry and taking advantage of a tragedy.

"We'll let Sylvia speak first." He handed the loudspeaker to the engineer.

Smith could see her trying not to roll her eyes.

She took a deep breath. "Everything that I've done, that has been done since we landed here, has been according to protocol. True, we

- 47 -

haven't spread out and explored as much as we originally would have, but we have limited resources. We lost what few modes of transport we had in the crash, and have no way to move out from this base camp other than walking. I'm not willing to risk anyone's safety just yet. We have enough for a few months, and my view is that slow and steady wins the race. Everything that I—that we—have done has been exactly what we were trained to do while we were back on the ship.

"Jonstin here would like you to believe—"

"Wait, wait. Let me speak for myself. Please. What I *know* is that this is not the ship. That this planet is not at all what the researchers on the ship told us it would be. And that we did not land where we were meant to. Not even close. We need to branch out, even if it is a risk, even if we have to walk dozens, hundreds of miles to figure out what's out there. We need to assess as much of the planet as possible, as quickly as possible, to learn what resources are at our disposal. And what dangers might threaten our survival."

Shouts of agreement came from far more people than Smith expected. Two weeks ago, nearly everyone hated the chief pilot. Although, even though Smith hated to admit it, Jonstin made some good points.

"So," Jonstin shouted, "what it comes down to is this: are we going to blindly follow protocol and training, or are we gong to do what we think is right for our futures?"

The crowd erupted in cheers, boos and taunts.

Sylvia pulled the loudspeaker from Jonstin and waved it in the air until everyone quieted down. "That is an oversimplification of what's going on," Sylvia said calmly. "What we have been doing is securing what little we have. We don't have the resources to go off exploring and discovering. We are *surviving*."

"Right." Jonstin raised his voice instead of taking back the speaker. "But, like I said, we could find more resources outside of the small perimeter we have confined ourselves to."

Sylvia nodded. "We could, we could."

Jonstin's face betrayed his surprise, but he quickly composed himself.

"Sylvia, are you agreeing with me?"

"I... I don't know." She put the loud speaker down. "Jonstin, can we go... deliberate? In private?"

He nodded and turned to the crowd. "Sylvia and I are going to go discuss some options. Smith, come join us."

As the three walked into an empty dome, the crowd broke into hushed whispers.

They walked in. Sylvia slammed the door shut, twisted the handle until a click indicated it was completely sealed. No sound would escape the structure.

"What the hell is your play, Jonstin?"

He looked at her innocently and lifted his shoulders in bewilderment.

"We all know there's more to your plan than what you're saying."

Jonstin looked at Smith, his face silently pleading for help.

Smith sat down in a chair and motioned for the other two to do the same. "Jonstin, we've heard you talk about what you would do if you 'were in charge.' Remember?"

Jonstin looked from Sylvia to Smith with raised eyebrows.

"What the hell are you talking about?"

"'H for H had it wrong,'" Sylvia said, repeating the rant they'd heard in that empty restaurant. "'Humanity is worse because we're trying to break down class and race barriers! Different is good, but different also means we all deserve different. Not all equal. Not all one.'"

"W-what?" Jonstin stammered. He stood and paced. "Where did you hear that?"

"You. The restaurant. With Smith, Ev and me."

"What? No, no, I don't believe that. Those... that's my dad talking. Did you find one of his pamphlets or something?"

Smith slightly raised his voice. "What the hell does your dad have to do with this?"

"He was"—Jonstin swallowed hard—"an extreme racist. He spouted shit like that all the time."

Smith and Sylvia exchanged doubtful looks.

"He did. But that's not me."

"Then why were you spouting it all those years ago?"

"When I was drunk?"

"Yeah."

"I was drunk?"

"Being drunk has never been an excuse in any court of law," Sylvia said. "And it's not for this, either."

"Look, look. My dad tried to indoctrinate me with all sorts of racist and bigoted shit since I can remember. When he was gone my mom always told me he was wrong. He was sick."

Jonstin sighed and sat down. He stared at Smith with watery eyes, pleading. "That's not me. Please. If I really was, would H for H have let me on the ship?"

Sylvia looked at the ground, then back up at Jonstin. "That is a fair point," Sylvia acknowledged. "But, look, you did say all that stuff. How you would reinstate segregation and a caste system based on race and wealth."

"My dad said that shit all the time." He shook his head and a few tears dripped out of his eyes, washing away lines of gray dirt that caked his face. "But that's not me."

Smith shook his head and looked at the floor. He had never liked Jonstin, in part, because he was so conceited. But his dislike had turned to a bitter distrust that night at the restaurant.

Sylvia looked him in the eye. "So you're telling us that you don't believe any of it?"

"I don't," he whispered. "I truly don't."

His eyes were dark with pain. They pleaded with Smith and Sylvia to believe him. Smith wanted to. He knew Evalee would believe him in a heartbeat, would have stood up and embraced Jonstin.

"Okay. Okay," Sylvia said. "Let's put that aside for now."

"What?" Smith's eyes flicked to Sylvia.

"Smith, please."

Smith looked away.

Sylvia continued. "Jonstin, there's a bigger problem with what you're trying to do. Sure, I'm kinda pissed about what you're doing. But, in all truth, you bring up some good points."

"Thanks." Jonstin wiped his eyes and straightened his shirt, sitting up taller in the chair.

Smith rolled his eyes.

"But, what you're also doing is dividing us. Whether you win a vote or I do, there will be a large group upset about the outcome. We can't have that division among us. Especially not now."

"You want me to step down?"

"No." She took a deep breath. "Actually, I think what would be best is if we led together."

"What, like the States used to have on Earth? A president and a vice?"

"Maybe," Sylvia said. "The issue though is what happens when we disagree. When we argue. What then?"

Jonstin nodded and scratched his chin.

Smith sighed, closed his eyes and then opened them again. Sylvia was talking like Evalee would have. Damn, if only she were there. Smith wished she would have survived the crash. Everything else could stay just as terrible as it was, but Evalee. *She should be here.*

"Smith?" Jonstin's voice pulled him out of his thoughts. "What do you think?"

"Huh? About what?"

Jonstin chuckled. "I think we need a third. Like a tribunal."

"I like that idea," Smith said.

"So you'll do it?"

"What?"

"Be our third," Sylvia clarified. "Our tiebreaker. Mediator."

"Uh, I... why me?"

"Nearly everyone likes you," Sylvia said. "You're calm. Collected."

"But harsh when you need to be."

"I have no... I...." He paused to catch his breath. "I've never led anyone before."

"You're Chief Farmer," Jonstin said.

"Was," Smith corrected. "On the ship. Now that's Tashon's job."

Tashon. He hoped the young man was doing okay. That the ship was accepting him as the youngest Chief Farmer. If only they had been able to get a signal to the ship after they crashed. Was anyone up there worried about them? Would the ship come back if they didn't get a message out?

"Smith." Sylvia snapped her fingers. "You here?"

"Yeah, Yeah. Sorry."

"Okay," she said. "I know you've never led, Smith. But they—we—all look up to you. We trust your judgment. You're fair. Objective."

Smith nodded a silent thanks and stood, turning his back to them. He sighed. "I need to think."

Sylvia stood and walked to him, placing a hand on his shoulder.

"I need to show you something. Jonstin, come too."

She walked to the door and opened it. Smith and Jonstin stayed where they were.

"Let's go, damn it!"

The two men quickly followed. Smith looked behind him to see if Evalee was coming, but she was not there. His heart dropped. Of course she wasn't there. But her absence still hung around him like the scent of a slowly rotting apple.

Chapter 8

Everyone who was selected to colonize a planet went through rigorous training. Physical, mental, emotional and academic. This on top of what they had gone through to even get on the ship—they had to ensure those colonizing were up to the task. It had always been considered an honor to be selected, and a privilege to participate in the training. It had been so since the first colony ship had left the Ship of Nations.

A few years after the secret to faster-than-light travel was discovered and implemented in small-scale research ships, the Ship of Nations was commissioned by H for H, with various other organizations contributing funds, materials and various workers. The drones and recon bots that were sent out using faster-than-light travel found something that surprised nearly everyone: there were far more habitable planets than expected. Even with faster-than-light travel, though, it would take decades, even centuries, to reach many of those planets.

But to H for H, and many others, it seemed like multiple chances for a fresh start. To begin human life again across the universe, in the hopes that at least some of the planets would not end up like Earth. H for H pulled the best people from any country they could, and recurved funding and aid from the wealthiest nations of the time: France, South Africa, China and Japan. The Canadians supplied what they could, which was mostly the design and outline of the political structure for those that would embark on the ship.

What seemed to be the most unique aspect of that political structure was that, even though many leaders from multiple nations would be living aboard, the ship itself would not be split into sectors based on nationality. Everyone agreed that this would be the best way to promote an environment of compromise, acceptance and understanding. The selected leaders from each nation served on the Board of Leaders. It totaled eleven in all, with leaders and people from countries of varying political and economic standings. They wanted every colonized planet to have a "healthy mix" of everything humanity had to offer. And many of the best came from the more struggling nations. Though they did stop the line at allowing criminals on the ship.

While the intricacies of that plan were worked out, the engineering of the ship was assigned to China and South Africa. It was estimated that the ship would carry one hundred thousand souls and they hoped the ship would stay active for at least five centuries. It had to be durable, self-sustaining and have the capacity to store and build hundreds of colony ships while in motion. And be able to travel at high speeds.

Leading up to the discovery of faster-than-light travel, there was a standard high school debate about what deserved our resources more: the exploration of space or Earth's vast oceans? Within the schools, a student's choice came down to what he or she was most interested in. In the real world it turned out that the ocean had to be explored first to gain the tech to explore space.

In the year 2103, renowned marine biologist Henry Flannigan found a section of the ocean that was deeper than any portion explored before. In a submarine made entirely of pressure-engineered glass, Flannigan and his partner, Matthew Lithen, slowly sank at an angle into what became known as Flannigan's Trench. With bated breath, the world listened to him live-broadcast the descent on various platforms. The recording was still listened to during training on the Ship of Nations. It tended to get everyone excited about what they might discover on a new planet.

"We're now deeper than any human has been before," is the point when everyone started listening to the recording. "It's so dark down here that I can barely tell our lights are on. They're shining into nothing. I mean, there's literally nothing down here for the lights to reflect off of. It appears empty, but I can't shake the sense that something is moving just outside our realm of vision."

It went silent for a painfully long thirty-one seconds.

"Oh crap!"

A few seconds of silence, then laughter.

"Ha! Did you see that, brother?"

"Hell yeah, brother."

"Okay, okay. What we just saw must be the largest bioluminescent creature ever seen. It looked like... like a large floating lizard. Webbed feet. Translucent skin with soft green, glowing stripes. I'd say nearly ten feet long. Damn, that was a beautiful sight."

For the next thirty minutes, the voices on the recording were calm. Periodically, Flannigan would say that it was still dark or wonder out loud if the creature would cross their path again.

"All right, we're slowin' it down. My sensors are telling me we're coming up on some sort of formation. I honestly have no idea what to expect. Stand by while we figure it out."

More silence. Sixty-seven seconds of it.

"Matthew, can you explain what we're looking at?"

"All I can say is it looks like a... ship or something."

"Yeah, yeah. But huge. It doesn't look—hold on."

Twenty-one seconds.

"It doesn't look to be man-made. But it's not natural, either. I don't know. I've never seen anything like it."

After dozens more scientists analyzed and studied the object, they classified it as "alien tech." It appeared to be a spaceship made with materials no one had seen before. After hundreds of hours of labor, three smaller ships were recovered, hauled to land, and subjected to every test imaginable.

On the first day, one of the scientists inadvertently hit a switch in one of the ships. The vessel flickered out of sight and was seen ten minutes later floating outside the South African Orbital Station. The scientist was still in it, alive and well.

Another hundreds of hours of research and experimentation later, the technology in those ships was successfully re-engineered. And humanity could travel faster and farther than ever before.

It soon became known as the tesseract engine. With a fast, high-pitched vibration, it would flash a vessel into the Fourth Dimension. For a moment, the passengers would catch a glimpse of their universe as seen from the Fourth Dimension—a view that disoriented most who saw it. They would simultaneously see in detail from where the vessel has left, where it was going and a paper-like version of the space between. Then they would move, and everything became bright and blurry. Soon, they arrived at their destination.

The way this was explained to those undergoing their academic training on the Ship of Nations was very simplified, but it helped passengers feel safer with the new form of travel.

"Imagine we are in a two-dimensional world," the instructors would say. "There are flat trees, buildings, plants and even empty space that slow us down or block us in our attempt to travel. The tesseract engine pulls us out and above this flat world, into the Third Dimension, in which we can travel across that same distance far more quickly than we otherwise would be able to. In simplified terms, that is how we now accomplish faster-than-light travel. Except we are currently in a complex three-dimensional space, and the engine pulls us into an even more complex fourth."

For those who cared to understand the Fourth Dimension on a deeper level, monthly lectures and discussions were held. Smith and his apprentice, Tashon, were fascinated by the Fourth and went as often as they could.

Each lecture began with a simple picture displayed on a wall.

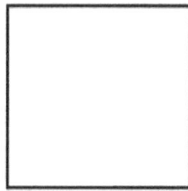

"This is a square," the facilitator, a heavy-set man with glasses, would begin. "A two-dimensional square."

With a smile, he walked back and forth in front of his students.

"For our purposes here, we can think of 'dimension' as 'direction.' So, this is a two-directional square. Its line can move in two directions: north/south and east/west. Or a combination of these, such as northwest."

"A three dimensional, or directional, square is a cube. It gains the extra dimension because it has a new direction to expand into. We call these up/down. But what would this cube look like if it had another direction added to it? We, who live in the Third Dimension, cannot not truly see one of these while we are in the Third. But we can draw a two-dimensional representation of it. Look."

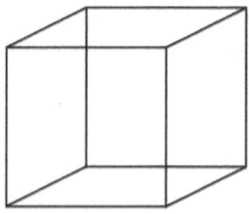

"A cube. Watch as we add representations of this fourth-dimensional direction. Which, by the way, we refer to as ana/kata.

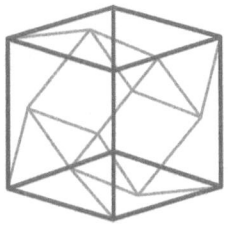

"The cube expands into what we call a tesseract, just as a square expands into a cube. Not only does being in the Fourth allow us to more easily maneuver around objects in the Third, it also provides us with a completely new direction in which to travel.

"While most refer to this as faster-than-light travel, that idea is only partially accurate. While in the Fourth Dimension, the ship only travels faster than the speed of light relative to the speed of light *in the Third Dimension*. In the Fourth Dimension, the ship, objects, waves and even light behave differently than in the Third Dimension. Technically, the ship travels just shy of light speed in connection to the speed of light *in the Fourth Dimension*. But when we drop out of the Fourth and back into the Third, the result is the same as if we had started in the Third Dimension and traveled faster than light while remaining in the Third."

After their first time attending the lecture, Smith and Tashon went out to eat with Evalee and Sylvia in the ship's entertainment sector.

"So the tesseract is the most basic fourth-dimensional shape," Tashon was saying. "Yet we can barely even grasp the idea of it with our three-dimensional minds. Can you imagine what pyramids, or spheres, would look like?"

"Or living beings?" Evalee suggested.

Smith laughed. "That would be something to see. A human body, each part of it stretched out in a completely new direction."

"But if there were beings living in the Fourth, wouldn't we have seen evidence of that?" Sylvia questioned. "I mean, the ship has already traveled through the Fourth."

"But only twice," Smith pointed out. "And think of how many uninhabited and uninhabitable planets we've found. Far more emptiness than life."

"True," Tashon said. "And if Fourth beings do exist, would we want them to know that we do? I mean, wouldn't they be able to destroy us if they wanted to? Like me taking an eraser to a drawing? Or a flame to a painting?"

"But why would these beings be violent?" Evalee wondered. "Just because humans might do that, what makes you say these Fourth beings would?"

"Well," Smith said. "Isn't that how most living creatures would react if something... inferior to them trespassed into their land? Their home?"

Tashon nodded in agreement.

"But they are in a higher physical dimension," Evalee retorted. "Perhaps they also have a higher sense of self-awareness. A higher moral code, a higher way of life."

Smith smiled and looked at his wife. Her perspective never ceased to amaze him.

"Sylvia"—Tashon clapped a hand on the table—"What do you think?"

"If there are beings in the Fourth," Sylvia said. "Then I hope Ev is right. But I think, if there are things alive in the Fourth, they can't all be good. There's no such thing as a perfect place."

***

Once the research bots made successful trips using small tesseract engines, the experts from Japan and South Africa spent over two years making it work for a vessel as large as the Ship of Nations.

The ship was designed to bring human life to the surprising number of habitable planets that had been discovered with the advent of the tesseract engine. When it left Earth, its lower level hangars held ten colony ships, enough to settle five planets. It also held two dozen single passenger ships for mining and excavation.

Anytime they passed an asteroid field or a moon that was in close proximity, the small ships would fly out. The pilots would search for and extract any issuable materials. Eventually, they would have enough materials to build new colony ships as the hangars emptied out.

The planet Smith was on was the sixth to be colonized. The first to use a vessel designed, engineered and built on the Ship of Nations. Most didn't even consider it a risk to fly the new colony ship. After all, it had been built on the most advanced space craft ever made by the greatest minds of all time. And yet it had gone down in flames.

Once the Ship of Nations was in motion, these hangars were on the bottom level, as the ship moved horizontally through the unknown. The level above held all the mechanics. Pipes and ducts that supplied oxygen, cooling and heating and any other gases or fuels they might need. At the very center sat the tesseract engine, surrounded by multiple walls made of pressurized steel alloy. The engine was built to be part of the ship. It wasn't attached but was itself an appendage to the ship, with no seams, welds or bolts holding it in place. During their studies, the engineers noticed this in the found tesseract ships. After trials, they found that the engine had to be this way. For it to move a vessel the way they needed it to, the engine needed to be fully integrated into the structure. Otherwise, only the engine would end up at the intended destination.

The next level up was the farm sector that Smith knew so well. It had been placed there, just below the many levels of housing. Pipes from every kitchen and relief room in the ship ran to tanks that sat under the topsoil. As time went on, soil was created from the decomposed waste and then moved to the top so that crops could continue to grow. On the surface, this seemed like a filthy idea, but dozens of biochemicals flushed through the tanks to speed up the composting and ensure the best possible soil was used.

The housing sector covered the next eleven floors. Just as the Canadians had planned, no one group, nationality or race was combined. There was no "China Town" or "French District" or "Little Italy." Every section of every floor had a "healthy mix" of human life. No one floor, no one housing unit was larger or of higher quality than another. The goal was to create a feeling of equality. A functioning society without greed or jealousy. But, as has been proven time and again, humans are often naturally greedy and jealous.

Even with these equalizing structures in place, everyone still had a role to play. Engineers were housed by educators, who were housed by ship security. No one group or person was intended to be higher than or lead another. Naturally, though, groups began to form. No one was forced to stay in a specific section or on a specific floor, so in many cases it turned into a hierarchy based on what one's role on the ship was.

This created a culture that had only been partially expected. Originally, the security and control personnel were meant to keep an eye out for anything that could lead to protests, riots or violence. And then they were to stop it before it got to that point. No one wanted a civil war to break out aboard a thirty-story state-of-the-art ship that could shift between dimensions and travel faster than light.

After a couple years, though, those in security became the rulers of the housing and business sectors. Sure, the board was around, but they only concerned themselves with big decisions like what planets to colonize and when to jump to faster-than-light travel. For a few months, it became a violent society with security controlling everything and everyone. Since there was no clear leader within each section, security took it upon themselves to put themselves in complete control. They remained undiscovered for a time because one of their roles was the control and monitoring of all surveillance.

But, as always seems to happen, a few of them flew too close to the sun. They tried to take out the board. To take control of the entire ship. They failed, and the board discovered what the security personnel had been doing. All who were involved were loaded into the first colony ship and sent to a planet that was barely habitable. They would live, but in extreme conditions.

It was then that the board decided having leaders and a hierarchy of power might not be a bad idea. People could be evil, but a position in and of itself could not. The difficult part was finding people who would be effective leaders. From then on, every occupation would have its own chief. And each chief went through a rigorous interview process before obtaining the title. In time, chiefs became some of the most respected individuals on the ship.

There were multiple chiefs throughout the ship: engineering, farming, communications, safety, food preparation and delivery, maintenance, mining, piloting, education, tesseract engine, physical health, emotional health and entertainment. Chiefs were given the responsibility to lead each sector. To delegate, control and police as they saw fit. If one chief did something another had issue with, it was brought up with the board. This rarely happened, as most chiefs respected each other's positions. The only chief to consistently receive complaints was the entertainment chief.

Many chiefs and citizens on the Ship of Nations were concerned that every Chief of Entertainment allowed prostitution. Every couple of years, the topic would land on the board's lap. Brothels were not discussed in the planning of the ship, whether for or against. Any unforeseen instance such as this was to be reviewed by the board and put to a vote. Of the eleven board members, five had home countries with legalized prostitution and five did not. The eleventh had legalized prostitution only in certain areas. For a vote to win, at least eight of the board had to agree. Since that never happened, the issue of prostitution would be put to the side until someone else brought forth a complaint.

But overall, the implementation of occupation chiefs was successful. It set forth an acceptable hierarchy that most citizens respected, and those who did not respect it tolerated it. Then, of course, there were those who directly went against it. Anyone who did so in a way that caused anyone harm was put in isolation for at least two days, all the way up to a decade, depending on the crime. As far as anyone knew, no one had ever been murdered. But if someone did murder, and was caught, all agreed that the murderer would be sent out an airlock.

Above all the housing, business, and occupation sectors was the top floor — the only one with windows and a view of the deep dark of outer space. It was always open to citizens, except for an hour before the Tesseract Engine would be engaged until an hour after the ship dropped back into the Third Dimension. This had also been implemented after the ship began its journey.

The first time that the Tesseract Engine was engaged, nearly everyone aboard the Ship of Nations crammed themselves on the top floor, anxious to see what it would look like. As expected, the engine performed flawlessly. But more than half of those who witnessed the shift to the Fourth suffered extreme vertigo. This caused vomiting and falling, which led to multiple head injuries. Since then, any citizen not directly involved with the operation of the engine was confined to their living quarters during Tesseract travel.

This was the history of the ship that chosen colonizers received at the beginning of their training. After that, they spent mornings undergoing intense physical training. During the afternoons, and often into the nights, they studied, analyzed and discussed the colonization plan, with little talk of what to do in the event of a crash landing. All they were told to do in such a situation was to stay as close to training as possible. Do not deviate from their given colonization plan unless necessary.

Each colonization plan was the same as the previous, with minor changes based on what they knew of the planet. On the first three colonizations, everyone wore full protective suits for at least seventy-two hours. No one knew how breathable the oxygen was, and they were each sent with ninety-six hours' worth. Plenty of time to get their domes set up, pressurized and oxygenated. Other than a few close calls, those first three went surprisingly well.

The fourth group to leave was sent out with protective suits that doubled as wet suits. Their preliminary tests showed that it rained often and at times 90 percent of the surface was covered in water. During the dry season, it dropped to 72 percent. This was the colony that suffered devastating hurricanes that destroyed more than half of their domes.

According to the video updates that were sent, the fifth group of colonizers to leave had the most success. They were the first ones to go an entire year with no casualties, despite a drought that limited their edible crops. To counteract that, they learned to hunt local wildlife.

Then there was the ship Smith and his family had been on. The first to not arrive safely. The first that ever had to question whether following protocol was the best move.

Chapter 9

Sides had already formed when the three walked back out into the crowd. Chants for Jonstin and Sylvia rang out. Sylvia gave a nod to the people and kept walking. Jonstin paused and waved with a big smile, telling everyone that they were going on a walk and would soon return.

Smith tried to follow Sylvia but was stopped by nearly everyone he passed. They wanted to know his thoughts. The one thing he didn't like about his position as a chief was the respect it gave him. He never felt he deserved it. But the more people began to stop and question him, the more he realized that he was going to have to play a more active role than he had planned. He and Jonstin were the only original chiefs left from the ship. And Sylvia, while having proven herself an invaluable asset, would be hard-pressed to gain the trust of everyone. Especially those who had been close to the original captain.

"I have to think it through," Smith told yet another curious family. "They honestly both bring up good points."

He pushed past them and went after Sylvia, Jonstin following close behind. She had gone toward the perimeter, and Smith caught a glimpse of her as she walked through the gate and toward where Smith had heard the screeching coming from. And where he had seen those smoke creatures running.

"Where the hell we going, Syl?"

"After you told me what you heard out here, I couldn't stop thinking about it. Last night I came to check it out."

"You did what?" Smith asked.

"You find something?" Jonstin asked, curiosity entering his voice.

Smith started paying more attention to where they were going. Ahead of them, the ground gradually rose to a small hill. Just high enough so that he couldn't see what was on the other side. The sun hung in the sky to the right of the hill, a glowing orange ball in the sky. Smith briefly squinted at it, trying to remember all he had studied about the planet back on the ship. The sun would set in three, maybe four hours. If the information they had about the planet's rotation around its sun was accurate. So far, what they had learned about the planet from outside its atmosphere had been far from correct. He strained his ears, listening for the smallest chirp. All he heard was the wind.

"I wanted to assess what happened. See if there might be a danger to all of us."

Smith sighed. "Yeah, and you could have lost an ear too."

"Smith, I'm fine. Come on. It's right over this hill."

"You want to tell us what 'it' is?" Jonstin asked tersely.

The farmer sighed and kept walking, scratching his scruff that had only grown longer since they landed. They started up the incline and he felt his legs strain against the pull of gravity. He wondered if he would get used that. Wondered if the ground where Evalee lay was slowly pulling her deeper and deeper. Imagined what it would be like to lie next to her as she did.

They got to the top. Smith looked down, hoping to see something that would explain everything.

It was a small crater, about twenty feet across. With a quick glance, Smith saw green and silver pieces scattered across it. He crouched down to get a closer look and found that there were hundreds of small chunks that had come from the biotech beetles. Instinctively, Smith pressed a palm against his head. Could one of them really be inside his head? His skull pulsed against the pressure of his hand. Smith stood up, shook his head back and forth. Told himself nothing was there, that it was all psychological. Still, a throbbing pain spread across his head.

Sylvia called for the two men to walk to the center of the scene. Smith jogged toward to meet her, while Jonstin stepped cautiously across the soil. In the middle of it all was a hole about two feet across. He peered into it, but there was no discernible bottom. A soft green glow emanated from the hole, slowly blinking brighter and dimmer, brighter and dimmer.

"And then there's this over here, Smith."

Jonstin shook his head. "Of course there's more."

They joined her on the other side. On the ground were six gleaming metal rods, an inch thick and rounded at the ends. One was three feet long, and the other five only half that length. They were arranged in a way that made them look like a kid's stick-figure drawing.

"Well, damn," Smith said. "This doesn't help us at all."

"Right. And it only makes Jonstin's points more valid. We don't know what's out past our little camp. Helpful or detrimental."

"Thank you for that, Sylvia," Jonstin said, hesitantly looking at the ground.

The three looked down at the metal stick figure. Smith crouched down, reached out to touch one of the rods. As his hand got close, he sensed a small vibration coming from it. He pulled away and stood up.

"This creeps me the hell out, Syl," Smith said.

"Yeah," she said, then laughed. "Never thought I'd see you scared of something."

Smith laughed. "Well, now you can die happy."

"That'd be funnier if I didn't feel like you might actually die from a biotech bug burrowing into your brain," Sylvia said.

Smith thought about that, scratched his scruff, and started to chuckle.

Sylvia glared at him, and then joined him.

Smith shook his head but couldn't stop himself. It wasn't a hysterical laughing. But the kind of laugh when one realizes the ridiculous state of his life. There he was, a few days after his wife had died, standing over a graveyard of biotech insects and the only suspect of their murder was a metal stick figure. Again, he felt the skin above his ear. Was that a bump? He slowed his breaths, tried not to think about it. Though it was impossible not to think how there might be a foreign body — an insect — living in his brain.

"I don't think I've laughed since we got here," Jonstin said.

Smith turned his gaze to Jonstin. "You've done plenty of smiling though."

Jonstin twisted a hand in the air. "Just politics."

Sylvia shook her head.

Smith rolled his eyes. He considered questioning Jonstin about the comment, but decided against it. Smith caught his breath. "What's the plan then?"

"Nearly everyone here respects you," Sylvia said.

"That's what everyone keeps saying."

"You know, back on the ship, we had more than just one leader. The board. All the occupation chiefs."

Smith nodded. It made sense to have the three of them work together to make decisions on what would be best for their small portion of humanity. "Okay. So the three of us."

"Exactly. I think everyone will go for it too. It's better than making nearly half the people upset that their person didn't win. And then Jonstin will have to go along with it."

"Okay, then. It's better than letting Jonstin run it all by himself."

"Exactly. And this way we can keep a close eye on him."

"Yeah. Enemies closer."

"I'm right here," Jonstin said and tossed his hands in the air.

"We need to put the tribunal to a vote, though," Sylvia said. "We can't give the impression that we're taking control away from the people."

Smith smiled, turned and started back toward the camp without another word. Sylvia quickly followed, and Jonstin soon caught up. None of them noticed that the metal rods had begun to hover slightly above the ground.

***

The vote was unanimous. The people agreed that having three leaders with differing views, who were willing to work together, made sense. That, in order to create an atmosphere of understanding, the leaders would first need to be that example. Although Smith doubted that Jonstin would be able to hold up his end as a respectable leader. Once the decision was made, everyone followed the three new leaders to the cemetery.

The sun was setting behind the red mountains to the east, casting orange rays through wispy clouds. It looked as though the mountains were burning, the flames reaching up to lick the sky. What had been a soft breeze grew into forceful gusts that sent shivers through Smith.

They arrived and everyone gravitated to the graves of those they'd been closest to. It was obvious that no one was unaffected by the deaths that had been suffered. Some stood, arms folded or in pockets, staring at the burning sky. Others squatted, their fingers brushing the gray dirt that covered the bodies of the lost.

Smith and the other two sat next to each other on a crate full of tools. Jonstin and Sylvia looked at him expectantly. He had suggested the service, but hadn't planned anything to say. He stood up with a cough.

"You know," he said. "I got lots of kind words from you all today. Thanks for that."

The crowd answered with nods and a few shouts.

"Look, if you know me, you know I'm not a talker. I keep more to myself. Even if I like you, I won't talk to you much. Ev was good at that, though."

More affirmation from the crowd.

"And I guess that's why I wanted us all to meet. To remember the 'was.' Ev was...."

He felt it all coming to the surface, wanted to shove it down. To turn and walk away, leave the speeches to Jonstin and Sylvia.

"Ev was kind!" someone yelled from the crowd.

"Strong!" shouted another.

"A badass!"

"Beautiful!"

"Great mom!" Smith heard Abe scream. "But sometimes a pain in the ass!"

The crowd erupted, all yelling what Ev had meant to them. Leader. Mentor. Healer. Hero. It lasted nearly three minutes before Smith finally lifted a hand to quiet them.

"Damn straight she was."

Smith walked to the grave closest to him, looked at the name scratched into a piece of shrapnel.

"Neeko was...." he began.

The crowd shouted for Neeko the same they had for Ev. This continued, Smith moving from grave to grave. The people sharing what that person was. Kind. Stubborn. Clever. Clumsy. Happy. Beautiful. And on and on.

By the time they got to the last grave, the sun had set, and the moon was halfway through its journey across the sky. But no one left. They stood there in silence, looking at Smith. The farmer had no words, so he turned to his fellow leaders.

Jonstin's cheeks were wet with tears and he stifled a cough. "Is Fritz around?"

Fritz shouted and waved a hand in the air.

Jonstin smiled through the grief. "Come up with the harmonica. Play something you think we'll know the words to."

Fritz slowly made his way to the front amidst a few shouts of encouragement. A woman followed close behind carrying a child-sized guitar.

"What're we gonna play?" she asked Fritz.

"That one from The Almost Homeless. 'These Damn Days.' Know it?"

"Hell yeah," she said. "Everyone, sing along if you know this one."

She began to slowly pluck out a melody that pulled tears from Smith's eyes after just five notes. The last time he'd heard the song had been just before the bomb collapsed his apartment building. The harmonica soon joined in, the two instruments weaving together a melody that, despite its simplicity, emanated a somber air that rolled through the entire crowd.

Someone choked next to Smith, and he turned to see Jonstin quietly sobbing. The pilot caught Smith looking, gave a smile, and turned away.

"Let's go." Fritz began to sing.

> Okay, okay, okay.
> What is there to say about these days?
> (These damn days)
> Everything moving in so many ways.
> But, but
> (Oh! These damn days.)
> All those ways seem to lead
> To places deeper, darker,
> Than we ever thought we'd see.
> (Damn, these days!)
> There's those knockin' down walls,
> Only to have some big man
> Put 'em up again.
> (Damn, Damn, Damn)
> And others fightin'
> To keep a job
> That pays just enough
> To live in some shitty shack,
> And feed your kids
> Half a meal a day.
>
> Man, damn these days.
>
> And then the powers,
> The powers that be,
> Bitch in their castles
> Over things they can't see.
> Every damn day.
> And the rest of us
> Eat
> Sleep
> Cry,

Fight
Bleed
And die.
Damn
These
Days.

The singing stopped. The instruments continued, the only sounds around. The sounds of a dying America reminded Smith of why he had left in the first place. And he wondered whether it was worth it. If he had never decided to leave, he never would have met Ev. He would still be on Earth, alone but not heartbroken and soulless. *Which hell is worse?* He looked through the crowd and saw Abe, tears running down his cheeks and a thin smile on his face. Despite the pain of losing his benevolent Ev, he knew which hell he'd rather be in.

The ground underneath their feet shook. The harmonica and guitar stopped as the people shouted and looked around, eyes wide and still wet with tears. As the speed of the vibrations increased, Sylvia yelled for everyone to get inside a dome, but it was too late.

A high-pitched, grinding vibration came at them from all directions. Smith looked in the direction of the crater. The pulsing green glow had become a vibrant dome of bright emerald light. The ground buzzed under their feet and before Smith could get to Abe, they were surrounded by vibrant light and speeding shadows.

PART TWO

Chapter 10

With Farmer Smith gone, Apprentice Tashon was to become the youngest chief the Ship of Nations had ever seen. He stood on the top floor of the ship with all eleven members of the board, the expanse of space spreading out behind him through the towering windows. A large crowd quietly observed the proceedings. He wore the ceremonial robes of the Chief Farmer. Brown and form-fitting, they were the humblest of all the chief robes.

The appointment of a new chief was one of the few times all members of the board were together in a public area. It had been this way since the rebel security team attempted their hostile takeover. But the chiefs were highly respected public figures, and no one would dare disrupt an appointment ceremony. At least no one ever had before.

"Apprentice Tashon," a woman said. She was thin and tall, with a tight face. The board member of Japan. "You realize the responsibility of this position?"

"Yes, Madam Tiffany," he formally responded. "To ensure that none on the ship go hungry. To ensure that all crops are vibrant and healthy, nourishing to both body and soul."

Madam Tiffany nodded and stepped back in line.

Another board member stepped forward, the one from France. His beard reached his waist. It was Johann, the man Tashon respected more than anyone besides Smith. The young chief had personally requested that Johann be the one to officiate the ceremony.

Johann had been friends with Tashon's dad when he was a kid. Back then, Johann was the chief of security. Tashon would stay up for hours, listening to Johann's stories of his time on Earth. The man had been a captain in the French United Army. A decorated hero. One of only five to receive the United Nations Medal of Valor. As a kid, Tashon asked to hear the story of that medal every time he saw Johann.

"It was another frozen night in the wilds of Russia," Johann would start in a whisper. "We'd been tracking the movements of the Georgian neo-Nazis for two weeks. Believe me, I wanted to jump out and start killing those monsters since we first found them. But they had about twenty kids with them that they'd taken from an orphanage in Moscow. They'd been taking orphans and turning them into soldiers for years. So we had to be careful.

"One night I was scouting out their camp. I saw a soldier slap a young girl across the face. This man's eyes were empty, dark. The kind of people who made me decide to leave Earth. He turned to a young boy and handed him a knife. Told the boy to slit the girl's throat. If he didn't, the man would shoot both. Like any good boy would, he refused. Before the soldier got his gun out, my knife was flying through the air. I was right behind the knife. It hit the man's neck, and I caught him before he hit the ground.

"I ran those two kids back to our camp. Took a few friends of mine back to the enemy camp. By morning, all those monsters were either dead or tied up."

Even though he was a board member with a graying beard, Tashon couldn't help but visualize the badass soldier he knew Johann had once been. Tashon turned his attention back to the ceremony.

"Tashon, we've known each other a long time," Johann said with his raspy French accent. "And I always knew you would do great things. But nineteen and already a chief? I never expected you to be this impressive."

Tashon and the crowd laughed.

"But here you are, with gleaming praise from our beloved Chief Smith. And so" — Johann reached a shaky hand into his coat pocket to pull out a small white box — "it is the pleasure, not just of the board, but the entire Ship of Nations, that you be our next great Chief Farmer."

He opened the box and pulled out a rectangular pin with the farming ensign etched into it — a stock of corn with nanotech circling it, forming the universal symbol for an atom.

"Unless anyone has reasonable belief that Tashon will not hold this position with honor, I name Tashon Tanger our new Chief Farmer."

The board clapped and the crowd cheered as the pin was placed on Tashon's robe, right over his heart. The young man stood up straight, nodded to each board member and turned to wave at the crowd.

"Thank you! Thank you," he said as he walked away from the board toward the back end of the ship, shaking hands as he went.

He made his way quickly to a back exit, where a young woman with vibrant red hair waited. The closer Tashon got to her, the faster he walked.

"Grace," he said, trying to catch his breath. "You find anything out yet?"

"No, nothing new. We need to talk about what to do next. Still good to meet at Wench's?"

"Yeah. Got Mister Johann comin', too."

"No way! Didn't think you'd swing that one, Tash." She roughed his hair. "I gotta stop by the lab. I'll see ya there."

"Hey! You mustn't mess with a chief's hair!"

"Hey," she scoffed as she walked away. "You'll always be my little bro. I can do whatever I want to your hair."

"See ya, sis." He waved after her.

Rubbing his hair back into place, Tashon took a deep breath and walked to the nearest elevator.

The ship was lined with elevators on both sides, spaced exactly one hundred twenty-five yards apart. Tashon sometimes wished they were closer, but knew they were that way for a reason. The same reason there were no moving walkways and the only forms of powered transportation were reserved for the ill and elderly—it was the engineer's way of keeping the ship's population more active and healthy. Although it was possible to live entirely in one's own living quarters, having food delivered daily. And some did. Tashon had tried that, but only lasted for two cycles before he needed to smell the farm again.

He got to an elevator, its cylindrical door protruding from the wall. With a sigh, he saw that his ride was currently on level 5. The elevators moved slow, and he was going to have to wait at least five minutes, or walk to the next one and try his luck there.

His wrist buzzed, and he looked down at the thin, rectangular screen. It was a voice message. He touched a button to listen. The bearded face of Johann lifted out of the screen. His lips moved, and Tashon heard the voice through the mini speaker attached behind his left ear. No one else would hear what was being said.

"Congratulations again, Chief Farmer. I—"

He was cut off by a voice in the background, and yelled at it to shut up. Tashon thought the voice had said something about a defect.

"Can't meet at Wench's. Same time, at Jenza's."

A soft beep, and the glowing face disappeared. *Jenza's?* Tashon thought. *Why the hell at Jenza's?* It was nearly eight hundred yards from Wench's and had far worse food. Tashon was sure he'd heard Johann complain about the place numerous times. And hadn't the old

Frenchmen even tried to get it shut down? The waitresses were prettier at Jenza's, sure. But that was the only thing it had going for it. Tashon shrugged his shoulders and sent a message to Grace about the change.

The elevator door notified him that it had only moved up four levels. Another twenty-one to go. It must have got stuck loading or unloading a large group. After all, each elevator could carry up to thirty-five people. He decided it made more sense to cross to the other side and walk the seven hundred fifty yards to the elevator closest to Jenza's. With a sigh, he turned and started moving.

Tashon hated walking. It wasn't that he was lazy. He would just rather spend his time crouching and bending over his crops. Ensuring they were growing just right. Taste testing them. Getting rid of any and all blemishes. He would never admit it, but he enjoyed the process because it made him feel better about himself in some way. If he couldn't fix his personal faults, at least he could make the crops perfect. As Chief Farmer, he now had access to the farm anytime he pleased. He wished he could spend his entire life with the soil, plants and nanotech. First, though, he had to figure out why Smith's colony hadn't sent a single update from Aethera in the two weeks since they left the ship. And more importantly, why no one on the board had made a single comment about it. It was killing Tashon. It had been hard enough sending his mentor off, knowing they would never see each other again. But then to not hear from anyone on the planet? To be left to wonder why no message had been sent, fighting to not imagine the worst? Tashon had to figure out what was going on.

The Ship of Nations had come out of the Fourth far enough away from Aethera to not risk entering its atmosphere. As with previous colony ships, it would have taken two days for Smith's group to land on the planet. Protocol and tradition dictated that they wait one day before jumping back into the Fourth and moving onward. And that's exactly what they did.

After that day had passed, the engineers set a course for the nearest resource belt they could find. They had just sent off their last colony ship and needed to mine for more materials. Thankfully, the belt they found had more than enough M-type asteroids to meet their needs. They had spent the last two weeks outside the belt while mining pilots flew drones to the asteroids to harvest nickel and iron.

Once the metals were back on the ship, they were sent to the manufacturing section of the hangar. Using these materials, an electron beam gun would form each part needed for the colony ship. Once each part was completed, the ship would be assembled manually by the engineers.

The top floor was the most open on the ship. With rounded ceilings that stretched nearly fifty feet high and nothing around but elevators and a line of benches down the middle, it seemed even larger than it was. If he had to walk, Tashon preferred doing it there. It was easier to avoid getting drowned in a large group. *Another plus*, he thought, *for Jenza's is that it's never crowded.*

The farther he got from the front of the ship, the more the crowds thinned out and the more he noticed the people around him. Some kids running around trying to tag each other, a woman watching and laughing. Further down was a small apple tree at the end of a bench. Tashon's assistants were assigned to take care of it, along with any other live plants not in the farm.

Next to the tree stood a few young men, all about the same age as Tashon. One of them was talking excitedly as the others hung on his every word. Tashon couldn't hear what he was saying, nor did he care. As he walked by two of the boys nodded and gave a quiet, "Congratulations, Chief Farmer," to which Tashon nodded back a silent thank you.

Soon, Tashon arrived at his favorite part of the ship, besides the farm. It had become known simply as "the hole." It was just that, a hole nearly ten yards across. It was in the exact center of the top floor, surrounded by a five-foot tall glass wall. The hole was in the middle of the top twenty-eight floors of the ship. Looking over the glass wall provided Tashon a sense of freedom he found nowhere else. He could catch a glimpse of nearly every sector, allowing him to get a sense of how vast and diverse the ship truly was. For a moment, he would feel as though he could see the entire ship at once: the family playing cards together, the young couple fighting, the old woman reading alone, the jaded man enjoying a drink with a friend outside his living space, the young boy learning that life is more complicated than he could have ever imagined. And countless others. Thousands of lives, a whole world, living inside a giant, man-made vessel floating across the vastness of the universe.

Tashon smiled, turned from "the hole," and continued on his way to Jenza's.

The elevator was packed on its way down. Tashon counted twenty-seven people other than him. All adults. Technically seven more bodies could have fit, but Tashon felt like there were fifteen too many. Someone tapped his shoulder. He turned around.

An old woman stood next to him, smiling. Her teeth were startling white, and her eyes a deep blue. She was broad, maybe an inch taller than Tashon. "Smith was the best chief we ever had," she said quietly, with a sense of reverence. "If you're anything like him, you'll be great."

Tashon nodded. "Thank you, ma'am. I would be happy to be half the man he is."

She nodded, then put her hand on his shoulder. "You seem good to me, hun."

He was about to thank her, but someone pushed through the crowd toward him.

"He don't seem good to me," a young woman hissed. She was about his age and wore a crisp suit that resembled the suit engineers wore, except it was a heavy gray. The color that, during the reign of the security officers, was worn by those lowest on the totem pole. This ensemble, with her jet-black pixie cut, gave her a deathly look. She wore glasses with an all-white frame.

She got in his face. "In fact, I *know* he's no good." She stepped back an inch or two.

She was still close enough for Tashon to see a small black speck stuck in between her gritted teeth and smell her sweet perfume. "Ma'am," he said.

"Oh, don't *ma'am* me."

He could feel his adrenaline rising. "*Girl.* You don't know me."

"Don't have to. You were trained by Smith. Sure you're just as bad as him and all the other chiefs."

"You watch your damn tongue, honey," the old woman chimed in.

The rest of the passengers had turned to watch the three.

"What?" Tashon didn't know what else to say. He'd never heard anyone disrespect Smith or any other chiefs, except maybe Jonstin. And that was just because he was conceited, not for any evil reason.

"You, all the chiefs. The board. Engineers. So-called scientists. You're all destroying the universe."

Tashon took a step back. "What are you talking about?"

In one blindingly fast motion her arm was outstretched, a small knife in her hand. The blade caught Tashon's collar bone and slid across his chest.

He felt the skin split apart, the blood trickle down his chest. It burned, stung. Throbbed. He pushed her away, then pressed his palm against the cut.

The old woman grabbed the girl's wrist with both hands. "Damn kids today. No damn respect." She quickly jerked the girl's hand one way and her wrist the other. The bone snapped with an audible crunch.

The girl let out a short, loud scream.

Some of the onlookers gasped.

The elevator dinged, and the doors swished open.

Silence. For a moment, no one moved.

Tashon glanced around. He realized that some in the crowd held their comm devices up, filming the scene.

"Go get yourself checked, Chief Farmer," the older woman said. "These idiots have been using poison. I'll take this specific idiot to Security."

She walked out, yanking the girl behind. It reminded Tashon of being a kid when his mom would grab him by the arm and pull him out of a store for misbehaving. He took a few breaths and stepped out, the ground feeling shaky beneath his feet. A man walked up beside him and put his hand on his shoulder. A woman steadied him on the other side.

"We'll help you get to medical, Chief Tashon," the woman said kindly.

"Thanks," he said through labored breaths.

It was strange, getting this sort of attention. Just the day before, when he wasn't chief, no one would have said hi while he walked around. It wasn't that he had been disliked, he just hadn't been someone of importance. But now, teens said hi and congratulated him. The elder generation told him how he looked like Smith did all those years ago. And now two complete strangers were helping him when he wasn't sure he needed the help.

There was no way it was a serious injury, he thought. The knife hadn't been that large, and Tashon could tell the cut wasn't that deep. He probably wouldn't even need stitches. And there was no way someone would poison a chief. Was there? *No way,* he told himself. And besides, his legs were probably just shaking from the adrenaline.

"You still with us, Chief Farmer?" The man broke into Tashon's thoughts.

"Yeah, all here. Hey," he said. "For now, just call me Tashon. Not used to chief."

"Uh, sure."

"Thanks."

"Not me," the woman said. "You are Chief Farmer Tashon. Better get used to it."

The man sighed and started to speak.

The woman beat him to it. "No, we will both call him by his proper title. Look, something just happened that never has. Sure, people have spoken out against the chiefs. But no one has ever assaulted one before. We can't let anyone else lose their respect for you or any other chief."

"Looks like I'll end up in the history books, ma'am." Tashon laughed.

"This isn't funny," the woman scolded. "If this girl is part of a larger group like she claims, we could have some big problems."

Tashon and the man fell silent, pondering her words. The intensity of it cleared Tashon's head and he stood up straight.

"I'm feeling okay. I think I can walk on my own."

The two cautiously let go of him, but he stayed upright.

"Thanks. Will you still walk with me, though?"

A sense of fear had entered Tashon. What if they went at him again? It didn't seem like he'd been poisoned. Maybe the girl had botched her mission and someone would try to get him again.

"Of course," the man and woman answered at the same time.

Tashon nodded and took a moment to actually look at his saviors. The man looked about ten years older and the same height as Tashon. He had no hair to speak of and brown eyes speckled with black.

"Name's James," he said.

The woman was about a foot shorter with white-blonde hair that hung to her waist. She had thin lips and a smile that comforted Tashon.

"And I'm Theresa."

Tashon simply nodded and looked around as he kept walking. They were on the eatery side of the entertainment level. Every building was the exact same size. Fifty by fifty feet inside, with a fenced patio half that size. This had originally been done to ensure equality among each establishment but, as could have been expected, some did better than others. After a couple decades, the more successful restaurants bought the failing ones that surrounded them. Soon, most restaurants spread across two to five buildings. Jenza's was one of a handful that still occupied a single building, continually refusing offers.

Tashon heard a whirling coming at him and his head whipped around, thinking it might be someone trying to take another shot at him. It was two men in red, riding a white, hovering tandem bike. Medics.

"Chief Tashon," one said as they rolled to a stop. "We've been ordered to give you a full workup."

Tashon looked at the med crates on their bike. "Sir, do you have everything you need to do that here?"

"Well, I guess. But we're supposed to escort you back to the main medic station."

"No, too far. I have a meeting with Board Member Johann in five. At Jenza's. Give me the checkup there."

"Sure, Chief. But, uh, what about other guests eating there? Don't you want some privacy?"

"Have you eaten there? I don't think we need to worry about other guests."

"Point taken. Uh, what about these two?"

"James and Theresa helped me right after. I think they should come so they can tell Johann what they saw."

He looked at the two to confirm, and they both nodded.

"Copy that, Chief. Let's get you checked out."

Chapter 11

The medics had gone. They'd found nothing irregular in their scans and blood tests, so they left Tashon at Jenza's with James and Theresa. Tashon had a small bandage on his chest and the bleeding had stopped. Tashon had asked his new friends why they thought it hadn't been poisoned. They couldn't think of any reason that made sense.

They sat in a small corner booth, waiting for Johann and Grace, watching a hologram screen that expanded from a small circle on the table. It was a newscast playing a steady stream of civilian videos showing the attack on Tashon. In every video, the attacker's face was obscured by a bright light. The glasses she wore had apparently been sending out a signal that hid her face on any recording device. Thankfully, the older woman apprehended her.

Tashon wanted to look away but couldn't. Over and over he saw himself slashed, heard his confused grunt, saw the fear and confusion in his own face. Saw himself do nothing but stand there and let the violent older woman take care of the problem for him.

The newscast turned to a spokeswoman. "We are still digging into this group. It is unclear at this point if the attacker is part of a larger group, although the older woman's comments seem to suggest that is the case. She has not yet been located, but many are applauding her actions."

The broadcast went on to a montage of witnesses who had been on the elevator.

"It was insane," a teen said. "I mean, this crazy bitch stabs the new chief. Like, who would do that shit? And that old woman. She was badass, man. She broke the bitch's wrist like it's nothin'."

"I'm still in shock," said a man who identified himself as a historical professor. "Our chiefs are great figures in our society. Why would someone risk, or even want, to attack one? Especially our youngest one, who will surely bring new ideas and innovations. Changes that the rising generation will surely approve of. It doesn't make sense. But thankfully that beast of an old lady was there. If it weren't for her, I bet the attacker would have gotten away."

Then a middle-aged woman, holding a toddler in her arms. "That lady was right, too many of these young kids got no respect for authority, even if it's someone their own age. I mean, that girl had to be nearly the same age as our wonderful new chief. I just hope it's not a sign of worse to come. Looking at that girl, she reminded me of the Anarchy Brigade back on Earth I learned about in my studies."

The focus was back on the spokeswoman. "This is a terrifying thought, and I know most of us hope that is not the case. It's time for us to go on break, but we will report more as updates arrive."

Tashon hit a button and the hologram disappeared back into the table.

James coughed. "Your sister and Board Member Johann were meeting you?"

"Yes, sir. They messaged me. Security is questioning Grace. Johann got called into an emergency board meeting. They should both be here soon."

Theresa shook her head. "Acts of violence are so rare on the ship. And against the most promising Chief Farmer we've ever had? It's more than stupid. It's insane. I'm convinced that girl is simply not right in the head."

Tashon nodded, unsure of how to take the compliment. He didn't feel like he was that promising of a chief, nor did he want to be. All he wanted was to improve on the exceptional farming system Smith had created and spend most of his time doing so. He didn't want all the attention that often came with being a chief, but it was looking like that would become unavoidable.

James wrapped his knuckles on the table. "Let's hope she's insane and this group of hers is just all in her head."

Tashon ran a hand through his hair. "Sir, now that is something I could drink to."

Tashon waved the lone waitress over. She'd been sneaking glimpses at Tashon while she pretended to wipe tables. In seconds, she was at his side.

"What do you need, Chief?" Her smile was vibrant, her eyes hazel.

She looked at Tashon in a way no girl ever had. Was she flirting with him? Pitying him? He couldn't tell.

"I've never drank," Tashon finally said. "Alcohol, I mean. But I hear it's good for times like this."

"I'll get you our house special. We brew it right on site with our mini distiller in the back."

James ordered the same.

Theresa shook her head. "I don't do intoxicants. Neither should you, Chief."

"Chief Smith always said that, too."

"And now he's gone and you're Chief Farmer, and you can do what you want?"

"I guess. But it's not...." Tashon faltered. "Look, someone just attacked me and it's all over everyone's comms and I'm kinda going insane and I don't know what the hell to do."

Someone walked toward them. "Well, you're sure as hell not going to be drinking."

Tashon turned toward the new voice. His sister. Of course.

"C'mon, Grace," he said.

"Hell no, Tash. I don't give one crap if you're a chief now." She turned to the waitress. "Don't you dare bring him anything but water."

Tashon sighed and dropped his forehead onto the table. The surface was sticky, like it hadn't been cleaned in a few days. But at that moment he didn't care. He closed his eyes but all he could see was that girl's face. The sound of her wrist cracking echoed in his ears. Grace sat next to him, wrapped her arm around his shoulders. *Don't cry,* he told himself. He coughed, balled his hands into tight fists, and managed to keep the tears at bay. Footsteps approached.

"Pick your head up, Chief," that familiar voice with the French accent said. "We've got work to do."

"Mister Johann, sir," Tashon said. "I don't think I've ever been happier to see that beard."

The old man chuckled. "Theresa, James, thanks for keeping an eye on our new chief here."

The two acknowledged him with a nod and a wave.

"Wait, what?" Tashon's words stumbled out.

"I had these two tailing you in case something like this happened. We've had tails on all our chiefs the last few days."

"So you expected me to get attacked?"

"Well, one the chiefs at least. I'm sorry it had to be you."

Tashon nodded in agreement.

Johann pulled a bar stool to the table and rested on it, his feet still on the ground. With a look of concern on his face, he reached into his pocket, pulled out a brush and quickly ran it through every inch of his beard.

"Sorry, I hate tangles," he said. "Now, Chief Tashon, you're the one who called this meeting. For now, forget about these last couple of hours. What did you want to discuss?"

Tashon shook his head and let out a small laugh. How could he forget? But he knew Johann was right. Just because a new problem had presented itself, the old problem didn't disappear or become less important.

He took a deep breath. "It's been over two weeks since the last colony left us. We were supposed to have received an update within five days. A film update. But we haven't received anything. Not even in type."

Johann nodded. "Yes, yes. I am aware of this."

"Are you sure? Because everyone has been silent about it. Nothing on the newscasts. Nothing from the board. From the engineers. From the comm team."

"That's because the board asked everyone to be silent."

In moments, Tashon's concern for Smith and fear for himself turned to anger at the board.

"Why... the... hell" — he began to stand — "would you —"

Johann pulled a cube out of his pocket and tossed it onto the table. "Because the only update we received was this," he said, indicating the cube. "It was sent the day they left, about the same time their ship was scheduled to touch down."

"Then why?" Tashon asked, raising his voice.

Johann quieted him with a glare and a raised hand. "Just watch."

He snapped four times in a specific beat, and a recording rose out of the cube.

It looked like the recording had come from one of the handhelds. The small camera was airborne above the planet's surface, spinning wildly. At first, the image just showed surface, sky, surface, sky. Then a flash of red was accompanied with a loud explosion. The spinning camera caught glimpses of the front portion of the ship falling from the sky, flames pouring from cracks in its hull.

Eventually, the camera hit the ground. Moments later, so did a body. And then another. Soon, there were six bodies within the camera's view. Silence, then the sound of footsteps. A few pairs of feet were running around, looking for survivors. Shouting. Trying to figure out what happened. A shadow covered the entire image, and the video went dark. Johann put the cube back in his pocket.

Tashon was dizzy, nauseous. His mouth was dry. The ship had crashed. Gone down in flames. But there had been survivors. Smith could have made it. He had to be alive. He was the closest thing to a father Tashon had ever had. And what about Evalee? Abe?

Grace was the first to speak. "Okay. I get why the video wasn't shown to anyone. But why keep the whole thing a secret? Couldn't you have just told everyone that there had been a crash? That there were survivors and we were just waiting for more updates?"

She seemed so calm. Tashon wondered how she could be so articulate after watching a film clip like that.

Johann clicked his tongue. "Do you believe"—he looked at Tashon—"that most of the people on the Ship of Nations are good people? That they value the lives of their fellow humans?"

Even though he'd just been attacked, Tashon didn't have to think. "Of course," he said.

"And what do you think, upon hearing the news of the crash, the people would want to do? That they would in all likelihood demand?"

Silence. The old man looked at each person sitting in front of him.

"We would say go back. Save them," Theresa said.

"Exactly."

"Okay, yeah. I would be signing that petition too," Grace agreed. "But why is that bad? Why would you be against saving our own people?"

"Under normal circumstances, I wouldn't be. The board wouldn't be. But with this new terrorist group...."

"Terror." Tashon choked on the word. "Terrorist? You mean X-Out? That bitch who attacked me?"

"Foul language doesn't suit you, Chief." Johann shook his head. "But, yes, the same group."

Tashon's mind reeled. He couldn't put together a coherent thought. Just images of terrorist attacks he'd learned about in his studies. So many of them had ended in massive casualties. But those had all been on Earth. One of those attacks on the ship? Where a few well-places explosives could suck the oxygen out of the entire ship? Unthinkable.

"Wait," James whispered. "Didn't that girl say we were destroying the universe?"

Grace nodded. "Yeah, she did."

"But what did she mean by that?" Theresa looked to Johann.

"They refer to themselves as Humans for Extinction."

"This has to be a joke." James ran a hand across his hairless head.

"These people really think the universe would be better if the human race were extinct?"

"Essentially, yes. Their viewpoint is that we're just moving our way across the universe, taking and destroying without giving anything back. That we are parasites sucking the life away from everything we touch."

"Okay," Tashon said. "Okay. But what do these psychos have to do with Smith and the others?"

Johann took a deep breath, stood up off the stool. Placed his palms on the table.

"Somehow," he said, "this group got a copy of the crash footage. They knew we would try to go back to save them."

"And what exactly does that mean?" James asked slowly, trying to understand.

"It's their belief that the crash is the start of the universe taking action against the human race."

"What, like that old-Earth idea of fate?"

"Very similar, yes." Johann flicked his fingers in front of the floating screen. "They sent us this, too."

Words began to scroll in a rotating circle above the cube.

There is no god, but one goddess, the universe herself. This universe gave us life. Gave us Earth, our home. This god, our god, gave us each other. She gave us love. She gave us all the good we have done, all the beauty we have seen, all the joy we have felt.
But....
We, the human race, have turned that joy into despair. That beauty into ugliness. That good into evil. And that life into death. There is no great evil power, no fallen angel, no Satan, that has brought about this darkness. Humanity, despite all our goddess has given us, has become that great evil. We have none to blame but ourselves.
We, the extinctionists, see these truths. And, with that sight, our goddess has called out to us. She is angry. Enraged at what her creations have become.
We will be the tools through which she exacts her revenge.

The screen went blank. The tension and fear grew within Tashon. Sweat formed on his forehead, his body tensed, his breathing quickened. These people truly believed they were doing right. That they were called by a higher power to destroy humanity. If Tashon had learned anything from his study of Earth history, it was this: There is no one more dangerous than those following the call of their own god.

"But that still doesn't explain why the more rational side of the human race can't fly this ship back and go save the survivors," James said.

Johann sighed and pulled out his comb again, this time running it methodically through his beard. For a moment, his eyes went blank and he seemed to be someplace else. "They won't let us go for the survivors," he finally said.

"Won't let us," Theresa shouted. "Like they can cont—"

"They have weapons," Johann said. "Guns, possibly explosives. At the mere hint of us jumping into the Fourth, they'll blow holes on at least eight of our floors. And shoot anyone who tries to stop them."

A weight settled over the group. No one made eye contact. For the first time since they'd started talking, Tashon forgot about Smith, Ev, Abe and all the other survivors. It dawned on him that Johann didn't say they would set the bombs off if they tried to save the survivors. They would set them off even for engaging the tesseract engine. Without the ability to travel through the Fourth, there would be far fewer opportunities to mine minerals and water from passing asteroids. Almost no chance of ever reaching another habitable planet to start one last colony. They would slowly run out of the materials needed to power everything in the ship, including the farm. Eventually, everyone on the ship would starve to death. Or the explosives got set off, and the ship ripped apart piece by piece. Thousands of lifeless, bloating bodies floating through that frozen dark.

James let out a breath. "Holy hell."

Grace shook her head in shock.

"How did this happen?" Theresa whispered.

Tashon thought of Smith again. Considered what his mentor would say. Thought of getting stabbed. How he'd stood there and done nothing but stare.

"Well," Tashon said. "What're we going to do about it?"

"Ha!" Johann slapped the table. "Now you sound like a chief."

***

Tashon had been six when his parents died. They'd both been on the top floor that first time the tesseract engine was engaged. It sent his mom into a seizure. Put her in a coma for nine days before her body completely shut down. It devastated his dad, who started drinking. Heavily.

One evening after dinner, Tashon's dad sent him to the neighbors to get more booze. Not knowing any better, the boy went.

Two hours later, his father stumbled his way into an airlock, opened the door, and let the black emptiness rip him away from the ship. Away from his pain. Away from his son.

The next time Tashon saw his father, it was his bloated body being hauled back into the ship in a vain attempt to rescue him. He'd been out for an entire minute before he was seen. By the time the medics got his body back in, he'd been out there for almost three minutes. Without oxygen, all of his organs had shut down. He had been pronounced dead as soon as he was back in reach of the ship's artificial gravity.

Tashon never stopped blaming himself for his father's death.

Later, Tashon sat on a small couch with Grace, his head in her lap. They were both crying. A kind woman took them to the Education Sector and placed them in what she called the "Kid Hotel." There were a few other children, and a man and woman.

As he grew older, he realized it was a live-in school for children who'd lost their parents. An orphanage. The ship continued to move through the universe, and more kids lost parents. More teachers came to work at the school. Occupation apprentices and chiefs volunteered as often as they could.

Tashon missed his parents, but he liked having more than just his sister to play with. More than just two adults to rely on.

Tashon was fourteen the first time Smith helped at the orphanage. The young boy was sitting at a desk, leaning over a large tablet, his fingers moving quickly across the screen. Smith pulled up a chair and sat next to him.

"Hey," he said.

"Hey," Tashon said without looking up from his screen.

"What're you working on?"

"Nanotech."

Smith looked around. "Where is the nanotech?"

"Not controlling it. Designing it."

Smith slid his chair closer to see the screen. Tashon moved slightly to give him a better view. The screen was split in half. On one side were strings of code, on the other, a visual example of what nanotech with that code might do. At that moment, it was an enlarged image of a single piece of nanotech. It resembled a minuscule egg covered with craters. As Tashon moved his fingers around the screen, the egg spun in circles and emitted rapid bursts of lasers.

"Woah, impressive."

"Thanks."

"What're those light blasts for?"

"Well, those don't actually work real-life. But what I want them to do is take thin layers off of, um, anything."

"Like, could I shave using it?"

"Right. Like that. Or maybe it could even take stuff off that's inside. That makes people sick."

"Huh. Like cancer?"

"Maybe. Or get in the brain and take away...." He went silent. He looked away from Smith.

"Take away what?"

Tashon shrugged. *Sadness,* he thought. *Addiction. Regret.*

Tashon indicated Smith's farming badge. "We could use them to weed out imperfections in the crops. Make them last longer."

Or imperfections in people, he added to himself.

"Now that, I really like. I never have perfect crops."

After that, Smith met with Tashon every week. Connected him with some of the engineers on the ship so that they could eventually implement his design into official use. While it never worked in the way Tashon secretly hoped, the nanotech worked wonders for the medical, engineering and farming occupations.

When Tashon turned sixteen and had the opportunity to begin an apprenticeship, Smith was sure he would pick engineering. To everyone's surprise, he picked farming. Almost no one in those days seemed interested in farming. It was an Earth activity, as many called it. Beneath them.

"Why not engineering?" Smith had asked.

"I like the smell of the farm."

"All right."

"And plants and crops are easier than people."

Smith laughed. "Agreed."

Chapter 12

Tashon and Johann sat in a large conference room. The table in the middle was an elongated, metal eclipse. The chairs were cool to the touch, sending a shiver down Tashon's spine every few minutes.

Eight of the twelve chairs around the table were filled. Johann sat in the middle of one long side, directly across from Tashon. Each of them was at the end of a line of four. The other six were reviewing the report of the attack on the elevator and everything known about Humans for Extinction. Johann worked his brush through his beard, as always. Tashon folded his arms tight against a cold no one else seemed to feel. He looked around.

Other than Johann, the people surrounding Tashon had rarely, if ever, acknowledged him. Hanat, the Chief Communicator who had replaced Evalee sat next to Tashon. She had thick curly hair and dark skin. Her ancestors had come from South Africa, and she still had a hint of the accent. A large tablet sat on the table in front of her, the screen black. Her chest rose and fell with deep, calm breaths. Tashon couldn't help but notice she had a face of complete peace and control. She looked at him and gave a warm smile.

Next to her was Zachary, the board member from America. He sat with a small comm device in one hand, the screen aglow with the report. His leg shook up and down. With his free hand he repeatedly rubbed his nose and adjusted the blue cap on his head.

At the end of Tashon's side of the table was Madam Tiffany from Japan, the woman whom Tashon had spoken with at his ceremony. She leaned over her screen, scrawling notes with her finger, eyes squinted in concentration.

Across the table, Johann whispered with his neighbor, Janise, the Chief of Security. Her long brown hair was always pulled into a tight ponytail. She wore a tight collarless shirt that showed off her massive biceps. As she leaned into her conversation with Johann, her pointed nose nearly poked the old man. Tashon tried to eavesdrop, but couldn't hear what they were saying.

To Janise's other side was the head medical apprentice, wearing the red and white body suit all medics did. As head apprentice, he had two white stripes down his sleeve and pants. His name tag read, 'Matisse, H.M.A'. He held a large cup of water his trembling hands, sipping every few seconds. Tashon spent the better part of five minutes counting how many times the medic brought the cup to his lips. He got to 192 before another shiver went up his spine.

The last occupied seat was filled by new Chief Pilot Winston, Jonstin's little brother. His hair was clipped as short as possible without being considered bald. He wore the blue jacket designated for the chief pilot with pride and confidence. Something Tashon wished he could do. The pilot caught the farmer looking and nodded at him with a slight smile. He may have been Jonstin's brother, but Tashon had always thought Winston was the better of the two.

The cold would not leave Tashon.

The door opened and two more people walked in. Board Member Hans from Canada. His dark skin contrasted greatly with the stark white jacket and pants he was known for. A few steps behind was someone Tashon did not expect to see: the bone-breaking old woman from the elevator.

"Sorry we're late," Hans said as he sat down next to Tashon. "We had to make sure the media didn't find our friend here."

The woman sat down by Johann.

"Why is she here?" Janise demanded.

"She helped Chief Tashon," Johann replied.

"No she didn't. She broke a civilian's wrist. If she were on my security team, she would be demoted or worse."

"Glad I'm not on your team then," the old woman said.

"Seriously." Janise looked at Hans. "Why did you bring her here?"

"Because" — Hans placed his elbows on the table — "she is the one who brought Humans for Extinction to our attention. She overheard her neighbor talking about it and gave him up to try to keep the people of the ship safe."

Janise huffed but didn't say anything more.

"And I wouldn't call a terrorist a civilian, Security Chief," Johann reasoned.

"Everyone has a right to fair and equal consequences for their actions."

"Well, I didn't have a knife to slice her back with." The old woman laughed.

Madam Tiffany stood up and walked to the head of the table. "Enough. We need to figure out what the hell we're going to do to stop these people."

"My name's Rosa," the old woman said. "In case anyone was wondering."

Janise rolled her eyes.

Winston laughed.

"Thanks for your help, Rosa," Tashon said.

Rosa nodded to him. "Of course."

"This is ridiculous," Janise mumbled.

"Moving on," Tiffany commanded. "We currently have two Extinctionists in custody. Rosa's neighbor and the girl who attacked Chief Tashon."

"Can we please just refer to her as 'the bitch?'" Winston interrupted.

Johann, the medic and the American laughed.

"I like him," Rosa whispered.

Madam Tiffany walked over and slapped Winston on the back of the head. "Almost as bad as your brother," she said. "If we don't handle this right, we could all die."

Silence.

Tashon was taken back to that childhood night, seeing his father's body after mere minutes out there. He imagined hundreds like that, with no one to pull them back in and try to save them.

"Madam," Tashon said, "what do we know so far?"

"Well, neither of them are talking. At all. The only information we have are their names, Cosima and Ashten. We had to learn that on our own. And we know they're part of the Extinctionist group. Still don't know for certain if they even have the firepower they say they do."

Winston stretched his arms up with a sigh. "See, that's what I don't get. How the hell would they even get guns? Or bombs?"

Tashon had been asking himself the same question. According to what he learned in school, only two guns had been on the Ship of Nations when it departed Earth. The security sector had a small factory with a 3D printer. It was able to produce, at most, two guns per week. Each gun was produced for a single person, designed to fit each user perfectly. Dozens of aspects were taken into account, from hand size and finger length to preferred grip. Each gun was finished with a fingerprint sensor on the trigger. To obtain a gun, one had to spend a minimum of eighteen months working in security and go through a rigorous stretch of evaluations with the security, physical health and mental health chiefs.

"Yeah," Tashon agreed. "There's no way they could have guns."

"That's what I'm sayin'." Winston slapped a hand on the table. "So why are we worrying about it?"

Tashon looked at Tiffany, who was looking at the security chief. Janise stood up and walked to the head of the table. Tiffany took her seat.

"There was an, uh...." Janise paused. "Incident. No easy way to put it. Our gun printer was stolen."

Gasping, scoffing and swearing came from around the table.

Rosa cackled and shook her head.

Tashon looked at her, and her smile seemed genuine.

"What?" Zachary pushed himself away from the table and began to pace the room. He took his cap off and feverishly ran his hand through his sweat soaked hair.

"How in the hell...?" Winston let out a high-pitched whistle.

Everyone except Tashon and Chief Hanat began demanding answers. After nearly a minute of incoherent frustration, Chief Hanat left her seat and stood next to Chief Janise. The communicator held her hand out to quiet everyone. The room fell silent. Tashon looked at her expectantly. She only spoke when she felt she needed to, and it was always in a voice that made listeners feel there was nothing to worry about.

She placed a hand on Janise's shoulder. "I have no doubt that Security Chief Janise is already torn apart with guilt about what happened. And I understand why everyone is upset and scared by this. But haven't we all, at some point in our occupations, faced something similar? A time in which something happened that should not have? Something that you keep telling yourself you could have prevented? Think about that time, and ask yourself this: would it have helped if those around you had attacked and questioned you? Think about that, and I'm sure each of your answers would be no."

Hanat moved closer to Janise, put an arm around the Security Chief's shoulders.

"It's okay," she said quietly. "We still have time to figure this out. I truly do not think this will be the end."

With that, she took a deep breath and went back to her seat.

After a moment, Winston broke the peaceful silence.

"Thanks, Chief Hanat," he said. "We can figure this out, but it's gonna be hard as hell. Let's start by figuring out how these people work. Chief Janise, how was the gun printer stolen?"

"It had been about four months since we had needed to make a gun," she said. "During that time, the printer was never used. It sits in the middle of our headquarters in a small room, always on guard. From everything we saw, it never moved. Nine days ago, it was time to make a new gun. When we went to do so, we found that the printer was a fake. Someone had stolen the real one and left us with a useless copy."

"It had to be an inside job," Winston commented.

"Exactly. And the main concern is we don't know when it was taken. Don't know how much time they've had to produce firearms."

Tashon quickly ran the numbers through his head. "So, they could have two guns. Or thirty-six."

Another moment of silence.

"Okay. And what about explosives? How would they get those?"

"I discussed it with one of the engineers. He doesn't think the terrorists actually have any explosives. But that's not what they're telling us."

"Then we need to figure how many guns they have and where they're stashing them. Have we found anything on the camera footage?"

"No. We've spent hours going over every millisecond over and over and over... nothing. They must have someone actively editing the footage."

Zachary stopped pacing. "We need the two we have to talk. I've read about techniques used in wartime on Earth to get information from war criminals."

"Torture, you mean?" Matisse spoke for the first time. "The chief medic would be against that, and so am I. Vehemently. Besides, this isn't a war."

Janise shook her head. "Isn't it, though?" she said. "It feels like it is to me. And I considered the option before Zachary even brought it up."

A laugh exploded from Rosa. "What? Ten minutes ago you were attacking me for breaking that girl's wrist. Now you're saying you're fine with torturing her?"

"Look, Rosa. Everyone. I'm not saying we should absolutely torture them. But what you did to that girl was in public, and on vids." She hesitated a moment. "But our... interviews with these two won't be seen."

"So what the public doesn't know won't hurt them?"

"Exactly," Zachary said as he dropped himself back into his chair.

"No way." Matisse folded his arms.

"I don't know," Winston said. "Seems excessive. But could we get the answers we need another way?"

"Obviously I'm okay with it," Rosa said.

Tashon shook his head and thought. The girl had attacked him, but he couldn't convince himself that torturing her was the right move. As he played that attack again his mind, he was sure he had seen something in the girl's face. Fear? Guilt?

"No," he spoke quietly. "No, I don't think we should."

Everyone looked at him, surprise or confusion on their faces.

"Look," he responded. "I'm pissed she stabbed me. But, come on. Earth was a disaster when the ship left. Because of how they did business. How they fought their wars. I just don't think we should return to that."

"Well said, Chief Tashon," Hanat said. "I will talk to them. I appreciate all you do, Chief Janise. But can we all agree that we should exhaust every other option before resorting to animal violence?"

Rosa stood. "But if that doesn't work, give me five minutes with them. We'll have all we need."

Chapter 13

Tashon sat in a small, stuffy room with Johann and Rosa, waiting for Hanat to finish speaking with the prisoners. With just the three of them, the room felt calmer. Johann had just finished brushing his beard and quietly fiddled with his comb. Rosa had dozed off, her chin gently resting on her chest, quiet snores flowing through her nose. She seemed too relaxed for someone who had just broken a girl's wrist and advocated torture.

None of it made sense to Tashon. If this group of Extinctionists genuinely wanted the human race to stop destroying the universe, why not just blow a few well-placed bombs and be done with it? They could kill everyone on the ship in an instant. There had to be something they were missing. But Hanat should be able to get the answers they needed. The only person more qualified for the task was Evalee, and she wasn't on the ship anymore. Might not even be....

Tashon ran a hand through his hair and sighed.

"I think it's time for a new comb," Johann said, breaking the silence.

"Huh?"

"New comb." Johann waggled his in the air.

"Oh, sure," Tashon said.

"But maybe not. You know, my mother gave me this comb. It's the only one I've ever had. I know it looks new, but look closer."

He held it out toward Tashon, who begrudgingly grabbed it. "See, when you look closely, it's not that nice of a comb. Fake, chipping gold. Some broken teeth."

Johann reached out and took the comb back.

"Okay? I don't know. I can't imagine you with any other comb."

"Hm. Interesting. I mean, I do like this comb. Love it, really. But I've had this itch to buy a new one."

"Does that really matter right now, Johann?"

"No, no. Not at all." The old man laughed, his beard moving up and down.

Tashon shook his head but soon laughed along with him.

"You're both insane," Rosa said without opening her eyes.

"Says the old ninja lady." Tashon laughed even louder.

"I should've let that girl stab you again."

They all chuckled, but the room soon grew quiet again.

"I wonder how the Smiths are doing," Tashon said.

"Still breathing, I'm sure," Johann said.

"You think?"

Johann began to run his comb through the thinning hair on his head. "I've decided to think that, yes."

Tashon met Johann's eyes. "Decided to?"

"Yes." The old man sighed, placing his comb on the table. "You see, there's really three ways we can wonder about how everyone is doing back there. First, that they're all dead or soon will be. They're gone, nothing to be done. Second, we can accept that there truly is no way to know if they're dead or alive. Logically, this is the best choice because, after all, there is no way to know for certain. But if we choose this one, we won't stop wondering if they're dead or alive. Our minds will constantly move through every possible scenario, good and bad. You'll drive yourself mad."

Rosa had opened her eyes and stared at Johann with a quizzical eye.

"Which leaves us with the third option: hope. We can choose to hope that they are doing okay. That they are surviving. And this, Tashon, is the most helpful choice. Do you know why?"

Tashon shrugged and shook his head.

Rosa cleared her throat. "Hope can give us a reason to fight back," she said.

Johann nodded. "Exactly."

Tashon let out a short laugh. *Easy to say*, he thought. But to do it there had to be a reason to hope, right? And he didn't see any.

"If you say so," Tashon said. He let out a long breath and closed his eyes. Kept seeing the video of the crash. Each body that hit the ground. His head began to pound with the loud thud of bodies slamming into hard earth. *Thud. Thud. Thud.* Smith. Ev. Abe. *Thud. Thud. Thud.*

All three of their wrist comms binged simultaneously. Tashon forced his eyes open. In floating red text, it told them to report to the main boardroom for an update.

***

The room was packed. All eleven board members were present, along with six chiefs. There were four security personnel, two at each door. A large, three-dimensional recording of Hanat's interview with the boy expanded from the center of the oval table. Only the boy's face was visible, Hanat's voice flowing from off-screen.

"So, Ashten," Hanat said. "You really want to die?"

"I will if I have to. I'll die to save the universe."

"Okay. And you think the only way to do that is to make humanity extinct?"

"Exactly." Ashten stared into the camera with a burning rage.

"Then why are we all still here?"

Ashten raised one eyebrow above the other and tilted his head to the side. "What do you mean, *Chief*?" he said with disdain.

"Your group claims to have enough explosives to destroy this ship in an instant. So why not just do it?"

Ashten laughed. "Does this glorious ship hold all of humankind, Miss Hanat?"

Hanat did not respond.

Ashten laughed again. "Of course, you know the answer to that. So, you tell me why we haven't blown this beautiful testament to the genius of humankind?"

"You want to travel back to the colonies. Make sure each one is taken out."

He stood up and crossed his cuffed hands across his chest.

"Humanity is pollution," he shouted. "Humanity is disease. Humanity is chaos. It is destruction. Humanity is death. And *we* will reign death back on humanity. This is our calling. The universe has spoken to us through its chosen vessel, and we will not be stopped."

The floating face flickered and morphed into the face of the girl who had stabbed Tashon.

"Cosima." Chief Hanat's voice was calm and caring. "How are you holding up?"

"Huh? I... I'm okay. Thanks?"

"Are you sure? That you're okay?"

Cosima looked down and didn't respond.

"Because you attacked a young man not much older than you. Sliced his chest."

Cosima looked up.

"It was for...." Her voice faltered. "For a great cause."

"I don't believe it was. And I'm not sure you believe it, either."

There was no sarcasm in Hanat's voice. No menace. She spoke as though she had found her daughter in a hopeless situation and she was simply trying to show compassion and understanding.

"But I do."

"And what cause is that, exactly?"

"You know what it is."

"Explain it to me. In your words. I want to fully understand what it is you're so ready to kill for."

"It's the cause of the universe. We need to save the universe from ourselves." Cosima swallowed hard and suppressed a cough.

"Okay. And what exactly are we humans doing that the universe needs to be saved from us?"

"We are taking far more than we are giving. Mining nearly every asteroid belt 'til there's nothing left. We know that every planet we left people at will eventually become a polluted cesspool like Earth."

"We *know* that, Cosima?"

"Destroying things is in our nature."

Hanat paused for a moment, perhaps considering Cosima's position.

"Do you think, Cosima, that people can learn from their mistakes?"

Cosima looked surprised for a moment, then bit her bottom lip in thought. She opened her mouth to speak, then closed it again.

"You see, Cosima, I'm not sure who has been telling you that we will repeat the same mistakes we made on Earth. True, we're bound to repeat some of them. But do you remember any of what you learned in your studies about the history of human technology? About the technology that nearly destroyed Earth, and the technology that we have now? We will not be turning more planets into cesspools, as you say we will."

Cosima continued to nibble on her lip. She ran a hand through her hair and looked up, directly into the camera.

"It's not just about the improved technology. Humans are imperfect. Volatile. Dangerous. It might be pollution, or war, or disease, or any number of things that could destroy each planet we colonize. But, in time, the human race will destroy everything."

"Hm. So you plan to fix this by being part of a group that is more volatile, more dangerous, than any group that has existed in the ship's short history?"

For a moment, her eyes opened wide and she seemed scared. She blinked rapidly and bit her lip again.

Tashon wondered what she must be thinking. Would she give up the information they needed?

She took a long breath, and slowly let it out. "I want to speak with Chief Farmer Tashon," she said. "Please."

Silence save for Cosima's breathing.

"I don't know that he'll—"

"Please. Please. I won't try anything. You can be in here. Hell, put two security guards next to me. I just... please."

Tashon closed his eyes and rubbed them. Exhaustion suddenly pressed down on him. He hadn't slept since before he'd become the chief farmer. It felt like he'd held the position for months, but it'd been less than twelve hours. He opened his eyes. Everyone in the room was looking at him. He sighed and stood up.

"I'll go," he said. "But I want the old ninja woman with me."

Rosa laughed. "Happy to, Chief."

Chapter 14

Tashon and Rosa stood in a square room. In front of them, on the other side of a table, sat Cosima, her hands cuffed behind the back of a chair. Two Security personnel stood next to her. The girl did not lift her gaze from the table. Tashon wasn't going to speak first. He stood, hand in the large pocket of his robe, wanting nothing more than to sleep. Knowing that even if he found his way to his quarters anytime soon, sleep would elude him.

Cosima whispered something unintelligible.

"Speak up, girl," Rosa said.

She looked up, her eyes wet with tears. "I'm sorry, Tashon."

"That's Chief Tashon to you," Rosa said.

Tashon waved her off as he sat down across from Cosima.

"Look." He paused, searching for the words. "I was—am—pretty pissed you stabbed me. But, look, I'm still standing, talking, walking. I mean, no real damage was done. I'm fine."

She sobbed. "For now," she said after catching her breath. "There's more coming."

"More what?"

"Attacks. On a larger scale. They—I mean we—have guns. They—we—have more planned. It cannot be stopped."

"Why did Chief Tashon get attacked and no one else?"

"We were supposed to get more," she said, her voice steadying. "Our attacks were supposed to be synced, but I don't know what happened."

More attacks. The room closed in on Tashon, and a cold gripped him. His head spun, stomach churned. Vomit exploded onto the table, spreading out until it dropped off the edge onto Cosima's legs.

"And that"—she coughed—"is from the poison."

Rosa pushed the table to the side and went at Cosima.

"What was it?" Rosa squatted down, her face inches from Cosima.

Tears filled her eyes. "I don't know. But Tash—Chief Tashon should be fine."

Tashon sat on the floor. "How do you know that?"

"I... we...." Cosima paused to compose herself. "We were all supposed to soak our blades in the poison. But I couldn't do it. All I did was dip the point in. I don't think the full effect will hit him."

"What happens if someone gets cut with a soaked blade?"

Cosima bit her lip. She looked to the ground.

"Cosima, I will break your other wrist."

"No, you won't," Tashon called from his spot on the floor.

Rosa looked at him. Then back at the girl.

Tashon could tell that Cosima regretted what she did, that she hadn't wanted to do it in the first place.

"Cosima, please." Tashon carefully stood up. "What does the poison do?"

"Coma," she said. "When they fall asleep, they go into a coma. Their bodies slowly die after that."

"You're sure?"

"That's what they told us."

Tashon nodded and turned to the door.

"Chief, what are you doing?"

"I need to get out." He paused as he opened the door. "Cosima, please tell Rosa anything you can that will help us. Please."

Johann was standing just outside the doorway and Tashon walked into him, nearly knocking the old man off his feet. He mumbled an apology and moved to walk around him.

Johann grabbed his arm. "Wait."

Tashon tried to pull away, but Johann's grip was surprisingly strong.

"There's been more attacks. Assistants this time. Civilians. Two have already slipped into comas. Come with me."

Tashon nodded and stumbled after Johann. As he walked down the hall, he heard Cosima sobbing.

"Where are we—"

"Shut up," Johann said.

Tashon obeyed and followed as Johann quickened his pace. They worked their way through tunnels that he would never have been allowed to walk without a chief robe on his shoulders. Where most of the ship was built to feel larger than it was, less confined, these walls seemed to press in around Tashon. The tunnels were built strictly to get people from one point to another, while avoiding as many eyes as possible. The ship's engineers had designed them to get important or threatened personnel through the ship in safety. Tashon had only heard them spoken of in rumor.

After four or five turns down more hallways, they reached a door. Johann pulled something out of his pocket and pressed it against the wall. Without a sound, the door slid up into the ceiling. Just through the opening was a steep set of downward stairs. Johann ushered Tashon in first and gave him a push when the chief hesitated at the descent. The highest stairs Tashon had ever seen were only five or six steps tall, at the theaters in the entertainment sector. But below him the stairs extended nearly fifty feet at an angle that disoriented him. With a deep breath he stepped down, feeling as though he could fall forward and crack his neck at the bottom. He realized with a shudder that a part of him liked the sound of that.

"Never thought everything would hit the fan like this," Johann said.

"Yeah, it's... yeah," Tashon said. No more words came to mind.

"Right." Johann nodded and kept walking.

They reached the bottom. The door slid up, this time with a soft squeak.

The room they walked into was small, rectangular. A long window on the right side overlooked a colony hangar. An unfinished colony ship sat on the ground. Through a smaller window, an electron beam gun was moving, forming a part of the next colony ship. Glowing red letters above the window read, "Vacuum enabled. Do not open."

On the opposite side of the room were two fold-out cots, both occupied. One was the medical assistant Tashon had met earlier in the conference room. He was shirtless, with an IV stuck in each hand. A small speaker next to him periodically read off his stats. Stable, for now. On the other cot was an elderly man Tashon did not know, hooked up the same way. There were ten others around the room. Two were medical personnel, a man and a woman. The woman was injecting something into a boy who wore the blue jacket of an engineering apprentice. The others were scattered around the room, whispering or pacing or sitting in a corner. Johann waved the other medical assistant over.

"Chief Tashon," the man said as he jogged over. "I'm Joel. I'm glad you're awake. We need to get your injection as soon as possible. You look exhausted."

"Injected?"

"Yeah." He pulled a syringe from behind his back.

"Wait, with what?"

"It's okay, Tashon." Johann patted his shoulder. "It's to keep you awake. These two didn't fall into comas until they fell asleep."

"But Cosima said I should be fine."

"You're going to the trust the girl who sliced you with a knife?" Johann nodded to the medical assistant.

"The substance is, technically, frowned upon. Desperate times, though, huh?"

"I hate clichés," Tashon said as he rolled up his sleeve.

The assistant held the syringe up, flicking the side of it. Tashon turned away, expecting it to feel the same as getting cut. But then Joel told him it was done. A warm sensation spread down his arm and into his fingers. In seconds, his entire body felt like it was vibrating. His eyes seemed to open wider. Everything he saw was of great interest. Deserving of keen observation. He walked to the window that gave him a view of the EBG.

The EBG was made of magnetic coils. Under these coils was a metal rectangle. On top of the rectangle sat a partially finished ship part. Tashon wasn't sure what it was, but it looked like it would end up being some sort of joint. In that moment, it was a half-ball with holes on either side. The coil stopped moving. A fine layer of metallic dust was released, resting on top of the joint. The coiled gun began to move again, slowly emitting electrons in order to melt the new layer to the existing portion of the sphere. This would continue, slowly, layer by layer, until the part was complete.

Tashon watched, transfixed. All that mattered to him was seeing that part completed. Time became not a measure of seconds or minutes, but of layers of metal added on top of each other. He counted each layer. Guessed how many it would be until it was finished. Adjusted his guess as the coils continued to meld metal to metal. He knew there were other small rooms just like this one, molding the parts needed for another colony ship. A ship that would probably never get finished.

His mind bounced suddenly back to the present. He looked around the room. A new woman was receiving the same shot he had. There were two others standing around that hadn't been there before. More people were getting attacked. *But how?* he wondered. *Shouldn't they have found them by now? The ship only has so many places to hide.*

"Johann," he called, jogging to the other side of the room. He was surprised at how much energy he had.

Johann finished a conversation he was having with an engineer. As he turned, Tashon noticed as he tried to hide a look of worry with a smile. It probably would have slipped past if he hadn't been injected with something that accentuated every detail.

"Wait, what's wrong, Johann?"

"Nothing, nothing. At least, nothing new is wrong." His smile beamed. "What do you need, Tash?"

Deciding to let it slide, he asked, "Any good news? Did Cosima give us anything? We catch any more of these people?"

"Well, the good news is that the personal attacks seem to have stopped. That woman who just came in is the only attack we've had in the last four hours."

"I've really been here that long? Staring at that beam gun?"

"Side effect of the drug. Cosima told us where she thinks the explosives are hidden. Security is looking into that. And, no, we haven't caught anyone else. How are you?"

Tashon nodded, then shrugged.

Johann nodded in response. "I do have some bad news, Tash."

"What happened?" Tashon's heart pounded in his chest.

Johann inhaled deeply. "I left my comb in the conference room. They won't let me out. All I have is my fingers. Honestly, it's driving me insane."

Before he could decide whether to laugh or smack the old man, a voice sounded over the ship's intercom.

"Hello, my fellow humans! All of you have been discussing what is happening on this glorious Ship of Nations. With all the attacks and the rumors, it's only human to do so. Well, I'm here to clear things up. To let you know what's going to happen."

"Whose voice is that?" Johann screamed. "Who is that?"

"The first thing to clear up. Yes, the Extinctionists exist. And, no, it is not just a few angsty teens. We have more in our cause than you know. In every occupation. In every housing sector.

"Second, do we plan on destroying this grand ship? No, not quite. You see, we are humble enough to admit what all of us know—we humans are a disease. We do, in fact, believe that this disease needs to be eradicated. However"—he stopped and audibly took a drink—"we must eradicate this disease *in its entirety*."

"He's insane. Absolutely shit brained." Johann reached into his pocket and pulled out an empty hand. He shook his head and ran aging fingers through his beard.

"Ah," the man on the intercom said. "I imagine you are all asking *why*. The universe, as a being, is benevolent. Gracious. She graciously gave life to all living things, including us. She gave us our very own planet, asking nothing in return. And what did we do? We demanded more! And then, when the universe, in her wisdom, did not provide, we went and took it. We hurt, murdered and stole. We built towns, cities and empires. Built them on blood, corruption and pollution. We kept building. Kept killing until Earth, that benevolent gift, was swallowed up by blood and pollution."

Tashon could almost hear the man shaking his head.

"We need...." He let out a long sigh. "We *must* atone for the sins of our race."

Static. No one spoke. The sound of distant shouting poured from the speakers.

"Aha! It seems they have found me. Let it begin, then. See all of you—" He was cut short by what felt like an explosion. The entire room shook. Tashon lost his balance and hit the cool metal floor. Pain erupted in his shoulder. He screamed. Tears filled his eyes, but he refused to shed them. Someone, the medic, maybe, ran to his side. Told him to take a deep breath. As he did, a hand gripped his shoulder. Another hand pushed hard and his shoulder kicked backward.

Tashon took a deep breath, realizing it had been dislocated.

"Tha-thanks." He wiped a tear off his cheek.

"No worry. And hey"—the medic gripped his other shoulder—"anyone asks, I'll tell 'em you handled this better than Smith would've."

Tashon nodded and stood up. Damn. Smith. How were they ever going to get back to him now? An alarm blared. Red lights flashed. On. Off. On. Off. The screens monitoring the two in comas started beeping. Johann and the medic ran to help. Tashon's heart pounded. Johann did chest compressions on one. The medic declared a time on the other, and gently closed the eyelids. An explosion shook the ship again. The patient in front of Johann flatlined.

"Damn it!" Johann yelled, throwing an IV bag on the floor. "We will *not* let these psychos take control of this ship!"

The door burst open. Three security personnel in full gear ran in. Gray, hardened boots with matching pants and jacket. White helmets with frosted visors. Each held a small pistol. Strong enough to do damage to a person, but not to any part of the ship.

The one in front spoke.

"Chief Tashon, Mister Johann, come with me. Adams and Sanjay here will stay with the rest of you."

"With pleasure, Captain," Johann replied. "Let's get these bastards."

Chapter 15

The three had been running non-stop through small, twisting hallways for nearly fifteen minutes. The drug they'd given Tashon was wearing off and he felt like his lungs might explode. Felt that if he just stopped running and fell to the floor, he could fall asleep forever and everything would be okay. In front, the captain stopped and held up a fist. Tashon nearly crashed into Johann. Then nearly fell backward avoiding the collision.

"Just around the corner is a door. Once we're out there, we need to walk."

"But what's the plan?" Johann asked. "Where are we going?"

"I've been ordered," the man said. "To get you two with the other chiefs and board members. Everyone needs to decide what the next step is."

"We're beyond deciding!"

Tashon had never heard Johann shout as much as he had that day.

"And besides, that is not our crisis protocol. All of us in one space? That'd make it too easy to—"

Johann took a step back.

The captain punched the old man across the left side of his face. Johann staggered back, turning his head away. He reached into his pocket. He pulled out a knife and whipped back around, thrusting it into the man's neck just below the helmet. The man's back hit the wall and Johann stabbed the other side of his neck. Blood drained from both holes as the body slumped to the floor. As it came to a stop, the blood bubbled out on one side.

Tashon turned and vomited onto the floor. "What the hell?"

Johann wiped the blood off the blade.

"I've been carrying it with me since you were attacked."

Tashon coughed and spit. "Didn't think to get me one?"

Johann chuckled and pulled a gun from his pocket.

"And pulled this out from when I was Security Chief. I was supposed to turn it in, but... you know." He shrugged.

Tashon shook his head.

Johann handed him the knife and told him to conceal it in his robes. He did the same with the gun.

"Let's go."

Tashon nodded slowly, thought to ask where, and then realized it didn't matter. He'd stay with Johann wherever he went. Besides, he realized there was no one else on the ship he trusted as much as Johann. Except Grace. But he had no idea where his sister was. Hadn't seen her since Jenza's. *Hope she's not dead like the Smiths*, he thought.

"Hope you're ready for a fight." Johann smiled as he pushed open the door.

"Wait, what?"

They walked through the door and into the eatery sector. Tashon didn't remember going up any stairs, but they must have. The area was packed with people. Men, women, children. Some were silent, others crying. A man leaned against a railing desperately yelling into his comm device, begging someone named Denow to call him back. Johann quickly closed the door and locked it with his thumb print. Men and women in Security uniforms paced up and down, ensuring everyone that they would be taken care of. Tashon knew that most of the Security team would not be a part of the Extinctionists, but he still wanted nothing to do with them. Johann waved the closest one over.

"Mister Johann," the young woman called as she walked to meet them. "You have any news?"

"That's what I'm asking. Tell me everything you know."

"I was here on lunch when that psycho came on the speaker. An order came to draw our weapons and stand on guard wherever we were. Then the explosion. Half of us were ordered to the site, the rest told to stay."

"To what site?"

"Oh. The engine room. They're trying to take control of the tesseract."

"Damn it!"

Johann broke into a sprint. Tashon followed and called after him. The old man only yelled back that he would not let it end this way.

Tashon moved faster and he wished the drugs were still pumping through his veins. He didn't know how long he could keep running. Ahead of him, Johann took a sharp turn into an emergency stairwell. Tashon made it through the door just before it slammed shut. His foot caught in his robe as he took the first step down. He tried, but failed, to catch himself. The shoulder he'd just dislocated hit first, the skin splitting on the cool metal edge of a step. Momentum flipped his feet over his head, which cracked against the next step. He rolled until he came to a stop on the landing. Warm blood trickled down the side of his face.

"You alive up there?" Johann called from somewhere below.

"Yeah." Tashon groaned as he forced himself to stand up.

"Good. Get down here. I can't do this on my own."

Tashon grabbed the railing and went down as fast as he could. Johann casually whistled a tune that vaguely reminded Tashon of a girl he'd met once. She had black hair and always listened to him talk about his nanotech ideas, even though he could tell she didn't care. What was her name? *Doesn't matter*, he thought. She and everyone else would be dead before long. He tried to force himself to move quickly, but each step became more difficult. Why not just lie down and sleep? Johann was the badass, not him. Leave the saving to the war hero, not to the young farmer. Not to the orphan. The kid that fed alcohol to his dad and killed him.

But he kept moving, though he couldn't say why. At the next landing, Johann stood next to a closed door with "Tesseract Engineers Only" etched onto its surface.

"It won't open."

"Huh." Tashon tried to shift his mind to the present.

"They must've disabled my access," Johann said.

As a board member, he had access to anywhere on the ship. At least he used to. For the Extinctionists to have disabled his access, they would have needed at least two higher ups, one in Security and another in Engineering. The more they moved forward, the more Tashon thought it was futile to fight it.

"What are we supposed to do?"

"Hand me that knife."

Johann started working the tip of the knife into the tiny crack between the door and door jam.

"I learned this back on Earth." He slid the knife mere centimeters farther into the crack. "Hey, put all your weight on the door while I'm working. I want to make sure we get it open."

Tashon pushed both palms into the door and braced himself with his feet. He felt his robe catch under his right foot. With a sense of freedom, he took his robe off and tossed it to the side. Now wearing black pants and a gray long sleeve shirt, which showed off what little muscle his thin frame had, he pushed against the door.

"Protocol says a chief must never be in public without his robes," Johann said as he shimmied the knife back and forth inside the door.

"Screw protocol." Tashon exhaled. "You were saying you learned this back on Earth?"

"I was still in Russia. Few weeks after we got those kids back home. It was just me and this new kid. We were supposed to be gettin' into this giant house, but we couldn't even get close. Electric fences, roaming drones that would shoot you with a tranquilizer on sight. Invisible trip lines that would set off any number of traps. I was about ready to call it when—hold on—"

Johann held his breath and slowly wriggled the knife back and forth. He exhaled, breathed in again, and gave the knife one quick push. The blade slipped out of the crack. The door stayed closed.

"Damn it," Johann muttered as he started over. "Yeah. I was about to call the mission when the kid noticed something. There were no human guards. The guy we were trying to capture was known for not trusting anyone. He'd killed his own daughter because he thought she was givin' his secrets to the Chinese. She wasn't, though. She was passing those on to us. This guy, though, he had a vast security system, but it all needed two things to run. Power and connection to a network. From everything we knew, he was the only one in there. The kid was some techie. Knew everything he needed to shut down the network and cut power to the entire block within thirty minutes. Damn it."

Johann wiped sweat from his eyes with his free hand. Ran his fingers through his beard and breathed loudly.

"This was easier back then. Do you want to—?"

"Shut up," Tashon whispered.

"Huh?" Johann whispered back.

Tashon put his ear to the door. Footsteps were approaching. Two voices were arguing. The steps stopped just on the other side of the door.

"How the hell are we supposed to stop this?" a man yelled.

"Quiet," a woman said, hushing him. "We're not going to let them take this ship. But we need to find some of the other chiefs."

"Isn't that—"

Johann knocked on the door. "Chief Janise," he called.

"Johann?"

"Yeah. Chief Tashon too. Can you open the door from your side?"

After a few moments of banging and scuffing, the door remained shut.

"Who's with you, Janise?"

"Apprentice Vinn. I trust him."

"Good. We need to get in the same room and come up with a plan."

"I know, I know. It's just... they have an insane hold on the engine room down here. Thankfully, they haven't been able to turn any of the tesseract pilots. That's the only reason we—" She paused. "Someone's coming down the hall," she said quietly. "Move away from the door. Be ready."

The two did as they were told. Tashon stood to one side, brandishing the knife tightly. Johann stood coolly on the other side, his gun at the ready. Running footsteps approached from the other side. Tashon tried to figure out how many sets of feet it sounded like, but he had no idea. *I hope just one or two*, he thought. Janise could take two out easily. A gun fired. The bullet hit the door with a loud *thunk* and Tashon leapt into the air. His heart pounded. More shots rang out and Tashon covered his ears. He knew the bullets weren't strong enough to pierce the door or wall, but he still felt helpless. Half expected one to bore a hole through the wall and into his head. But soon the sounds stopped, and Tashon was alive. His head throbbed and his ears rang but he was alive. He exhaled, realizing he was happier at the fact he had not died than he would have expected. The door he stood next to slowly slid open. Tashon raised the knife. Johann gripped the gun tighter and let his finger hover over the trigger.

Something fell through the doorway and hit the ground. Tashon looked down. The lifeless, bloodied face of Security Chief Janise stared up at him. His stomach churned inside of him. He clenched the knife tighter.

A foot came out of the doorway, stretching over the body. A head, reaching about the same height as Tashon's, soon followed. No helmet. Tashon lost awareness of himself. He took one step forward. Held the knife up at eye level. The blade pointed outward, ready to stab. He turned quickly to look at the face. Then Tashon brought the knife down to the head. Fast. It pierced above the ear at a downward angle. Tashon didn't realize what had happened until he let go of the handle and the body dropped to the floor. Blood dripped from where the knife stuck into the skull. He looked through the doorway.

Tashon hadn't heard gunshots, but Johann must have fired. Another body with two holes in its head slumped against the doorjamb.

"Don't forget the knife."

Tashon nodded and reached down with one hand. The knife wouldn't budge. He gripped with both hands, placed a foot on the head and pulled. It popped as if he had just pulled a stubborn carrot out of the ground. He looked down at the face, noticing the eyes for the first time. They were blue-brown. Same as his dad's. He thought for a moment about his father, floating lifeless outside the ship. *This is the second time I've killed someone*, he thought. A hand touched his shoulder.

"The first time," Johann said. "The first time I killed someone nearly took me out. I puked for over an hour. Couldn't stop."

"This is my second time."

"What?"

"My father."

"Tash, that wasn't your —"

"Let's keep going."

Tashon stepped over the lifeless form. The knife tight in his hand. He crouched, snatched another knife from a dead man's boot. He had to keep moving. Moving forward was the only way to forget what he had done. To forget that he had made himself an orphan. That he had probably just made another child fatherless. He broke into a jog. The sound of Johann's quickened footsteps followed him. Tashon thought the old man called after him. He didn't care.

Chapter 16

Fifteen minutes had passed. They stood in a small storage closet, trying to catch their breath. Tashon leaned forward, hands on his knees. He'd been dry heaving. Johann stood tall with the back of his head resting on the wall, eyes closed. Neither one had spoken since they found their hiding spot.

Tashon spit and sat on a crate. He pulled the knife out and twisted it in his hands. A thin line of blood had dried on it. He didn't want to keep going. Didn't want to hurt anyone else. But if he didn't, what would happen to everyone else? If he didn't hurt those who were trying to hurt others, even more people would die. He wondered if that justified the killing. The murdering. Something told him that it must. Yet that didn't ease the pit in his stomach. It didn't calm his mind. He didn't want to move forward. Didn't want to live. But he didn't want to die. He was stuck, floating through a fog of purgatory. A scream exploded from him and he slammed a fist on the wall. Johann opened his eyes and turned to him.

"You can stay here if you want." Johann sat down next to him. "I bet I could take these psychos alone."

Tashon rubbed his eyes. He wasn't in the mood for banter.

"No. I'll come," Tashon said. "Besides, we can't be the only two pushing back against them."

"Sure as hell hope not."

"Yeah," Tashon said and stood up. "Let's hope your hope is enough for the both of us."

He hit a button and the door slid open. They walked out. Down the hall they went, side by side. Johann holding his gun at the ready. Tashon with a knife in each hand, arms at his sides. They moved at a quick, steady pace. Shots rang out in another corridor, the sound echoing toward them. Red lights flashed. An alarm blared. They stopped at a three-way split.

"Which way?"

"If they're shooting, they're shooting at someone," Johann said. "That's good for us."

More shots rang out, echoes bouncing from the corridor to their left.

"What the hell? Left it is."

Johann broke into a sprint. Tashon paused to take a deep breath, raising his knives. He ran after the old man. As they got closer, the shooting stopped. A few seconds of silence, followed by screaming. They turned a corner and entered a square room. There were two doors on opposite sides. Both were held open by what looked like dead bodies. On the left, a woman crouched on one knee, her gun pointed at a man across the room. He pointed his back at her. Both wore security uniforms. Neither one moved their gaze as Johann and Tashon came in.

"Johann. Chief Tashon," the girl spoke calmly. "I'm glad to see you two alive."

"Shut your mouth, traitor," the man said.

Silence again. Tashon looked back and forth, his gaze shifting between the two. There was no way to tell which one was with the Extinctionists and which one wasn't.

"Screw you." The girl sneered. She raised her gun.

"Drop your weapons." Johann stepped between them, blocking their line of fire. "Both of you."

The man immediately crouched and placed his gun on the ground. The girl slowly adjusted her aim. Tashon shouted Johann's name, but by the time he got it out Johann had already turned and fired at her. She dropped, her head coming to rest on the stomach of the body beneath her.

"Update, Officer," Johann said to the man.

"Oh, um, just apprentice."

"I used to be Chief of Security. You're an officer now. Update?"

"Oh, uh, thank you, sir." The man tried to gain his composure. "They haven't made it into the main engine room yet. Three more doors to get through, and none of the tesseract engineers are giving in. They've executed two already."

"Okay. We still have some time then." Johann scratched his beard and pursed his lips. "How many do they have down there?"

"Eight fighting for them," the officer said. "Three engineers held hostage. We should have five opposite the engine room. Or, we did ten minutes ago."

"We should have many more," Johann said.

"Spread thin, Mister Johann. Extinctionists are wreaking havoc across the ship. Starting fights. Tossing smoke bombs in the education district. Starting grease fires. Any kind of distraction they can. And they've disabled at least half the access doors. Same with the elevators."

"Damn it." Johann shook his gun at the ground. "Your name?"

"Modell."

"Officer Modell. In your opinion, how did these Extinctionists bring so many to their cause? I just don't get it. Makes no sense to me."

Modell sucked in a breath with a whistle as he thought. He stretched his arms above his head. He was tall, and as he reached his hand to the ceiling, Tashon felt for a moment like a child standing at the feet of a stranger.

"We've been debating that ourselves, sir. The majority of those fighting for this insane cause is under the age of twenty-one."

"Which means?"

"Most of them have little or no memory of the world before."

"But we learned that in education," Tashon pointed out.

"True," Johann agreed. "But do you remember what it felt like to choke on the fog of pollution? Or wonder every time you took a sip of water whether it had been contaminated?"

Tashon shook his head slowly and gave a look that showed he understood. He didn't experience life on Earth the way many had. In truth, he could not compare a life on the ship to a life on Earth.

"But why would that make them join a group set on destroying everything?"

Shots and screams echoed from another hallway. The three stopped and looked at each other. Each tightened the grip on his weapon.

"Knowing why isn't going to stop them from taking the engine," Tashon said. Though he wished it would. He wanted to be a part of stopping them, but he wasn't keen on running off to commit more murders. However, the three took off with Johann and Modell side by side and Tashon right behind.

They took a right, a left, and another left. As they got closer to the main engine room, the walls became thicker to protect the engine. Which meant the hallways grew narrower. They were forced to run single file just as more screams rang out. Tashon stopped cold. Of all the screams he'd heard recently, that one sent his stomach into his throat. It was a wailing, stretched out scream that sounded like a man slowly being pulled apart. The three paused for a moment, then ran around the next corner. They had reached the tesseract.

The door to the main engine room stood ajar, the rectangle tesseract emitting a soft green glow. Two men in security uniforms stood in front of the open door. In front of them, three engineers knelt on the ground. One was holding his wrist. Blood leaked through the grasping fingers. Tashon looked to the ground and found a severed hand resting in a pool of blood.

One of the men had his helmet off, sweat-soaked hair sticking to the sides of his face. His eyes were dark. His mouth tight, open just enough for Tashon to glimpse his gleaming white teeth. He held a large knife in his hand. Blood dripped down its side. The other man stood to the side, hands clasped in front of him, unmoving. Neither seemed to notice the three that had entered the hall merely fifty feet away. They ducked behind a storage crate. Tashon's heart pounded. His ears ached. He tried to quiet his breathing, but could not. He could either turn and run, or stay and face the monster he saw before him. Neither appealed to him. The man crouched and placed his fingers under the engineer's chin. He gently lifted it up.

"Apprentice engineer." His voice was surprisingly soothing. "Please. We need the launch codes."

"Need them." The engineer laughed and spat blood on the floor.

The man simply smiled and shook his head.

"The universe needs it. Have you not been hearing what we've been telling you?"

"All I hear," the engineer said, "is a madman spouting bullshit to excuse his own insanity."

"I am sorry to hear you say that, friend."

The madman turned to the man behind him. "Gar," he said with tears in his eyes. "Please proceed."

Gar unclasped his hands and reached for the gun on his hip. Before he had it out of the holster, Johann had jumped into the room and fired one shot. It struck Gar in the left eye. The body wobbled for a moment, fell through the doorway, and landed with a thud next to the tesseract.

The dark-eyed man looked up with surprise in his eyes.

Johann and Modell walked toward him, guns centered on his skull. Tashon followed a few feet behind, his knuckles turning white as he gripped the blades. Something about the madman seemed familiar, but he couldn't place it.

"Friends." The man dropped his knife and raised his hands. "I see you're upset. Let's talk, okay?"

"We don't have shit to talk about," Modell said with a hiss.

"Oh, of course we do! Have you heard what we're trying to do?"

"Kill us all," Johann answered.

"No, no, no." The man laughed. "You've got it all wrong. Okay, look. My name is Aleron. And you're Johann, and that's Tashon behind you. Who's this other young man, pointing a gun at me?"

Johann glanced at Modell. He didn't answer. His eyes didn't even flinch.

"Aleron," Tashon said. "Former Chief Pilot Aleron?"

"Ha! Chief Tashon, you recognize me."

"B-barely," Tashon stammered. "You used to be one of the ship's most beloved chiefs. Now you're, what, leading some crazed cult and killing innocents?"

Chief Pilot Aleron had been a revered pilot in the ship's first decade. He led dozens of excavation missions. Each brought in more material than expected, allowing them to build the first three colony ships ahead of schedule. But, on his final mission, he crashed into a large asteroid and got thrown from his ship. His suit gave him thirty minutes of oxygen out in the open. He barely made it back alive. Tashon had thought the man still lived in the medical ward.

"Chief Tashon, you are incorrect on two points." Aleron help up a finger. "First, I do not lead this so-called cult. No, I do not have the mind for such things. Second, we do not kill anybody because death is, in fact, an illusion. So, if no one can die, how, then, can one kill?"

"You're batshit," Modell stated.

"Ah." Aleron smiled. "Insanity is also an illusion."

"It's easy to justify anything if everything is an illusion," Johann said.

"Perhaps," Aleron said. "Friends?"

Two more men in security uniforms emerged from inside the engine room. One held a gun in each hand. The other, knives.

In a sudden movement, the one flung his arm forward. A blade flew out of his hand. Modell ducked out of its path while firing a shot into the thrower's forehead. The blade continued toward Tashon. He tried to move but wasn't quite fast enough. The edge of the blade sliced the left side of his cheek as it flew past. He inhaled with a hiss and pressed the back of his hand to the wound.

Johann nodded, silently asking if Tashon was all right.

Tashon nodded back.

"Look." Johann aimed his gun at Aleron. "I don't know what your game plan is, but I will not let you take down this ship."

"Well," Aleron said. "Good thing I don't plan on destroying it."

"Or use it as a military vessel for your insane crusade."

He looked down at the three engineers. The one with a missing hand had passed out on his side. Another stared blankly at the hand in the floor. The third moved his lips as if he were praying.

Modell took a step forward. "Fed up with this bull—"

Aleron's bodyguard raised and fired his gun in one effortless motion. Modell's head snapped back and he collapsed. With one glance, Tashon could see the officer was dead. Johann fired two quick shots to drop the bodyguard then turned his attention back to Aleron. He walked closer to the man until the gun was inches away from the sweat-soaked forehead. He pulled the trigger, but all that came from the gun was a soft *click*.

"Damn." Johann punched the man across the face.

Tashon walked up and gently pushed Johann out of the way. "I want"—he coughed and wiped blood off his cheek—"to talk to him."

He pushed Aleron into the wall with one hand and pressed a knife to his cheek with the other. His entire body trembled. This violence, this bloodshed, was all new to him. It felt like he'd been walking through bodies, knives and gunfire for years. But it had only been a couple of hours, maybe less. He stood there, unmoving, trying to focus on Aleron's eyes. Wanting to shout at him, or stab him. Do *something* to him. But all he could do was picture his father's lifeless body. See the blank stare that came over the other man when he stabbed him in the skull. He let his grip loosen, though Aleron stayed still, his eyes wide. Tashon turned his gaze for a moment and caught a glimpse of the tesseract engine and its soft green glow. He shook his head, and his mind began to clear.

"Wait, wait," he said to Johann. "The engine."

"What?"

"The engine. Smith. We could go help them."

The engineer who had been praying looked up. "Is something wrong on Aethera?"

Johann sighed. "They crash landed. Haven't had any updates. We kept it secret while we dealt with this onboard threat."

Tashon shoved Aleron at Johann, who promptly knocked him out with the butt of his gun. Aleron slid peacefully to the ground with a slight grin on his face.

"Can you get us back there?" Tashon crouched to the engineer's level. "Please."

"You know," the engineer said, "as a chief, you could just order me to."

Tashon grasped his hand and looked at his name tag. "Thank you, Bodhi."

Bodhi limped to the engine. He pressed a button and the top of it slid open. Inside was what looked like a chaotic array of wires, buttons and switches. With one hand, he dropped a small comm device into the center. It projected a two-dimensional hologram on top of the array, providing labels for every aspect of the engine. He quickly turned dials and flipped switches, stopping only once to confirm that he pressed the correct button. Tashon thought to question him, but decided he'd better not. With a flourish of his hands and a big grin, Bodhi flicked one last switch and picked up the comm device. A pre-recorded voice came over the ship's speakers.

"Attention, five minutes until our jump to Fourth. Please proceed to the nearest safe jump location." It continued to repeat the message.

Tashon let out a sigh and laughed. "Glad I didn't just lie down in that storage closet to die," he said.

Johann gave him a quizzical look, then walked over and hugged him. "Me too," he whispered.

"Heathens!" Aleron screamed from outside the room.

Tashon turned to see the large knife leaving Aleron's hand. It struck the engine, sending sparks and severing wires.

Tashon's body tensed and his mind swirled. The one chance he saw to save Smith and his family, gone with the single throw of the knife. He looked at Aleron lying on the ground, coughing and smiling. With no regard to the guilt he'd felt minutes before, Tashon jumped on Aleron and raised his knife above his head. The two stared at each other. One with eyes full of conceited victory. The other with eyes blinded by rage. What would it matter, really, if he killed just one more person? Just drive the knife down one more time, let Aleron float off into whatever it was that came next. Tashon still did not move. Aleron had caused the death of countless civilians on the ship. Destroyed the only chance they had of going back for Smith. Possibly stranded them in a vessel that would become the floating grave of thousands. Still, Tashon's arms stayed above his head.

Screaming, he dropped the knife and stood up, keeping his eyes away from Aleron. He paced back and forth. Thought Johann said something to him, but ignored it. Without warning, the ship shook violently. The engine whirred loudly. Tashon's body lifted off the ground, then gravity grabbed hold and he fell on his back. With a smile, Tashon realized a damaged tesseract engine could still make the jump to the Fourth.

Chapter 17

While the Ship of Nations was being built, many theories formed concerning what would happen if a compromised tesseract engine made its jump into the Fourth. Some imagined it would stretch the human body in ways impossible in the third dimension, pulling it apart until it broke completely. Others said the opposite would happen, that our bodies would be pushed on and crushed down to mere atoms. Then there were the psychologists who were concerned with the psychological effect such an experience might have on a person. For, if they ended up stuck in the Fourth somehow, and were able to observe what it looked like, their minds would collapse. As third-dimension beings, they might see fourth-dimension objects beyond their comprehension. This, some said, would be too much for the human mind to handle.

From Tashon's perspective, they were all wrong. Particularly the psychologists — the human mind is far stronger than most give it credit for.

His body slammed on the floor, knocking the breath out of him. With a laugh, he realized the engine had, at the very least, not been completely destroyed. But something was different. When the ship had been in the Fourth before, he could feel the momentum of the ship. Technically, everyone was to be in a sitting position during the entire trip. Tashon stood up.

He sensed that they were somewhere different than they had been. But he did not have to lean forward as he walked to keep from falling. It felt as though they were gently floating. With a shake of his head, he looked for the others.

Johann sat over Aleron, tying the man's hands together behind his back. Bodhi stood in the engine room. The comm device was on the wall, projecting stats and readouts of what the ship was doing. Tashon walked over and looked at the numbers, though they meant little to him.

"We're moving slower," he said.

Bodhi flicked his finger through the hologram, numbers moving up and down. "About thirty percent what we would normally do."

Tashon nodded. He couldn't help but wonder what it looked like outside the ship. A completely different dimension, far more complex than his native one. And at the slow speeds they were moving, if he got a glimpse outside he would be able to truly see what lay out there.

"Looked at the exterior cameras yet?"

Bodhi's hands went still. With a grin, he turned to Tashon. "I hadn't even thought of that. At these speeds, we could actually get a full view of what's out there."

"Right."

Bodhi pulled out a different comm device, this one a cube. He walked out of the engine room and placed it on the floor. With a verbal command, the room lit up with a projection. For a moment, what floated there made no sense. Tashon walked around the projection, trying to understand it. Johann and Bodhi did the same. No one spoke.

It was mesmerizing. Full of color. Shapes and forms unimaginable to any who had spent their entire lives in the third dimension. After nearly ten minutes, the shapes made sense to Tashon. The lines, the curves, the faces. He could not have explained it to anyone, but his mind understood. It would be like a two-dimensional circle traveling to the Third and finding a sphere. It would spin round and round the new shape until it made sense of what it was seeing. When it returned to its two-dimensional friends, they would ask what it saw. All it would be able to say would be, "I saw circles like us. Only they were more round. More... complete."

And that's how Tashon felt. The world he was seeing was somehow more complete, more *whole*, than the one he lived in. Something sped across the image. Tashon only caught a glimpse, but whatever it was looked alive. A tall, narrow figure, it still appeared round. A biped, perhaps? Its entire form glowed softly. Toward the top of it, two dots shone brighter than the rest. Eyes? A live being, in the Fourth? Tashon stared, waiting and hoping for the being to make another appearance. But nothing came.

An alarm blared from the engine room, breaking his trance.

Bodhi swore and ran back to the engine room. Tashon and Johann followed.

Bodhi moved his hand wildly, staring at a large circle radar projected on the wall. "No. No." His hands shook, his eyes opened wide.

"Bodhi?" Tashon asked gently.

No response. Bodhi stared at the radar. Tashon followed his gaze. A long green rectangle moved across the circle—the Ship of Nations. Other shapes were outlined, all stationary. Then there was an oblong eclipse, smaller than the ship, moving quickly. Directly toward the Ship of Nations.

"Bodhi!" Johann shouted, a hint of worry in his voice.

"Okay, okay." Bodhi took a deep breath. "Something is moving toward us."

"Is that something new?"

"Yeah. I mean, when we're moving at full speed all we really have to do is make adjustments, so we don't hit any objects. I've never seen signs of something alive in the Fourth. People theorize about it, sure. But whatever we saw from that camera? And now this?"

The object on the radar continued its unwavering path.

The ship shook violently to one side, knocking Tashon and Johann off their feet. Bodhi caught himself on the engine. Tashon sat up and looked around wildly. He noticed with a slight smile that Aleron had rolled into a corner and got stuck between the wall and a pipe.

"Did it get us?" Johann stood up.

In reply, Bodhi simply pointed at the radar. The object was still moving in its same line, only it had passed the ship and continued on. The ship was moving to the left. No, Tashon realized. It was being *pushed*.

"Can you get us the starboard cameras?" Johann asked.

Bodhi looked on the floor and after a few minutes found the cube he had used earlier. Bodhi held the cube in his hand and flicked it on. He flipped through each starboard camera until they could see what was moving outside the ship.

Tashon gasped. Johann and Bodhi swore in amazement.

The glowing being they had seen floated outside the ship. From its sides, four appendages that vaguely resembled arms were outstretched. It was pushing the ship, the light from its body flying out behind, like hair blowing in the wind. What Tashon assumed was its head swiveled around and seemed to see something. Its form tensed, and it burst into a higher speed. Again, Tashon was knocked off his feet. He hit the ground but kept his eyes fixed on the image. Whatever was happening out there was beyond his control. Beyond anyone's. The alarm in the engine room roared back to life. In response, Bodhi set the cube on the floor and expanded the picture for a larger view.

A multitude of fourth-dimensional beings were chasing after the ship and their new pilot. These did not radiate color and light like the first being. Instead, they emanated a glowing darkness so dense that Tashon could barely comprehend it. As soon as he saw them, he shivered and felt like vomiting. He hoped with everything he had that the dark forms would not catch them.

He hoped in vain.

The forms hit the ship with such force that Tashon flew off the ground and was slammed into a wall. From his perspective, the forms had begun pushing the ship downward. On the projected image, a ball of light expanded from the body of their would-be savior. If one of the dark forms touched the glow, its form disappeared. But there were too many of them. The ship was under their control.

One of the black forms pulled away from the group, floated above them and toward the bottom of the ship, closer to engine room, and then it disappeared from view. The ship shook and spun quickly nose over tail, sending Tashon back through the air into another wall. The cube slammed into the wall opposite and shattered, taking the image with it. They were blind to the outside.

Tashon's breathing quickened, his heart pounding in his ears. Where had that lone black figure gone? The ship shook and twisted again, throwing Tashon back onto the floor. Then everything went still. Quiet. Tashon looked at Bodhi and Johann, apprehension on their faces mirroring his own.

The wall Tashon had just been pressed against began to vibrate. A small square of pure... darkness appeared in its center. The square widened to nearly three feet. It spread up and down from the center, forming a wide line of black nothing that moved down, across the floor and up, across the ceiling and met at the opposite wall, encircling the room. The entire ship shook, creaked and then ripped into two pieces in an explosion of metal and wires.

The black dissipated. Tashon suddenly felt the tiniest bit heavier, as if gravity had increased. He cautiously stood and looked around. A few feet in front of him was the new "edge" of the ship. There was a gap over ten feet wide that separated the section Tashon was on from the section Bodhi and Johann were on. They stood there, so close yet so far, staring back at Tashon the same way Tashon stared at them. As if they would never return to the Third, as if that were okay if only for the chance to truly see the Fourth.

Tashon took a deep breath, and blew it out. How could he breathe? He stepped right up to the edge and looked down—up?—into the fourth dimension. No human had ever seen it. The space below, to the sides and above was filled with shapes, colors, waves and lines, all unimaginable until one laid eyes on them. Tashon had thought the only difference between the Third and the Fourth would have been the shapes and the added directions of ana and kata, but here he saw colors more vibrantly beautiful than anything he'd ever seen. The air itself seemed to take on its own color and shape, a silver spherical swirling that weaved in, out and through the impossible shapes.

He looked back at his companions. They had drifted farther away. Now, two hundred yards of fourth-dimensional space spread out between Tashon and the only other humans in sight.

He sat down and let his feet hang out into the unknown. He looked down and stared, trying to make sense of the evermoving shapes and colors. After a while, he began to see a floor or, perhaps, ground. It was a large surface that looked to be the Fourth's equivalent of "flat." It was an indiscernible distance below him, but he could not just sit there. He pushed himself off, and fell.

Slowly. Far slower than gravity would have pulled him had he been in the Third, even with the lessened gravity aboard the ship. Floating down, he was able to get a better look of what was around him. Small cubes, towering rectangles, trapezoids, spheres. At least, the Fourth's version of those shapes. He knew he'd been told the right names, but couldn't remember them. In the distance were figures like the ones he had seen outside the ship. Some glowing white, others filled with a deep darkness. But most of them emanated varying shades of gray. Flying in directions new and familiar to Tashon. And flowing in, out and around all of it, the silver air churned.

As his feet touched the surface, he bent his knees and stood up straight, then fell slowly onto his side. Gravity in the Fourth, he realized, pulled from more than one direction. The surface he lay on was semi-translucent. He pushed himself to sit and peered through it. Behind him and to his right, where the back end of the ship was, he could see the asteroid field where they had been when they first jumped into the Fourth. It did not look flat, as everyone had said it would. It simply looked less dimensional than the world that surrounded him. And much smaller than it truly was. Or, perhaps, it was that small in comparison to the vastness of the Fourth. In front and to the left, farther ahead and beneath the fourth-dimensional surface, floated Aethera. It slowly orbited its sun as two moons orbited the planet itself. And between the two moons, dozens of other planets uninhabitable by human life.

Tashon pushed himself back to his feet and slowly began walking to Johann and Bodhi, who had also ventured out of the ship. Thankfully, the distance between them had not continued to grow. But it was still a painstakingly difficult journey. He fell at least once every twenty steps, and the resistance of the silver wind made him feel like a paper cutout trying to walk vertically through a park on a windy day.

Eventually, he arrived at a cliff. The surface he walked on quickly curved downward and became a vertical face. Tashon stopped and looked down. He saw the bottom, but its distance from him seemed to shift, at times a mere six feet away and at other times hundreds of yards. He looked closer. The surface at the bottom of the cliff seemed to rotate slowly. As it turned, the distance between he and the bottom changed. Patiently, he waited for it to show a side closer to the top of the cliff. It rotated so lazily that he had more time to examine his surroundings.

The structures he saw in the distance looked deliberately placed, as if each one had its own purpose. As if it were a city. But if that were the case, then that meant the Fourth was far more alive than anyone had ever expected. If the beings were floating around, moving in and out of structures with specific intent, then the Fourth was alive with its own cultures, its own societies. *Maybe*, Tashon thought, *the Third was truly just a shadow of the Fourth. A shadow of something higher and more beautiful.* He looked back to the other half of the ship.

Johann and Bodhi walked toward Tashon. With each step, their half of the ship followed behind, as if it were attached to the two men by invisible ropes. Tashon looked behind him. Floating just above the surface, five feet behind him, was his half of the ship. The simple act of moving forward was bringing the two halves of the ship closer together.

The distance to the bottom of the cliff had lessened to a few feet. Tashon jumped and floated down until his feet touched. The spinning shape stretched forward for hundreds of feet and ended at the base of another cliff. In the middle of the shape, floating inside of it, was the unconscious body of Aleron. And just behind him was the tesseract engine.

Tashon paused and stared. How had the engine been taken from the ship? The side of the shape he walked on turned vertical, but he did not fall off. As if the spinning of it kept pulling him toward its center.

It dawned on him that he was walking on the outside of a fourth-dimensional rendering of the Ship of Nations. It had far more faces, just like the Fourth's version of a cube would, but it was a copy of the ship he knew as home. With a deep breath he continued forward.

Soon, he was standing directly above the engine with Johann and Bodhi. All three tried to speak, but no sounds escaped their mouths. Bodhi knelt, gripped a handle and pulled. A hatch opened. Tashon peered in. Save for Aleron and the engine, the ship appeared to be empty. The Fourth had not created a complete copy of the ship. Quickly, one at a time, the three went through the opening.

Inside, the source of gravity was the engine itself. They were pulled closer to it at an even slower rate than Tashon had floated down off the ship. Tashon watched Aleron, expecting the man to come out of his daze, break his restraints and come after them.

But it was not the man that threatened them.

A black being slammed into Johann, sending him flying out of Tashon's view. Then, Tashon was hit, pushed by a deep darkness that he could feel inside his bones. It seemed his very soul would burn with the cold that enveloped him. Another grabbed him on the other side, wrapping its appendage around him. He was being embraced by Death itself, he knew it. His fingertips went numb, then his hands, arms and shoulders soon followed. The numbness crept down his chest, closer to his heart. Up his neck and face, slowly dimming his vision.

All he could see, all he could hear, all he could *feel*, was utter darkness. He floated through darkness. The darkness floated through him. His mom's face exploded into his mind, followed by the floating and lifeless body of his dad. Grace's body, falling off the ship, bones shattering as she hit the ground. The dead, stunned eyes of the man he stabbed through the skull.

Nothing else entered his mind. Nothing but complete hopelessness in his heart. He floated for minutes, maybe hours, the despair slowly tearing his soul apart, piece by piece.

He felt the forms that held him scream, and they let go him of him in a flash of light. Tashon landed on a hard surface and opened his eyes. He lay on his back in the middle of dozens of towering structures. Up close, they were far larger than anything he had ever seen. The smallest one, a sphere, was double the size of the ship. In front of him was an enormous tesseract, with what looked like doors spaced along its entire bottom. Behind that, the top of a pyramid reached into the air.

Around him, a battle raged. The figures of darkness were being pushed back by a handful of white forms. Fighting alongside them were dozens more of the in-between gray figures. Explosions of light, dark and every shade of gray sent figures slamming into the surface, into structures, scattering chunks of four-dimensional rubble everywhere.

Johann and Bodhi sat nearby, eyes wide in fear and amazement. Two forms of darkness slammed a floating form of light into the ground and then quickly made their way to Tashon. A thin tentacle snaked out of one of the forms and touched Tashon's temple. His body turned cold. The tendril pierced his skin. Tashon felt his conscious mind being pulled away. His will to fight, to survive, to do anything for himself, began to wane.

A gray being flew over Tashon's prone body and slammed into the dark one. The force of the hit sent it flying, ripping the tendril out of Tashon's head. He gasped and sat up. The figures of darkness were slowly overpowering the others. The one that had been draining Tashon's will threw its attacker into the air, and sped back toward its victim.

It was fifty feet away.

Thirty.

Ten.

The tentacle stretched out again as it neared.

A white being appeared in front of Tashon. The tentacle slid through the glowing body and out its back, then stopped. It, along with the body attached to it, glowed red, then blue, then white. In an explosion of burning light, the dark form disappeared. Tashon's savior turned to face him.

Tashon was instantly filled with warmth. In front of him a figure of pure, white light floated. Something about it felt... familiar. Comforting. It turned its head toward him and, for a moment, a human face appeared. Evalee, her face and eyes bright with her beaming smile. Another being of shiny white, this one with a hint of gold, joined her. Tashon turned and looked at the newcomer. He jumped to his feet as he saw the face—Grace. His sister. Tears formed in his eyes. He moved to hug her but was stopped by a voice in his head telling him they could not touch. Two gray beings appeared beside Grace and Evalee. Tashon fell to his knees as he recognized their faces. His mother. His father. His tears spilled out and down his cheeks. For countless minutes he knelt, overcome with pain of his losses, but comfort in seeing their faces.

What he did not notice were his two companions on their knees, in front of similar figures, overcome with the same inner turmoil.

Eventually, the beings flew away, and the three were again pulled to the engine. Johann got to it first. As soon as he touched it, the ship slammed back together, and they all lay on the floor of the engine room.

Tashon cursed as his head hit cold metal.

"What the hell?" Bodhi screamed.

Tashon turned his head to see Aleron's unconscious body. Above it, a loan black figure floated. Tendrils streamed out of its body, injecting themselves into Aleron's back.

Before anyone could react, a prerecorded voice sounded over the ship's speakers. "Attention. Please prepare for reentry into the third dimension." The prerecorded message repeated its warning several times.

"Bodhi," Johann shouted in a panic. "Where are we coming out?"

The engineer ran to the engine to investigate. Tashon sat up, his eyes focusing on the forms outside the ship.

Bodhi laughed. "We're coming out over Colony Six," he said. The smile fell from his face. "Oh no. No. No, no, no."

"Bodhi!" Johann shouted. "You need to keep talking."

"We're uh...." He tried to catch his breath. "At Colony Six. But we came out too close. We, uh, we...."

He stopped talking.

"Damn it, Bodhi!"

"We're out. *Right* over Aethera. We're in its pull. We're —"

"Going down," Johann finished.

They were back in the Third. Back at Colony Six. Gravity pulling the ship toward the planet's surface.

PART THREE

Chapter 18

Smith, Jonstin, Abe and a handful of others sat in the gray dirt. Some spoke, some cried. Sylvia lay away from the group, asleep. Her gentle snore reminded Smith that she hadn't died. The glowing light and dashing shadows had disappeared nearly as quick as they came, leaving only destruction in their wake. In front of the small group was a massive crater, the pulsing green light shining from deep within. They had spent the better part of the day digging through the large hole, pulling out materials, survivors and bodies. Thankfully, there weren't many of the latter. But after all they'd been through, it felt like far too many.

Two of the colony homes remained. One was missing a large section on the side closest to the crater. Smith and the others had packed it full of the remaining supplies. The other had only cots and pads for sleeping, though it was not large enough to hold everyone.

Smith saw beetles everywhere he looked. He was the *only* one seeing beetles everywhere. Had been since the funeral. Crawling across the ground, over the bodies of those sleeping. One, larger than his head, floated around in aimless circles. Others were too small to be seen, yet he felt their presence, moving like armies across the earth. Smith closed his eyes, inhaled, and then opened them. The beetles were gone. He knew they would be back.

Jonstin stood, walked to Smith and sat down.

"There goes the neighborhood," he said, pointing to the crater.

"Huh?"

"Nothin'. Something I heard on an old Earth film."

"Um-hum."

Smith jumped in surprise as two beetles appeared in front of him. They fought intensely, mandibles slashing back and forth. One pinned the other down and ripped it in half with a spatter of blood. Smith turned away, trying to pretend nothing was wrong. He wasn't going insane. There wasn't a beetle living in his brain. Wasn't. Wasn't. It was just the stress, the grief of recent days. It would pass. The winning beetle walked into the distance and disappeared. The other decomposed before his eyes, the natural process sped up in the hallucination, and was gone. Just like Evalee's body. Slowly breaking down, skin drying out, flesh falling apart, until nothing of her remained. Or was her soul somewhere else, like she had always believed?

"What now, Smith?"

The farmer sighed and stretched his arms above his head, looking up at the sky. The sun was almost behind the red mountains, casting the now familiar red glow. Dark clouds hung in the sky to the west, nearly stretching the distance from the ship's wreckage to the far edge of the mountains. From the maps Smith had memorized of the planet, he guessed the cloud system was nearly one hundred miles long. They looked like they held millions of gallons of rain and he hoped they would stay far away. He pulled his gaze away and looked at Jonstin.

"I really don't know," Smith admitted with a shake of his head.

"Yeah, but we have to do something."

Smith nodded and rubbed his hand over his head. Checking for bumps and scabs, any sign that an alien beetle was living in his head, had become a habit. So far, the worst he'd experienced were minor headaches, though he wasn't entirely sure those weren't just psychological.

"I know," Smith nodded. "But where're your ideas? You wanted to take leadership of this colony." Smith tried to keep his voice calm. But so much had happened.

"Smith," Jonstin sighed. "I really was just trying to help."

Smith looked at the man, locked eyes with him for a moment.

"I believe you." Smith turned away. "But did you had to improve your image while you did it?"

Jonstin sighed. "I can be a vain man, I suppose."

"Well, it takes some humility to even say that."

Jonstin nodded once. They sat in silence for a few moments. The wind had picked up and Smith shivered.

"Did I really say all that?" Jonstin inhaled. "All that racist shit?"

Smith eyed Jonstin before responding. "Yeah. You did say all that racist shit. You really don't remember?"

"No. Nothing."

Smith wanted to believe him. Wanted to believe Jonstin was a good man, even if it meant he had been wrong about the pilot for the last decade.

"My life," Jonstin said, "back on Earth was the shits. A lot of stuff... my dad.... It was the shits. My dad was a racist bastard. Always said it was a travesty the wall was never finished, that when construction on it stopped was the turning point toward the States' demise. Shit like that."

"You don't agree with him?"

"Hell no. But for years I had to pretend I did. The old man once caught me riding transit home from school with a few Latino kids from my class. I must've been seven, maybe eight. He ran onto the street train, grabbed me by the collar. In front of everyone. Yellin' about how it was the beaners that had ruined our country. That I was betraying our country by even breathing the same air as them. He dragged me home. Belted me. Indoctrinated me every day after dinner 'til I moved out. Beat me anytime I made a hint of disagreeing with him. I can't believe I said all that. Why didn't you report me?"

"You're the Chief Pilot. The chaos that would've caused? What if it caused race battles on the ship? Or led to your murder? We confided in Johann and kept an eye on you. Nothing else you ever did worried us."

"Thanks, Smith."

Another ten minutes of silence. The pain in Smith's skull adjusted its position as if huddling in for the night. Again, he rubbed his hand over it. Again, he felt nothing. But it had to be there, right? He tried to push the thought away, tell himself it didn't matter. That there was nothing he could do about it, anyway.

"It's getting cold," Smith said. "We can't all fit in that one home, though."

Jonstin stood up and raised his voice. "Listen up! Young ones and their mothers get first call on sleeping in the home. After that, we'll start with our eldest and work our way down 'til it's full." Jonstin motioned to a group of teens. "You kids. Go to the storage crates and get blankets, jackets and anything else that will keep the rest of us warm out here."

He paused and looked around, his eyes wet with tears.

"I know we have all lost so much. Damn near everything, it feels like. But look, we can make it. Tonight, I want us all to try to sleep. Dream of what this planet will one day become. We already have patrol schedules planned so we have eyes watching all night long. But I honestly believe that we will have a safe night. In the morning, I want to hear everyone's ideas on what we can do moving forward. Sleep well, everyone. Let us dream."

Smith smiled. He had to admit, Jonstin could be a great leader.

***

The sun was nearly up. The beetles had returned, disappeared and returned again. Smith stared at the looming rain clouds. Some survivors stirred, but most still slept. Or had no desire to wake up and remember what had happened.

Smith's head was still intact. On the outside, at least. No physical signs of anything living inside of him. The more nothing happened, the more he became convinced that it was an intelligent biotech beetle with a deep understanding of human psychology. Physically, it did nothing to him, but the mere idea of it living in him would drive him mad. Maybe there wasn't even anything in his head, and the leftover beetle half was left only in attempt to drive him so insane that he cut into his own skull in search of something that wasn't even there. He wiped exhaustion from his eyes. A few beetles floated down from the sky as if they were raindrops. Each time he looked directly at one, his head pulsed. Like the beetle in his head wanted to get out and join its nonexistent beetle brothers. He looked to his son. The beetles disappeared, but the pain stayed. It was becoming a constant companion.

Abe sat next to him, casually digging small holes in the soil and scanning the chemical makeup. Just like before, the soil was decent. Crops could grow in it with enough care and effort.

"I'm going to go see what seeds we recovered," Abe said.

"Okay, son. Thanks."

Before he woke, Smith had been dreaming of his wife.

In the dream, he had been harvesting crops all day, and had just finished delivering them to the dozens of colony homes. With a smile, he carried the last basket of orange corn and purple apples inside to Evalee. She stood, her back to him, lighting the small stove. He quietly sat the basket on their small table and walked up behind her, kissing the back of her head. She turned and placed a warm hand on his face. When he looked down, he saw that she was pregnant. He immediately knew it would be a girl and he looked back up to see Evalee smile. But she had disappeared. He screamed for her, and awoke to the sound of his own shouting, beetles crawling from his open mouth. His heaving had brought Sylvia to him, and he told her it was nothing. She didn't need to know her last connection to her sister was going insane. *And*, Smith thought, *slowly dying*.

Smith wiped a tear from his cheek and watched his son walk away. He knew Abe must be struggling too, but hadn't had the chance to really talk to him about it. And if he did, he wouldn't know what to say.

That they'd been dealt a bad hand? Or that it would all be okay, that they'd get over it? Maybe that they would see her in heaven again? But none of those seemed right, though he knew he should say *something*. With a burst of willpower, he stood up and called after him.

Abe turned around.

"Wait up, son. I'll help."

Smith tried to run, but with the strength of the gravity it was more of a jog. By the time he got to Abe, he was dripping sweat.

"Damn, Dad. You need to run more."

Smith laughed. "Ah, shut up." He put an arm around Abe and squeezed. He thought about keeping his arm there, but it felt odd. He pulled away. "So, if we only had one type of seed left, what would you want it to be?"

Abe laughed. "As long as it's not the green carrots, I don't care."

"Your mom always had to force you to eat those," Smith said.

Abe nodded but said nothing.

"Abe." Smith looked for words but found none.

They stopped walking. Abe coughed. He leaned forward, hands on his knees. Bile sprayed from his mouth, churning the gray dirt to mud.

Smith patted his back and helped him sit down.

"You know, Abe." Smith sat down next to him. "I hate this. I hate the hell out of this."

Abe wiped his face with the back of his hand and looked at his dad.

"Me too. It's bullshit, Dad."

Smith stopped himself from telling Abe to watch his mouth.

"It is," Smith said. "It is."

Sylvia walked toward them and waved. She sat down on the other side of Abe and grabbed the boy's hand.

"Do you think we'll get the chance to see her again?"

Smith's breath caught in his throat. He turned to Abe, and looked into the boy's eyes. His voice sounded steady, but his eye seemed to be pleading for guidance. For reassurance. Beyond his son, Smith saw Sylvia nod with a reserved smile. But Smith couldn't lie.

"I really don't know." Smith pulled his son in close. "I sure as hell hope so."

Abe looked at the ground. The puddle of bile had already dried.

"For now, though, you got me. And I'm not going anywhere."

Abe nodded and stood up, reaching out a hand to help his father stand.

"Thanks," Abe said. "But I would've really preferred if it were Mom."

Smith smiled and wrapped his arm around the boy's shoulders.

"Yeah," he agreed. "That would be better."

***

The remaining survivors sat in one group, each sharing a prepackaged meal with at least one other person. They were discussing ways to secure their survival.

"We need shelter," Sylvia said. "Those clouds are closer, which means the rainy season is coming soon."

Many nodded in agreement. They had all seen the footage sent back from the scouting drones. Massive raindrops pouring down at high speeds often turned to hail the size of a child's fist.

"We want to hear any ideas," Jonstin said. "Thoughts?"

Smith looked closely at the people, waiting for an answer. He could tell some had already given up, their eyes glazed over. Others talked among themselves. In the back, he saw Abe and Winona, a teen girl, looking at a comm device. She had no hair like Abe, yet she was still beautiful. She'd lost both of her parents to the crater, and Smith was happy to see Abe keeping her company. He turned to say something to Jonstin and Sylvia, but Abe stood up and announced that they had a plan. Smith called them both to the front, but Winona shook her head and sat down. Abe joined his father by himself.

"Okay," Abe said. "It's not an easy plan, but Winona and I think it will work long term." He took a breath and glanced at the screen in his hand. "We were supposed to land on the other side of the red mountains. The recon drones showed signs of a cave system in the mountains and vegetation on the other side."

"But how the hell are we gonna get there?" a father with two young children asked. "That's gotta be nearly fifty miles!"

Abe nodded his head. "Just over sixty, actually. But where else is there shelter?"

Everyone looked around at what they had in front of them. One broken colony home with supplies to last a month, maybe a bit longer. And one intact home that could house about a third of them. There was no arguing—they needed to go somewhere.

Sylvia cleared her throat and moved next to Abe, patting his shoulder with a smile.

"It's a good idea, Abe. But how're we going to get there? We need to take the supplies with us, and none of our land transports survived the crash."

Abe nodded and looked to his dad, then back to the others.

"We have ropes and storage containers. Full and empty ones."

Smith shook his head and laughed. "That's going to be tough going," he said. "But I think it's the best chance we have. Anyone have another plan?"

No one spoke.

"Then let's get to work."

***

They'd been walking for what felt like hours. Beetles flickered in and out of his vision, still unseen by everyone else. The sun would soon set behind the red mountains, another day of survival behind them. Smith and Jonstin led the group, walking side by side. Each had ropes wrapped around their shoulders and waist. Behind each of them, the ropes stretched back and connected to a train of storage crates. Jonstin pulled three, all filled with various supplies. Smith pulled five—two filled with supplies, the other three carrying younger kids. Periodically, he would sprint a few feet, just so he could hear them laugh. Others behind them and to the sides did the same, nearly a dozen trains slowly making their way to the red mountains.

The rest walked in something that resembled a wide line. Some of the kids ran up and down, throwing soft chunks of dirt they'd found near the crater. Sylvia walked among the group, talking with the people. Learning their thoughts, their struggles, their strengths.

"If we get through all this," Jonstin said to Smith through heavy breaths. "Sylvia really would be the best one to lead us."

Smith looked at him in surprise.

"Oh, don't give me that look." Jonstin laughed. "Though I can see why that's unexpected."

"'Cause you're kind of a prick?"

Jonstin laughed again and shook his head.

"I know I can be difficult, Smith. I'm just saying that, after everything, I see Sylvia still standing strong, connecting with the people. She cares about them, and they *know* that she does."

Smith nodded. With a smile, he sprinted ahead and the children in his train laughed.

To the children, it was a game. But Smith was trying to get away from the beetles that lingered more and more. They kept pace with him. After Smith slowed, they wandered around him for at least another hour.

***

The sun had set, and the group rested. The sounds of whispers and snores filled the night. Abe and Winona had walked a bit away from the group. They laughed, and Smith couldn't help but wonder what they were talking about.

The three leaders sat in a small circle, back to back, keeping an eye out for any sign of danger.

Smith breathed slowly, enjoying a calm respite from the beetle hallucinations. He was beginning to realize, or at least believe, that something inside his mind was causing the hallucinations. And when the beetles weren't making him questions his sanity, he was overcome with memories of Evalee, real and hoped for. With a drop in his gut, he thought yet again of how the place that was supposed to be their home had become a place he never imagined he would have to live. No, not live. Survive.

"Sometimes it feels like I've lived a thousand lives," he whispered.

"Or like we've been on this planet for our whole lives," Sylvia responded. "But also like we only got here yesterday."

Smith nodded. He thought of his life back on Earth, living amid the smog and pollution. He remembered when men in uniforms first brought gas masks to his grandma's house when he was five. After that, he was never allowed to go out without one. Then, the first time he saw Evalee cry as they sat in a greenhouse. He sighed and shook his head.

"Smith, I ever tell you about the first time I saw you?"

"You mean when we trained together just before the ship left Earth?"

"No, at the brothel," Jonstin said. "When you went to save Sylvia."

Smith could feel Sylvia stiffen. She moved away from Jonstin.

"What the hell are you saying?" Smith tried to stay calm. "Were you seeing her?"

"No! No. I was... I was high. My father had gone mad, killed my mom. Left me with my brother. I was lost, looking to feel something. Anything. I didn't care what or where from. I was about ready to give up on my piloting career. You didn't notice, but I walked into Pixies right behind you. You were a ball of...." He paused, twisting his finger in the air. "Righteous rage. I saw them knock you down. I tried to get them off you but I was, you know, under the influence. I got knocked out in one hit. But after I sobered up, I said to myself, 'That's the kind of man I want to be.' I got myself back together after that."

"Really?"

"Really, Smith. Why do you think I'm always trying to earn your respect?"

Smith shrugged. "I just thought you hated if anyone didn't like you."

"Yeah, that too."

Sylvia turned around. "I'm sorry about your mom."

A blinding light lit up the night. They all turned to see the Ship of Nations breaking into the atmosphere on the other side of the mountains. Smith had forgotten how massive it actually was. It fell at an angle, covering an entire space of sky from the top of the mountains to the stars high above, hiding the moon completely. It seemed to fall slower than it should have, as if it were a boat sinking to the depths of a great ocean. Smith screamed as he watched it disappear behind the mountains. The only sign it had hit the ground was the shaking of the earth beneath their feet.

That ship had been his home for over a decade. Tashon was on that ship. So many they cared about. He screamed again, hoping to wake up. But what he had seen disappear behind those mountains was real. His home—perhaps every human that had been on it—was gone.

Chapter 19

Tashon closed his eyes tighter and gripped his hands around his head. He felt like his skull would shatter at the slightest turn of his neck. Cool metal pressed against his back, and he realized he had rolled into a wall. He opened his eyes. At some point he had lost his grip on the pipe. His body was crumpled in a corner. As his eyes began to focus he realized he was looking *up* a hallway toward the engine room. The angle was dizzying and Tashon would never be able to climb up it, even if he hadn't just fallen from the sky.

He let out a wordless scream, his voice hoarse, and waited for a response. None came. With grunts and curses, he slowly sat up. His head spun with the effort, the ship seeming to shiver around him. He screamed again.

Someone above him coughed. "Tash?"

"Yeah."

"I lost...." The voice fell into a coughing fit.

Tashon caught the accent through the gurgled voice. "Johann," he said.

"I lost my damn comb," Johann said.

Tashon smiled. Then he coughed and spat. The saliva was red with blood. "Who else?"

"Bodhi's up here." Johann paused. "The others too. But...."

Tashon could hear Johann stumbling around above him.

"Damn it. Bodhi's the only one breathing."

Tashon bit his lip and closed his eyes. They'd made it to Colony Six, at least. Barely. That urge to lie down and let it all fade away crept back into his mind. Instead, he slowly slid himself up the wall until he was standing, his back against the wall, staring up into the hallway. He had to find Smith. And, if he really had seen Evalee, would he also see her on the surface? There was no way to know.

"Can you get down here?" he called to Johann.

More stumbling and grunting from above. Then Bodhi's head popped out from behind a wall, dangling toward Tashon.

"I'm going to let him slide to you." Johann counted to three and let go.

Bodhi's body slid slowly, his jacket squeaking loudly on the floor. The sound made Tashon wince. His head pulsed. Bodhi came to rest just to the right of Tashon, his feet pointed down the next hallway. Above, Johann let out a *whoop* and slid down in a sitting position.

Tashon grabbed Bodhi's arms and started pulling him down the next hallway. Johann grabbed the feet. With no flat surface to walk on, it was slow going. Tashon had one foot on the wall and one on the floor. He dragged Bodhi along the corner where the two surfaces met. They arrived at another hallway that went up to the left and down to the right. They slid down and continued through three more hallways until they reached a door. They took a moment to catch their breath.

"He's heavy," Tashon said. "I think it's your turn."

"Nah. Too old."

"Not too old to take on a bunch of terrorists."

Johann nodded and shrugged. After a moment, he gasped. "Hell." He shook his head. "Aleron's body wasn't there."

"What?"

"It wasn't there."

Tashon leaned his head back against the wall. If he was wandering around the ship, there was no telling what damage he could do. How many people he might kill. Tashon was certain the man was crazy. And there was no telling what an insane fanatic might do when he's failed at what he thought the universe called him to do.

"He's insane," was all Tashon said.

Johann nodded and knelt over Bodhi. He grabbed the engineer's collar, lifted his head off the ground and slapped him across the cheek. Bodhi grunted and shook his head as if to say, *No, just let me sleep.* Johann slapped him again and shouted his name. Bodhi opened his eyes, blinked and sat up with a start.

He looked around, breathing heavily. "What happened?"

"Made it to Colony Six." Johann spread his arms out to the sides.

Bodhi looked around. "We better get out of here fast. Don't know what damage the ship sustained. Or how long it will sit still."

Johann pulled Bodhi to his feet. Tashon swung the door open and stepped into the dining district. The sector was a disaster. Dozens of chairs and tables had slid into a giant pile on the bottom wall. A fridge dangled from a wire with its door open, the contents splattered everywhere. The sound of shouts echoed toward them. Tashon carefully let himself down and began to crawl toward it. Johann and Bodhi followed. It was disorienting to be in such a large, angled space. They kept slipping and eventually decided to slide all the way to the bottom and use the wall for support. It wasn't long before they found a group of survivors tucked into a turned over restaurant.

"More survivors!" Johann beamed as they joined the small group.

"Mister Johann," a man with long hair and a thin face said. "You're the first leader we've seen, which is good 'cause we can't agree on what to do."

"Well, are any of you engineers?"

None of them were.

"Engineer Bodhi here has indicated that the best option is to get out. We don't know the status of the ship, or how stable it is."

Some grumbled, but none would argue with the board member.

"Okay. Now, what's our quickest way out, Bodhi?"

"An airlock would be ideal, if it will unseal. But we don't know how high off the ground we are. It's possible that the nearest airlock is hundreds of feet above the surface, or buried underground."

"What about the exterior cameras?" Tashon asked.

Johann nodded and pulled a cube out of his pocket. He held it out in his left hand and turned it on. The camera leaned to the right, showing the tops of massive yellow trees. He flicked his fingers. The next camera showed the same trees from a lower angle. Thick branches grew all around the trunks.

"Those look climbable," a man noted.

"My thoughts," Johann agreed. "An airlock over there?"

Bodhi nodded. "Right between those two cameras, actually."

Johann motioned for Bodhi to take the lead.

"We won't have to climb up at all," Bodhi called back. "Just one level down. Not too far."

Tashon nodded gratefully as he fell in line behind a woman carrying a small child. A boy. Tashon gave him a smile but it looked like he was asleep. The woman slipped and almost dropped the little one. She quietly swore.

"You want me to carry him, ma'am?" Tashon asked, though he'd never held a baby before.

"No, no. Thank you though, Chief Tashon."

Tashon nodded and kept walking. The group got to the airlock without incident, but discovered the window with three-inch thick glass in the door was shattered, leaving a hole the size of a grown man in the airlock. All that could be seen were the thick trunks of the trees, their branches angled upward and covered in large yellow leaves. Curved red lines ran up and down the bark like veins. Thin rays filtered through, as if pure light were raining from up above. One branch was mere inches away from the hole. A cool breeze blew in, and Tashon greedily breathed it in. He was anxious to get out and find Smith, but the group stopped at the opening. Bodhi examined the hole.

"What's wrong, Bodhi?" Johann asked.

"I don't know," Bodhi said. "But I don't think this is from the crash."

"Then what?" A woman asked with a sense of fear.

Aleron, Tashon thought. He was about to say it out loud, but Johann locked eyes with him and shook his head.

"But it could have been from the crash, right?" Johann stared at Bodhi.

Bodhi seemed to catch on. "Yeah, it could. Just surprised by it, I guess."

"Okay. Let's start getting everyone out, then. Like you said, don't know how stable this thing is."

Bodhi nodded. After some discussion, it was decided the engineer would climb out first. Then one man would wait on the branches halfway down, and another at the top to ensure that all made it down safely. Johann insisted that he, as a board member, be the last one out.

As Tashon stuck his leg through the hole and placed his foot on a branch, his heart seemed to stop. It was his first time outside the ship. Despite all that had happened, he felt an almost overwhelming excitement. He wrapped both arms around the trunk, pulled his other leg out, and looked up. He saw only slivers of the sky through the thick yellow leaves. It was a soft orange. He smiled and began to climb down, slowly. It wasn't until later that he realized he would probably never be in that sky again. His feet touched soft dirt, and he lifted his legs up and down as if to test the solidness of the ground beneath him. Tashon had never stepped on ground that sunk under his feet. It was only a few centimeters, but for a moment he felt as though a hole had opened and he would be pulled in. He shook the feeling off and took a few steps back. Soon, everyone had made it safely down.

They stood, staring at the shell of what had been their home for decades. It stretched high above them. The back end had sunk into the earth. The ship had ripped apart a few hundred yards above the broken airlock. The front portion of the ship had broken off and was now level on the ground. The mom who had been carrying the child softly cried, as did a few others. The little boy sat on the ground, excitedly playing with the soft earth, sticks and fallen leaves. Tashon looked down at him and smiled. In that moment, the two had much in common.

It was the first time either had breathed air that hadn't been filtered and recycled on the ship. The first either had stood on something not made by human hands, or stood under the rays of a beaming sun, or in the shade of trees hundreds of years old. Or any shade at all. Over fifteen years separated the two, yet they were experiencing the same firsts. For a moment, he felt like a child again. Like everything around him was new, fresh and exciting.

"Okay," Johann called. "We need to send a group out to circle the ship and look for other survivors. Right now there are far too few of us."

Tashon's childlike gleam faded.

"And we need another group to go back into the ship for supplies and to look for anyone else." Johann pointed to Bodhi. "You know the layout and design better than any of us, so you'll lead that group. Any volunteers?"

Tashon looked again at the young boy playing in the dirt without a care, and for a moment wished to join him. But he knew he couldn't, so he raised his hand.

"I'll circle the ship with a small group." Tashon took a few steps forward. "We'll look for signs of Colony Six while we're out."

Johann nodded. After checking that there were at least two working comm devices in each group, two groups of six left the clearing. Johann stayed back with five others.

As the only chief in his group, Tashon led the group. Walking with him were twin brothers Elric and Sanga. They both wore their blond hair long, neither one making an effort to distinguish himself from the other. To be certain who was who, Tashon had to wait for one to speak. Elric had a stutter. Then there were two men about Smith's age. Doran was a hefty man with no hair. On the ship, he'd been the manager and cook at one of the restaurants. He still had his chef belt on. It held two knives and a spatula. The other man, Heth, was short and thin. He hadn't said a single word since they got off the ship. Last to join their group was Linoa, who had been in Security. She was a few years older than Tashon and walked with an air of confidence that was mesmerizing. Tashon couldn't help but watch as she ran a hand through her short brown hair.

"Let's take a wide circle around the ship," Tashon said. "Move in if we see something."

Everyone nodded their agreement and off they went. It didn't take long for Tashon to get used to the soft ground underfoot. What was stranger to him was the vast space around him. There were trees around and above him, but he was not enclosed in anything other than the planet's atmosphere. The openness of it made him nervous, and he tried not to jump at the slightest sound. And the sound around him was constant. The forest seemed so alive, yet he couldn't discern where any of the noises were coming from. The rustling of leaves to his right. The snap of a twig to his left. A whisper of unknown words just above, yet every time he looked up, there were only leaves and branches.

The group kept silent as they walked. Tashon was glad for it. He didn't want to talk about what had happened, what might happen. A shadow moved out of the corner of his eye. He stopped walking and looked toward the ship. Nothing there. He took a few steps forward and looked down, trying to catch his breath as he stared at the dirt. The dirt began to move. No, not move, come alive. Tashon quickly stepped back, keeping his eyes on the ground. Multiple forms began to take shape in the deep brown of the earth. Black and brown speckled insects, dozens of them, traveling across the forest floor. He crouched down to watch them. This was the first time he remembered ever seeing an organic bug in person. He'd been a young child when his parents took him from Earth on the ship, and he remembered nothing of the life before. The larger insects either carried smaller insects on theirs backs, or little plants. At the front of the line was the largest of the group. It reached a tree and, instead of going up or around it, it lifted its back legs into the air and sunk into the dirt, leaving a hole behind it. The line of insects followed. Within a couple of minutes, they were gone.

A swift breeze whipped through the trees, sending a shiver down Tashon's back. He stood up and continued forward, the others following. Then, movement. This time to his right, at the front end of the ship. Someone was standing on top, waving their arms. Without a word, the group broke into a jog.

They covered the distance quickly to find a girl standing on the ship thirty stories above them. She was shouting something at them, but from that distance, Tashon couldn't make sense of it.

"We need to get her down," Doran said.

"Maybe you can use your spatula." Linoa smirked.

Doran looked down at his belt, as if seriously considering it. Then he shrugged and looked to Tashon.

Tashon held up a hand and didn't speak. He walked away from the group to the torn edge of the ship. He turned the corner and stopped short. What lay before him was a scene of unmoving destruction. The floors of the ship were visible, all level with the ground. Wiring and chunks of metal hung everywhere. One thick wire gently swung back and forth, sparks shooting from the end.

At first, Tashon didn't notice the bodies. They were hiding in the shadows, some hanging off the torn floors. Too many for Tashon count, and he sensed there were many more that he could not see. For a moment, he blamed himself. What if he *had* killed Aleron when he had the chance? Then the engine wouldn't have been compromised. They would have made it safely. The death and wreckage he stared at would have never happened. He took a few steps into the shadows, then fell to his knees. In front of him were the bodies of James and Theresa, the two who had helped him out of the elevator after the attack. How many innocent deaths had he caused by leaving Aleron alive?

Something in the shadows, against the far wall, caught his eye. Red hair. A white ribbon held it in a tight ponytail.

"Grace!" He broke into a run.

She lay half concealed in the shadows, her body pressed between a storage crate and the ship's outer wall. Her arm was broken at the elbow, bent opposite of its natural direction. Her chest was covered in blood, and as Tashon's eyes adjusted, he realized she hadn't died in the crash—her throat had been slit. He screamed her name. Cried it. Whispered it. She did not wake. He yelled wordlessly as tears and snot poured down his face, drenched his collar. He could not pull his eyes away from her. She looked so uncomfortable, with her arm like that. With a deliberate gentleness, he slowly bent it the right way and placed her hand over her heart, then did the same with the other arm, crossing her chest.

Footsteps came up from behind, and he turned to see the rest of the group joining him.

"Those ba-bastards," Elric whispered through clenched teeth.

Sanga put a hand on his brother's shoulder, squeezing tightly.

Heth let out a short string of swears and then went silent again.

Linoa stood, her face betraying no emotion. Silence for a few moments. Doran screamed and threw one of his knives at a nearby tree. It sunk deep into its flesh. A thick line of red liquid dripped down underneath the knife. A short, soft squeal emanated from the tree. Tashon wondered if it was somehow in pain. The entire group stared as Tashon and Doran slowly walked to it. Tashon placed his hand on the warm bark. It pulsed rhythmically underneath his skin like a heartbeat. He moved to a tree a few steps away, placed his hand on it. It beat just as the other one, and Tashon was sure if he could touch both at the same time the rhythms would be in sync.

Doran grasped the handle of his knife and pulled. It came out with a squishy *pop*. The top half of the blade was gone. It hadn't been broken. Melted, its edge still glowing red from the heat.

Doran stared at his knife. "Where the hell are we?"

"I don't know." Tashon tried to pull his thoughts together. "Okay. We, uh, need to focus on the living. I mean, we should, right?" He nearly choked on the words as they came out. Countless people, gone. Because of him. His sister. Damn it, his sister.

Voices echoed from inside the ship. Laughter. Three men in security uniforms stepped into the sunlight, each brandishing a knife. As soon as they met eyes with Tashon and the others, their bodies stiffened, their stances widened. They spread out and each broke into a sprint, directly at the survivors.

Doran whipped out his second knife and threw it, hitting one of the men in his left eye. Another man yelled as he neared Linoa. She sidestepped and stuck her foot in front of him, sending him headfirst into a tree. He fell to the ground, unconscious.

The remaining terrorist reached Sanga and sliced his throat open in one quick motion, sending drops of blood at Tashon's face. Sanga's limp, lifeless body collapsed to the ground. Elric screamed and jumped on the back of his brother's killer, ripped the knife from his hand and stabbed him in the chest one, two, three, four times until both fell to the ground.

Doran ran over and pulled the body off Sanga. They all stood motionless and silent. Slowly, each turned to Tashon as if seeking advice. Comfort, even. Tashon wondered why, then remembered he was a chief. In their eyes, the highest authority they had in that moment. It didn't seem to matter to them that he'd held the title for less than twenty-four hours.

"If they...." He paused to consider his words. "If they survived, other Extinctionists did too. We have to be careful. Anyone we come across could be one of them."

Chapter 20

Smith, Jonstin and Abe made their way to the red mountains, to the fallen ship, as fast as they could. They had left Sylvia in charge, with no complaint from Jonstin. Smith looked at his son. Smith had wanted to stop Abe from coming, but after everything, he couldn't tell his son no.

The sun had risen. They were already a few miles ahead of the others and continued at a relentless pace. Smith and Jonstin took turns carrying a large pack that had water and food. The three ate and drank as they moved, stopping only when their bodies forced them to. They didn't speak. Smith was almost always at the front, his breathing heavy but his stride steady. He found that the more he moved, the less he thought, and the less he thought, the less the beetles seemed to appear. The more he strained his body, the less he felt. The less he noticed the dull pain in his head that seemed to move every hour. So, on he went, Abe and Jonstin following close behind.

Hours passed. The sun began to set. Smith stopped to hand the pack to Jonstin. He turned to start walking again when, suddenly, the ground in front of him was covered in the same prints that he had seen that first day. This time, however, there were dozens of them. In front of them. Behind them. On both sides. The footprints began to move, circling the three travelers. Smith closed his eyes, and then opened them again. The footprints remained, but he saw no beetles.

"Smith?" Jonstin called.

"What?" Smith tried to ignore the footprints.

"You see those prints?"

Smith paused. It wasn't a hallucination. At least some of the insanity he'd been seeing was real. The realization lightened his mood, gave him a surge of confidence.

"Yeah, I see it."

"And?"

"Keep moving." Smith took a few steps forward. "Abe, you good?"

"Yeah. Pure O_2."

They slowly moved forward. Smith tried to step on the prints, but they moved before his foot touched down. He didn't feel or see anything moving around them. No wind. No dirt being kicked up. Yet the prints began to disappear and reappear faster and faster. The three pressed forward, the circle of prints following them, neither growing nor shrinking. Smith decided to ignore the prints. Nothing he could do about them, anyway. And, whatever they were, they didn't seem to want to harm them. He spent several minutes debating whether he should try running past the circle, but decided not to. The more they walked, the more comfortable he began to feel with the footprints.

The sun set. The sky glowed a silver-blue as the moon and stars appeared in the sky. Still, they walked. Still, the circle followed them. For Smith, the walking felt natural. As if he wouldn't be able to stop even if he tried. His sole focus was on the simple task of reaching the mountains. He would worry about getting past them to the ship when they came to it. As long as he walked, his mind held no thoughts of the past. He put one foot in front of the other, again and again. He knew they needed to rest, so he stopped and sat down. Abe and Jonstin did the same. The circle continued to move around them.

"You two rest," Smith said. "Jonstin, I'll wake you up to switch in two or three hours."

"Are we really not going to talk about—" Jonstin pointed to the circle of prints.

"What's there to say about it?"

"I don't know." Jonstin tossed his hands in the air. "Like, what the hell is it? Is it a herd of invisible beasts? An illusion? One invisible animal with dozens of feet?"

"Does it matter?" Abe asked.

"What?"

"Does it matter?"

"What? Of course it matters!"

"Why?"

"It matters because we need to figure out what it is."

Smith smiled and shook his head. He wanted to hear what his son had to say. He turned to Abe.

"I'll admit I'm curious," Abe said. "But how are we going to do that?"

Jonstin was silent. "I don't know," he finally admitted.

"Right. So we could talk about what it might be, what it might mean. But I would rather sleep. Besides, we'd probably be wrong anyway."

Jonstin shook his head. "There's no way you're going to fall asleep with these things walking around us."

Abe shrugged, lay down and then closed his eyes.

A loud laugh burst from Smith. It was one of many moments that reminded Smith how much he loved his son. "He's got a point."

Jonstin shook his head. "There's no way I'm falling asleep. You get some rest. I'll keep watch."

"Maybe." Smith pulled two food bars out and tossed one to Jonstin.

They ate in silence. Smith looked at the stars, then at the dark clouds that still hung in the distance. They were a long way off, but Smith was sure the storm was still moving toward them. He brought his gaze back to the ground to look closer at the circling footprints. After a few minutes, he realized every footprint was identical. Same shape. Same size. Each and every one. Were the footprints connected to the beetles? Smith lay down on his side and watched the footsteps pass him by, over and over, until he fell asleep.

***

Evalee stood in front of Smith. Her eyes were wet with tears, but her lips curled in a gentle smile. Smith tried to speak, but no words came out. Evalee stood next to an open grave. She looked down into it, then back at Smith. She waved to him, turned her back to the grave and let herself fall. Smith ran to the grave and fell to his knees, staring into the hole with wet eyes. The grave had no bottom. It went on and on, swallowed up by darkness. Smith screamed and opened his eyes.

He lay on his side in the gray dirt. The sun was just cresting over the red mountains. He rubbed his eyes. The circle of prints had turned into a circle of visible creatures. He jumped to his feet and backed into the middle of the circle. They were black, dog-like. He realized they were the same as the one he had seen the night his eardrum blew. The creatures that had rushed past him, toward the deafening sound. Was he the only one seeing them, or were they real?

Abe and Jonstin stood beside him. Neither spoke. The three stared at the creatures. They were real. Smith thought something was wrong with the dogs. Their fur didn't seem quite like fur. It looked like black smoke, gently moving along with the creatures as they ran in the circle. And there were no facial features to be seen. No nose, mouth, eyes or even ears. Whatever they were, they didn't seem to be alive. They only resembled a living creature. But Smith thought again about that first night he had seen them, and got the feeling the creatures were not there to harm them. If they were dangerous, wouldn't they have hurt him already?

"I'm pretty sure they're not going to hurt us."

"*Pretty* sure?" Jonstin whispered.

"Yeah." Smith shrugged. "And even if they are going to attack and devour us alive, what can we do about it? We're surrounded. Better to keep moving forward."

Abe nodded. "Hell yeah."

And they kept moving. Just as the prints had, the creatures continued to circle them while also moving along with them. After a time, they decided to run, but the creatures kept pace with them the entire day. Eventually, Abe decided that they needed to name the creatures.

"Smoke dogs," Abe said.

"They don't look like dogs," Jonstin said, still nervous about their presence.

"Closest I've seen in real life," Abe pointed out.

They kept walking. The sun had reached its peak and was beginning its slow descent behind them. Smith found it oddly comforting to hear his son talk about naming the creatures. It made him feel as though they would all be around for a long time. If their time on the planet was going to end soon, why bother naming things?

"I got it," Abe announced. "Smokies."

Abe crouched down as he walked and reached his hand out. "Isn't that right, my little smokies?"

Smith chuckled and rolled his eyes.

"Your kid is insane, Smith."

Abe smiled. "I got that from my mom."

Smith slapped Abe's back and then squeezed his shoulder.

Abe turned and gave him a bittersweet smile.

A beetle crawled across his son's bald head, and Smith had to force himself not to slap it away. They walked the next few hours in silence.

***

The last rays of sunlight were about to dip behind the horizon. They continued to walk, though their pace had slowed significantly. The circle of smokies continued to match their speed. Smith noticed a slight trembling in the ground. He stopped walking, as did the others. A high-pitched whine screamed at them from the red mountains. The smokies squeezed tighter around the group, pushing them together until their shoulders touched. The screeching grew louder. Closer. Smith looked toward the mountains.

Dozens of lines raced along the ground, small clouds of gray dust rising above them. As they got closer, Smith realized that each line was made up of hundreds of biotech beetles. His heart pounded in his chest. He hoped it was only in his head.

"What in shit's name are those?" Jonstin screamed.

"Ah, shit," Smith whispered. They were real.

As if reacting to Smith's adrenaline, the wall of smokies moved faster and faster. The black smoke that made up their bodies began to spread out, morphing into one spinning wall of black wind. The lines grew closer. Smith clenched his fists as the first beetle hit the wall with a spark and a *pop*. It didn't make it past the barrier.

Soon, the screeching was replaced by a constant battery of electrical pops. It went on for what felt like hours. Abe shouted something in his dad's ear, but Smith couldn't make it out. Suddenly, a hole appeared in the wall next to Jonstin. The smoke filled it quickly, but not before one got through and latched onto Abe's forearm.

He screamed and tried to swat it off, but it didn't budge. It began to sink into his skin. A small pool of Abe's blood squished out from beneath it.

"Dad!"

Smith grabbed his son's shoulder with one hand and ripped the foreign insect out of his flesh. He threw it on the ground and smashed it under his boot. Abe dropped to his knees, his eyes riveted to the hole in his arm. It was an inch long, and half that across. A thin yellow line ran across the outside of the wound. His dad sat next to him and pulled a roll of bandaging out of the bag.

"Damn it," he whispered. "No antibiotics."

He wrapped Abe's arm tightly and tugged it to make sure it would stay.

"You okay, son?"

"Yeah." Abe shrugged. "Does Sylvia really think one of those made it into your brain?"

"Maybe." Smith pushed his fingers to the back of his head. "Sure as hell hope not." *Pretty sure one's in there right now*, he thought.

The air around them began to change, a howl emanating from the wall of smokies. Smith looked up as the black air rose higher and then curved inward until they were encased in a dome of smoke. His feet trembled beneath him and he looked down to see a thin crack appear directly underneath the wall. The smoke continued to spread, this time into the ground. Somehow, Smith knew they would soon be inside a sphere of black air. The howling intensified, and the entire structure shook and moved. *Upward*, Smith thought. But that couldn't be right, could it? Then, without warning, the sphere sped off, knocking the three to the ground.

"Dad?"

"Smith?"

"Abe." Smith rolled to his side. "You all right?"

"Crisp, Dad." Abe sat up and scooted to the curved wall. He stretched his good hand to touch the smoke.

"Abe!"

He stopped for a moment. "It's okay," he said.

Just as his fingers were about to touch it, the smoke parted. His hand went through unharmed. He slowly moved his hand in a bigger and bigger circle until the opening was over a foot across. With a soft grunt he moved onto his knees and peered out through the hole.

Abe gasped. "Woah."

Smith and Jonstin looked at each other.

Smith stood up warily, realizing the sphere had carried some of the gray earth up with them. He walked to his son and looked out of the opening.

"Damn."

They were speeding thirty feet in the air over the gray earth toward the red mountains. The wind rushed against his face and he couldn't help but smile. He stepped back and waved Jonstin over. With a cautious nod, Jonstin shuffled over to the hole. From a distance, he peaked out for just a moment. That was all it took. With a cough, he fell to his knees and vomited onto the floating dirt.

"Jonstin!" Abe shouted, taking a step back. "And they called you a chief pilot."

Jonstin shook his head and let himself fall onto his side. The hole in the smoke closed and the sphere began to slow.

Smith stood up, his body tense. He thought the smokies were friendly, but he had no idea what was coming. The sphere shook and settled. The smoke spanned in opposite directions until the smokies, in their dog form, were back. The three had been carried to the base of the red mountains.

Smith had imagined a hill that gradually rose to the peak, but instead what they found was a cliff that stretched thousands of feet above them. The rock was a deep red. Vines of nearly every shade of green slithered upward. Smith touched one, wondering if they could use them to climb, but pulled back when a hooked thorn caught the skin between his thumb and forefinger.

"How the hell are we supposed to get over that?" Jonstin asked.

Smith shook his head and looked to either side. If they walked one way long enough, they could probably find a safe spot to ascend. But there was no telling how long that would take. And the smokies had brought them to that particular spot. Smith had a feeling the creatures were aware they wanted to reach the other side of the mountains.

As if reading his thoughts, one walked to Smith and sat at his feet. He looked down. They really did look like dogs, but with an airy quality Smith couldn't quite describe, as if they weren't completely real. Slowly, he reached out a hand to let it smell him, like a real dog would. In response, the smokie turned away and walked alongside the cliff. Smith followed it about twenty feet. The creature stopped, turned to the cliff and sat.

"Abe, Jonstin," he called. "I think we have something."

The three stood next to the smokie, staring at the wall. For a moment, the spot looked no different than the rest of the cliffside. But then Smith noticed a section of vine that was all one shade of green. It was a dark green rectangle, the size of a large door. He stepped toward it and reached out to touch it.

"Dad," Abe said cautiously.

"Yeah," Smith stopped and turned toward his son.

"What the hell is going on?"

Smith chuckled. "No damn clue."

"Okay, so we're all on the same page," Jonstin said.

"Yep," Smith said. "So, are we going where these things guide us?"

Jonstin shrugged. "Let's do it. They haven't killed us yet."

Abe agreed and Smith turned back to the cliff. He grabbed one of the off-colored vines. It felt cool to the touch. Some sort of metal, then. Smith gripped and pulled. The door swung open. The smokies rushed in as a group. Smith took a few cautious steps into the black opening, holding his breath. When nothing happened, he waved the other two in. They joined him. The door closed silently, and they were swallowed by darkness.

Chapter 21

Tashon sat on the ground, slowly drawing circles in the dirt. They had walked around the entire ship and the only survivor they found was Liu, the girl on top of the ship. They didn't find any sign of Colony Six. *I should've killed that bastard when I had the chance*, he told himself for the hundredth time. But if he had it all to do over again, he didn't know if he'd be able to do it. If he would actually take another life. And for what felt like the thousandth time, the image of the man he killed falling to the ground replayed in his mind. He saw the light leave his eyes as the last bit of oxygen left his body. He choked back the tears and looked up. Johann was walking toward him.

"It'll be dark soon." The old man reached out and pulled Tashon to his feet. "And cold. We should take shelter inside the ship."

Tashon nodded. "Where? I don't want to sleep by all of the bodies."

"There's an airlock farther down that Bodhi got open. He found a handful of more survivors in the ship too. They're all taking supplies into the airlock—food, clothes and water. What else do we need?"

Tashon nodded again but didn't speak. He had just realized something that terrified him.

"You okay, Tash?"

"Johann." Tashon looked at him with wide eyes. "I still can't fall asleep, can I? I'll end up in a coma, won't I?"

Johann exhaled. "I was thinking about that. You got knocked out in the crash, right?"

"Yeah, I did."

"And you woke up fine. So maybe Cosima was telling the truth. She didn't give you as much as they told her to."

Tashon knew it was just a guess. But he also knew he needed sleep. And if he didn't wake up? He wasn't sure that would be the worst thing that could happen.

"Think any more Extinctionists survived?"

"It's possible." Johann squinted into the sky. "But we never knew who they were. So I think we should keep a close eye on everyone. But not tell people the person in the cot next to them might want to destroy all humanity?" Johann shook his head. "It'll just cause paranoia."

Instead of responding, Tashon walked to the ship to join the rest of the survivors.

As Tashon walked through the airlock and into a large room, he was shocked to see over fifty other survivors. Bodhi had found far more survivors than Tashon had. They had set up cots using storage crates and blankets. A large stack of usable food was pushed against one wall. A small group of kids were playing a game. Around the outer edges, others whispered and cried together. But in that room, there was a sense of warmth to the whispers. The smallest shiver of hope seemed to run through the group. Tashon couldn't explain it. Someone jogged across the room calling Tashon's name. Bodhi.

"Hey!" He gave Tashon a hug. "Thanks for dragging me out of the ship." He lowered his voice. "And, you know, saving me from that psycho."

"Yeah," Tashon said. "Yeah, anytime."

He suddenly remembered that Aleron's body had been missing after the crash. He had to be alive, then. But where was he? Tashon scanned the room more carefully but the zealot was not there.

"Chief Tashon, you okay?"

Tashon considered lying. "I probably shouldn't say...."

Bodhi gave him a reassuring look and nodded.

"Ugh. It's Aleron. I think he's still alive."

"What?" Bodhi shouted. A few people turned and stared. He waved them off and pulled Tashon outside.

"How?"

Tashon looked at the trees that surrounded them. "I don't know. He was gone when we woke up after the crash."

Bodhi clicked his tongue, shaking his head. "Hopefully he crawled out and died somewhere."

"Yeah," Tashon agreed. Though he couldn't help but feel the madman was still out there, alive and well.

***

Despite his deep exhaustion, Tashon lay on the cool floor, unable to sleep. The sounds of snores, whispers and tears surrounded him. But that was not what kept him awake. He continued to wonder if he made the right choice not killing Aleron. He knew that if he had, they would probably not be in the mess they were in. But he also knew that if he had killed Aleron, he would always wonder if that had been the right choice. He again thought of the man he killed. Let the guilt sink into him, focusing on the image of his lifeless face. Then that image morphed into the dozens of lifeless faces he had found earlier that day. Then Grace's face, her blood-soaked throat and chest. No matter what he told himself, he had killed those people as well. He had been the cause of his sister's death. He almost screamed, but stopped himself. Instead, he quietly rose and walked to the closed airlock. He leaned against the glass and stared outside.

A bright moon cast down a silver light. The branches and leaves swayed gently. Other than that, the night was still. There was an unusual, chaotic beauty to the landscape. Tashon was used to the plants on the ship's farm. Perfect, symmetrical, identical. But in that new place, no two trees, no two leaves, seemed the same. To Tashon, it seemed unnatural, though he knew that thought was ridiculous. A figure joined him at the window. He turned to see a familiar face.

"Rosa!" Tashon hadn't realized how much he missed the violent old woman.

"Chief Tashon." She nodded to him with a grin. "I hear you held your own against those bastards."

Tashon shrugged. "Not as much as Johann."

Rosa laughed. "You did more than a lot of people. Good work."

"Thanks," Tashon whispered.

He tried to feel proud of what he'd done. Of the fight he'd made against the ship's enemies. But all he felt was sick. Sick that he'd stabbed the man in the brain and killed him. Sick that he hadn't killed Aleron, and instead killed countless more when the ship crashed.

Rosa looked him in the eye. "No, really. I know what you did and how hard that can be. But, Chief Tashon, you were fighting to save us all. Please know that none of us hold that against you."

"Yeah, okay," Tashon said sincerely. "Thanks, Rosa."

Rosa nodded and smacked Tashon's back. He couldn't help but wonder what Rosa's story was. He never would have expected her to talk like that and, in that moment, she was not the same woman that had snapped a girl's wrist on an elevator. He looked back out through the glass just in time to see a shadow disappear behind a tree.

"Did you—" Tashon said, but was shushed by a finger in his face.

The two stared out into the night. Tashon's heart pounded. His mind raced, wondering what it could have been. The wind picked up, and more shadows rushed through the trees. Tashon's breath caught in his throat. Then he sighed with relief when he realized what the shadows were.

"Leaves." Rosa laughed. "Damn leaves almost gave you a heart attack, Chief."

Tashon chuckled awkwardly. "You were scared too."

"Don't tell anyone."

Tashon nodded and laughed.

"Get some rest, farmer."

"Yeah, thanks."

He slowly walked back to his spot on the floor and, finally, fell asleep.

Chapter 22

Smith, Abe and Jonstin had been following the smokies deeper into the mountains for almost an hour. The way was dimly lit by small, glowing spheres that floated listlessly. There was a single tunnel carved carefully out of the blood-red rock. They had passed no intersecting tunnels. The walls and floor were perfectly smooth. Not a single crack could be seen. Smith felt like they were moving slowly upward, but couldn't be sure.

He kept thinking about the ship. Why had it crashed? Smith knew they must have come back to help Colony Six. But something had obviously gone wrong. He just wanted to get to the ship. To know who survived. To simply be there to help. To have something to do to keep him from thinking. Moving from objective to objective, focusing only on actions to be completed.

"Hey, Dad." Abe's voice pulled Smith back to the tunnel. "Is that a door up there?"

Smith looked ahead and squinted. Maybe fifty yards away was an opening. Not a door, exactly, but more of an entryway. It was a large, ornately carved arch. As they got closer, Smith could see a large room on the other side of the archt.

"How did this all get here?" Abe wondered aloud.

"No idea," Smith whispered.

They kept walking.

"Why does it seem like all the information we had before coming here was wrong?" Jonstin asked.

Abe shrugged. "Because it was."

Jonstin scoffed and shook his head.

In front of them, the smokies ran through the archway and disappeared. Smith stepped over the threshold and stopped short, his eyes wide with amazement.

They were inside a massive, perfectly square room. It was still carved from the red rock, but the walls and ceiling were striped with thin white lines that illuminated the area. In the center of the room, a large white rectangle rose out of the ground. Smith walked to it. On the top were multiple indents in sets of five. Each one resembled a stick figure, the exact same size as the metal one Smith and Sylvia had seen at the crater. Suddenly, each of the smokies lay down and went completely still.

"What—"

Smith shushed Jonstin.

A soft whoosh emanated from each creature. The black smoke that made up their bodies began to move inward. As the smoke thinned, Smith saw that at the center of each smokie body were five metal rods. A small slit had opened in the middle rod of each creature and the smoke was being sucked into it. Soon, all that was left of the smokies were their metal skeletons. Silently, each rod rose off the ground and floated over the rectangle, and then dropped into the precisely cut indents. As each piece found its resting spot, they were outlined in a glowing green light.

All three stared at the table. Abe walked to his dad and stood next to him.

Abe spoke in a hushed reverence. "Is that nanotech?"

Smith scratched his beard and nodded. "Yeah. I mean, what else could it be?"

"And those beetle things?"

"Biotech, I think."

Jonstin sat down on the ground. "Nothing how it's supposed to be," he said.

Smith looked at the pilot but didn't know what to say. He decided to give Jonstin time to wrap his mind around whatever was going on.

Abe continued to stare at the metal rods. "None of this is natural. It has to have been made by something. Someone."

"Yeah," Smith whispered. "Kind of amazing."

"Amazing?" Jonstin stood up. "This is insane."

"That too," Abe agreed. "Insanely amazing."

Smith looked around the room again. On the opposite side, past the smokie's resting place, was another door. He walked around the rectangle, dragging a finger on the corner as he did. Other than the rectangle and the resting smokies, the room was empty. No manuals, paper or electronics to reveal the purpose of the room or the smokies. No screens. No answers.

"Let's get to the ship then," Smith said.

They walked through the doorway and entered another hall. The hallway was nearly identical to the first, though this one had doors on either side every few yards. They tried to open the first several they came across. Each one was locked, and trying to force their way in proved useless. So they kept going straight. No one spoke. What could be behind all those doors? More nano and bio tech? Or maybe supplies that they could use? *Or the remains of whatever creatures made the tech,* Smith thought. *And, if so, how had they died?* Smith sighed. At that moment, he needed to focus on getting to the ship.

The floating lights around them began to buzz. Or they always had been buzzing, and Smith didn't notice it at first. He wondered if the creators of that place were still alive, merely sleeping or eating or working on the other side of the locked doors. Unaware of the aliens walking through their halls. Or they were aware, and had sent the smokies to retrieve the three humans and were now funneling them to some unknown location. No. He had to focus on getting to the ship. If something else tried to stop them, they would deal with it then.

"How far you think we've gone?" Smith asked.

"Far," Abe said. "I started counting my steps when we got to this hall."

"And?"

"Six hundred and forty" — he paused — "seven steps."

Smith nodded. That was far, and he was pretty sure they'd been in this hallway almost as long as they had been in the first. If the room had been the center point, they should be at the exit soon.

"Jonstin, how far do you think the ship was?"

There was no response.

"Jonstin?"

"Do you see that? The lights are getting —"

The floating white lights blinked off, leaving them in complete darkness. A ringing alarm sounded. The balls of light flashed back on, this time glowing orange. They blinked on and off in rhythm with the alarm. A dotted line along the center of the hallway floor flashed brightly in the direction they had already been heading.

The three looked at each other. Smith's heart pounded, his ears ringing against the alarm. He wondered if it sounded even louder to Abe and Jonstin, with both of their ears working.

"Follow it?" he shouted over the blaring.

Abe held his hands up and shrugged. He tried to look calm, but Smith could see in his eyes that his son was scared. If he was being honest, so was he. They were inside a mountain with tech they didn't understand and couldn't control. There was no telling why the alarm was sounding or what waited for them at the end of the glowing line. But he had to assume that whoever created the place would not direct people into harm's way. So, yet again, he began to walk.

Abe and Jonstin followed, the latter shouting something that Smith didn't hear. And he didn't care. He was growing tired of Jonstin's opinions and worries. Yes, he knew they were valid. But Smith also saw no point in spending so much energy focusing on the insanity of their situation. Besides, the most insane thing to him was that Evalee was not by his side.

Ahead of them, the lit path took a sharp left down a new hallway that crossed the one they walked. They stopped for a moment at the intersection. Again, Smith considered the possibility they were being led into a trap. He looked at the others. Jonstin shook his head as though he didn't care. Abe suggested they continue to follow the lit path. They turned left and continued on.

The new hall was narrower and shorter than the other. Unmoving lights hung from chains every few feet. They flashed between orange and white. The alarm continued to pierce Smith's ears. He felt like he had begun wincing to the rhythm of it. He imagined the sounds were alive. That living waves were swimming their way into his brain and they would soon make his head implode. Just as he thought his other ear drum would burst, the hallway ended at a large door with a wheel lock. Abe reached out, gingerly touching one of the spokes. The alarm stopped. The wheel spun on its own. The door swung inward with a puff of air. A soft green light reached toward them.

"Jonstin," Abe motioned to the opening. "You want the honor?"

"Hell no."

Abe smiled and moved out of the way. Smith stepped in and Abe quickly followed. They turned to Jonstin, who slowly stepped inside. Once all three were through, the door swung shut. Smith's mouth went dry. His stomach suddenly felt heavy, threatening to pull him to the ground. With a deep breath, he took a step forward. From out of the shadows, a woman emerged. Smith swore and jumped back, raising his fists. The woman's only reaction was to speak in a language none of them understood. It sounded almost like a song with a wide range of notes, many of them higher and lower than Smith would ever be able to make with his voice. Some of the notes lasted for seconds. It was beautiful, really.

Smith cautiously lowered his fists and tried to speak to her, but she continued her monologue as if they were not there.

"I think...." Jonstin walked around the woman. "Yeah, this is a recording."

"It looks real," Smith said.

She was shorter than all three of them, with a thicker build. Her short hair and eyebrows were yellow. *Not blonde*, Smith thought, *but strikingly yellow*. It reminded him of the yellow sauce he put on his food on Earth all those years ago, but he couldn't remember what it was called. Her eyes were a vibrant blue. Her nose pointed at the end and she had the thinnest lips Smith had ever seen. Her skin was a pale green. She kept talking.

Abe took a step closer. "Is she human?"

"No," Jonstin answered quickly.

"Not exactly." Smith scratched his cheek. "Close enough."

"What?" Jonstin asked. "She's obviously not human."

Smith shrugged. "She looks human to me."

Jonstin opened his mouth to protest, but the woman lifted her arm up and pointed into the dark. As she did, there was a loud *click* and the room filled with light. Smith squinted against the brightness, but his eyes soon adjusted.

Jonstin opened his mouth to protest, but the hologram woman lifted her arms into the air. Bright white light burst from the ceiling, illuminating the large room. A deep square had been carved into the floor, with stairs leading down. Smith and Abe cautiously walked down. Lining the walls of the basement square were crisp white, metal boxes. They were long. A bit longer than the hologram woman was tall, as if they were—

"Coffins," Smith said.

Abe, as if he hadn't heard his dad, stretched a finger out and touched the side of one of the rectangle boxes. A hologram picture jumped out and hovered off the ground. The man seemed to be the same species as the woman. Characters of some unknown language floated beside him. Smith assumed it was the man's name, birth and death dates, and anything else the species considered important.

"Like a 3D obituary," Abe said.

Smith nodded and turned in a circle. There were hundreds of coffins surrounding him. An alien species, and it seemed they were all dead. Like the planet didn't like keeping intelligent species alive. He looked down. An intricate carving stretched across the floor. An interlocking jumble of shapes in a measured zigzag pattern. Smith had no idea what it meant, but got the feeling they were intruding in a sacred place.

A swarm of beetles crawled out of every crack and crevice. Dozens of them. They charged at him, forming a circle. They weren't there for Abe or Jonstin. They were there for Smith. Vibrant. So alive. He needed to move. Get out into fresh air.

"Let's go find the ship." He turned and walked up the stairs, stepping on the beetles only to have them reappear behind him.

The swarm followed him up and out of the alien catacombs.

Chapter 23

Sylvia and the other survivors continued their slow walk to the red mountains. It had been a day since she lost sight of Smith, Abe and Jonstin in the distance. Nearly as long since she had seen a black ball rise into the air and fly off. She thought of Jonstin and how he had wanted everyone to journey past the red mountains from the beginning. How, if they had, they would probably still have all of their supplies. And they wouldn't be racing against the looming black clouds that grew ever closer. But she let the thought linger for only a moment. If there was one thing she knew in life, it was that she could not let guilt or regret guide her.

Back on Earth, it was her ex who had forced her to work at the brothel to pay off his debts. Twisted her love for him in a way that made her feel guilty for his gambling problem. And he used that guilt to send her to the brothel. She was thankful every day for Smith barging in and pulling her to her senses. Otherwise, she'd be stuck on a pollution-filled Earth with men who used her. No matter what insanity that new planet gave her, she knew without question that it was better than being back on Earth.

Three claps of thunder burst into her thoughts and she stopped short. She looked up. Somehow, the clouds were hundreds of yards closer than they had been only a few hours before. Close enough to see the thick strings of water pouring out and splashing onto the gray earth. A fierce wind hit, threatening to send supplies into the air.

Sylvia turned and looked at her people. All thirty-six of her responsibilities. Eight of them under the age of ten. She glanced back at the oncoming storm. The raindrops looked as though they were turning into hail. And there was no way they would make it to the mountains in time.

She called everyone into a tight circle and started going through the bins for anything they could use. Sixteen weatherproof suits. They could fit two small kids in a couple of them, but that still left at least fifteen people that were going to get soaked, and it was getting colder by the second. She looked back at the wall of falling water to see it had turned to hail. She shouted for everyone to find something, anything, hard to cover their heads. They huddled together as close as they could, and waited for the storm to hit.

Two hours passed. Fist-sized hail pounded the ground, at times bouncing up a yard or more. Sylvia clutched a small cooking dish over her head and tried to make herself as small as possible. A fierce wind blew and Sylvia had to fight to not lose grip of her small shield. Her head and face were untouched, but the rest of her body ached from the constant pummeling. She shivered against the wet cold that felt as though it would freeze her bones.

Around her, everyone else did the same. They had emptied some of their storage crates and flipped them upside down to cover a few of the children. From her position in the middle of the circle, Sylvia was able to slowly turn herself around and keep an eye on each and every person. So far, everyone seemed okay. But it was what came after that worried her. It would be night soon. Without the sun to dry out clothes or warm anyone up, the chances of hypothermia were high. She would have to worry about that when the time came. With a grunt, she turned her body forty-five degrees.

A crate sat upside down just a few feet ahead of her. A large pack sat on top of it to keep the wind from blowing it away. She knew the young girl who huddled underneath it. Heather had lost both her parents in the initial crash, as well as a brother. Just next to it was Heather's older sister, Rae. The older girl held a handle on the crate with two hands and wore a helmet, her long red hair whipping in the wind. A massive gust of wind ripped past Sylvia and sent the pack flying off the crate.

The crate slid across the ground. Rae tried to crawl on top of it, but the wind was too strong. Another gust hit and the crate lifted into the air. Rae held on for a few moments, but the crate was ripped from her hand and lifted into the air. Heather clutched her small hand over her head, her eyes wide with terror.

Sylvia moved instinctively. She flattened herself and rolled to the young girl, using the wind to quicken her pace. Within moments, she had the girl zipped inside her jacket. Sylvia was barely aware that her head was no longer protected as she covered Heather's face with the dish. At least, not until a piece of hail slammed into her right eyebrow. She shut her eyes tight, wanting to press a hand against the pain but refusing to loosen her grip on Heather.

The ground began to disappear under a layer of ice chunks and the hailstorm showed no signs of slowing. Another hailstone hit the ground just in front of Sylvia then bounced into her nose. She felt a crack, followed by a warm stream of blood flowing down her lips and off her chin. She choked back a scream and looked down at Heather. The little one was breathing and there was no blood on her. *Good*, Sylvia thought. *Good*.

Another hailstone hit the right side of her forehead, breaking the skin. Her head spun, and her vision grew blurry. The ground vibrated as hail continued to fall.

The last thing she saw was the ice around her turning red with blood.

The last thing she thought was, *I hope this isn't the end.*

Chapter 24

Tashon stood atop the Ship of Nations, watching a storm rage on the other side of the red mountains. Above him, the night sky shone bright with stars, casting a dim silver light into the forest below. Johann stood next to him, using his fingers to brush his beard. Rosa sat on the edge, her feet dangling over the side. They had spent the entire day looking for signs of Smith and Colony Six, but found nothing.

Tashon saw a slight grin on Rosa's face as she swung her legs back and forth. Johann stood still, his hands pressed deep into his pockets. Occasionally, he commented on a large streak of lightning or the force of the wind.

Tashon could not tear his eyes away from the deep blackness of the clouds. Watching for the merest hint of a figure breaking away from the storm. But the clouds remained just that, clouds. While his eyes focused, his mind went back to the same guilt and shame that had been tormenting him.

"Tash." Johann took a step closer. "The first time I killed someone, it was for a good cause, but it was still... painful. For him and me. And—"

He kept talking but Tashon stopped listening. Johann had good intentions, sure, but at that moment it didn't matter. Tashon admired Johann. The problem, though, was that Johann had killed many more after that first one. If Johann really knew what Tashon was feeling, that first kill would have been his last.

Johann stopped talking.

Tashon looked at him and managed a tired half-smile. "Thanks," he whispered.

"I'm heading down. You coming?"

"Soon. Can't get enough of this air."

Johann gave him a quick hug and disappeared into the ship.

With a sigh, Rosa stood up and joined Tashon, staring out into the darkness.

"It does get better," she said.

Tashon didn't respond.

Rosa simply stood, as if waiting for him to speak.

Tashon gave in. "How do you know?"

"What do you know about me?"

"You like breaking the bones of teenage girls?"

"Rumors." She faked a smile. "Before all of this, back on Earth, I lived in Mexico City."

Tashon turned to her.

"What? Were you there when—"

"The bombs hit? Yeah. I was about your age, actually. It was chaos afterward. No law. No protection. And I had to kill someone. He...."

She paused and looked away. "I guess, all I'm saying is, it's a good sign you feel guilt for taking a life. Because... honestly? I didn't. Not even my first time." She turned and slowly walked back into the ship.

And Tashon was alone. The one thing he wanted to be but knew he shouldn't. He walked to the edge and looked down. In the dark, he could barely see past the tops of the gently swaying trees. He could jump and not even see the ground coming. Just jump into the darkness. He inched closer until his toes hung off the edge. He teetered between jumping and stepping back.

The idea of simply ceasing to be called to him. But after seeing Evalee's face in that fourth-dimensional creature, he wondered whether death would truly be the end of his existence. So, if he were to jump and be reborn as some ethereal being, would he not suffer even more guilt for killing himself? Or would he gain a different understanding of what his current life was, and thus be rid of all his guilt? And added to it all, he couldn't help but think of how life in that other plane seemed far superior to his current plight. He took a breath and told himself to jump, but his body would not move. He told himself to step back, but his body remained still. If only he could tear his body apart straight down the middle, one side falling to the ground below, the other remaining alive on top of the ship.

A black form darted through the trees beneath him. His breath caught in his chest, and he jumped back. He was sure it wasn't a leaf this time. And he was also sure that it had not been on the ground. Whatever it was, it had been moving through the highest branches of the trees. It rushed past again in the opposite direction. Tashon's heart pounded. This time, he could tell that whatever it was had been flying between the trees. With a flash of terror, Tashon realized he recognized the figure. For a moment, he considered falling, letting everyone else deal with it.

No. Within seconds, he was rushing down the stairs inside the ship to find Johann and Bodhi. He slammed through the door into the sleeping quarters, causing a murmur of curses aimed at him. While muttering apologies, he walked toward Johann's cot in the far corner. It was empty. A gasp from across the room drew his attention. He turned to see a small group huddled near the airlock, staring out the glass. Johann and Bodhi were among them. As quietly as he could, Tashon jogged clumsily to meet them.

Before he had the chance to speak, Bodhi hushed him. There was a sense of terror in the engineer's eyes as he discreetly pointed out the window. Tashon turned to look. A short scream leapt from his throat. Aleron stood just outside the airlock.

The mad man still wore his security uniform. A long gash split open his forehead. His hair was plastered to the sides of his face with blood. He hovered nearly a foot off the ground. A black form floated out behind him, seeming to grow out of his body like a cancer. Tashon knew the figure. Knew without question it was the being from the Fourth that Evalee had not been able to get rid of.

Aleron floated motionless. Behind him, the trees gently moved back and forth. Tashon didn't remember feeling any wind outside. He wondered for a moment if the trees breathed. If they had some type of heart and lungs.

But those thoughts of curiosity were cut short as he turned his attention back to Aleron. No facial expressions betrayed his thoughts or intentions. He stared, eyes still and unblinking. The dark shadow behind him attempted to mimic the human form, but it was too tall, too wide, too round. As though it couldn't quite grasp its three-dimensional surroundings. A black light pulsed out of it. The onlookers all jumped back, but it soon dissipated. Tashon waited for Aleron to do something. Ram into the glass. Scream at them. But for ten minutes, nothing happened.

Aleron and the shadow remained still, staring blankly at the onlookers. More survivors stood near the airlock, nervously keeping an eye on the man that had destroyed their ship. Their home. Tashon sat, his back against a wall, hugging his knees. He rubbed his palms into his eyes.

Someone sat next to him. He looked up to find Doran, the chef, smiling at him. He gingerly held the half melted knife between his hands, slowly spinning it around. He handed it to Tashon, who grabbed it carefully, holding it as though it were a sacred artifact.

The blade had cooled. He brought it close to his face. Its new edge was perfect. Clean, sharp, as though it were a new knife that was unusually short.

"Did you sharpen it?"

"No." Doran shook his head slowly. "When it cooled, that's how it was."

Tashon nodded and handed it back.

Aleron was in the same place, but the figure behind him looked even darker than it had earlier. As if it were sucking in the light that surrounded it. They couldn't stay like this forever.

Rosa walked over and sat on his other side.

"Chief Tashon," she said. "Doran."

"Miss Rosa," Doran said with a grin. "How are you this strange evening?"

"Fine as always, Doran," she said. "Chief Tashon, how are you holding up?"

Tashon shrugged. "Fine, as always."

"Chief Farmer, I don't think you've been anything close to fine since Cosima cut you."

Tashon tried to think of a response. One sentence that would prove he was fine, that no one needed to worry about him. Nothing came.

"Hell," Doran said. "I don't think any of us are fine. Not even you, Rosa."

"Probably true," Rosa whispered.

"I killed on the ship." Tashon's voice cracked. "Murdered a man."

Doran looked up in surprise.

"You did not murder him," Rosa said firmly, as if it were a fact. "He was a terrorist, Tash. He would've killed you."

"Maybe." He leaned his head against the wall.

"Chief Tashon," Doran spoke calmly, as if he were trying to provide comfort.

Tashon wanted none of it. "Doran, it's fine. Rosa, I hear you. I just never thought I'd be able to do something so... so brutal."

Tashon realized then the real reason he had not killed Aleron. The violence, the sheer brutality of what he had done to that man, scared him. He feared that if he let that savagery out again, he would not be able to stop it. That he would fight and kill until he died.

Was letting himself become that worth saving humanity?

He told himself that it should be, yet he still questioned what he would do if another time to kill came. But given the sheer instability of their plight, he knew such a time might come.

Someone by the airlock screamed. Tashon and Rosa jumped to their feet. Aleron and his shadow had moved to the airlock, the man's nose pressed against the glass. It was cold outside, and his breath should have fogged the glass, but the glass remained clear.

"Aleron!" a voice screamed from outside the ship.

Aleron and the shadow turned to the source. A man slowly came into view through the glass.

"It is!" The man smiled, then laughed. "Oh, our goddess has turned you into something amazing!"

The man fell to his knees, lifted his arms straight into the air.

"Oh, goddess, universe herself, I desire only to bring about your retribution. Please, let—"

He was cut short as a black tentacle burst out of Aleron's chest in a spray of blood. It sped at the man's face, wrapped around his head and pierced the back of his neck. The man's eyes went blank.

Across the room, Bodhi and Johann yelled for Tashon to join them. He did, and they jogged away from the group of horrified spectators. Out of earshot, but close enough to keep an eye on the airlock.

"Is it what I think it is?" Bodhi bounced up and down on his feet.

"Yeah," Tashon confirmed. "It's from the Fourth. Johann? What do we do?"

Johann sighed and yanked on his beard. "Need my comb," he mumbled.

"Johann?"

"We should try to get them," Johann said. "Before he does... anything else."

"Get them?" Bodhi questioned.

"Capture them. Kill them. We'll see how it pans out."

Tashon opened his mouth to protest, but decided not to.

"I'll keep a group by the airlock," he said instead. "Hopefully it stays focused on us while you guys do whatever you're going to do."

"It?" Bodhi looked at Tashon.

"I don't know," Johann said to the engineer, "if Aleron or the others are still in there."

Tashon looked back out the airlock. The man now had countless tentacles piercing his body, extending out to a second shadow identical to the one behind Aleron.

Two martyrs for the universe, two dark figures seemingly from the Fourth, all connected into one new being.

"What?"

"It doesn't matter right now. Are there any other airlocks we can get through?"

"Uh, yeah. A few. I'll have to manually override the codes."

"Good. You get on that. I'll get anyone with security experience. We'll want to come at them from every angle possible."

***

Tashon tried to stay calm as he and an even larger group stared out at Aleron and his new appendages. All had remained motionless. By that point, nearly all of the ship's survivors were awake and aware of what was happening. The children had been taken further into the ship, as far from any airlock as possible. There was an air of anticipation and fear that hung over everyone and everything. Tashon had to fight the urge to pace the room or chew his fingernails. He didn't know how aware the thing was of its surroundings, but he didn't want to risk it noticing his nerves and realizing something was about to happen to him. Tashon looked at the time on his wrist comm. It should have happened already.

Johann had gathered eleven men and women who had been in security. Two were going to come at the hybrid creature from either side, two from an air lock above them, and the last five were circling out into the trees to come at it from behind. They should have made their move already. Tashon sat on the floor, feigning boredom so that he wouldn't go insane. He kept Aleron in the edge of his vision and tried to take slow breaths.

It didn't help. As he stood up, he caught a glimpse of Johann and four others behind Aleron. They slowly made their way forward, pausing to duck behind trees every few yards. Soon, they were almost on Aleron. Johann lifted a hand in the air and all five stopped. He quickly dropped his hand down, and the attack began.

Two women fell from above. One looped an arm around Aleron's neck and brought him to the ground. Another followed an instant later, bringing the other man down. The shadows moved their right arms in unison, and the human arms followed. Each grabbed a woman and effortlessly tossed them to the side. They slammed into two of the others. And just like that, eleven became seven. The shadows and their puppets floated back up.

From the other side, two large rocks flew through the air. One slammed into the side of Aleron's head, the second struck the other man in the temple. Both fell to the ground, unconscious. The shadows remained attached to their bodies, hovering above them.

The seven rushed the bodies and shadows. But just before they got there, the shadows lurched into the air and flew off, carrying the limp bodies of Aleron and the other Extinctionists beneath them.

After a few seconds of piercing silence, the room erupted in shouts and curses.

Chapter 25

"So you're not going to refer to them as aliens?" Jonstin asked again as they walked through another red tunnel inside the mountains.

"Why would we?" Abe retorted. "This is, or was, their home. They're native to this land, this planet. Why not refer to them as natives?"

"Because they're alien *to us*."

"No, to you. To me, they're just different. Doesn't mean they're alien."

"Isn't that what alien means—different than us?"

"Come on, Jonstin." Abe shook his head. "You took the same Earth history courses I did. In America, after the Immigration Wars, 'alien' became equivalent to the N-word."

"But we're not in America," Jonstin replied, though he remained calm.

"If anything," Smith said, "*we're* the aliens."

Abe laughed.

Jonstin huffed but didn't argue.

Smith was glad for the silence. So much had happened in so little time. All of it nothing like what had been planned for or expected. So many gone. Lost forever. And, somehow, even the great Ship of Nations had joined the disaster. And Evalee, whose sad smile was always there. Hovering behind him, above him. Everywhere. But then, they had found an entire alien existence. One that, in that moment, only three humans knew about. And his Evalee wasn't there to share it with him. He looked at Abe. More than ever, Smith saw his wife in the boy's eyes. But there was a heaviness there, too. One that Smith knew was in his own eyes as well. He shoved Abe with his elbow and gave him a smile. Abe shoved back and let out a quiet laugh. The boy's face lit up briefly with Evalee's smile. It was all Smith could do to keep from crumpling to the floor.

The pain in his head moved again, slowly growing closer to the left side. The size of the pain had grown too, he noticed. If an alien beetle were in there, could it be feeding off his brain, slowly growing larger inside his skull? If it were inside his head, was there any way to get it out that wouldn't kill him? The white lights that hovered around them transformed into floating beetles. Some complete, others the front or back halves. He looked to the others to see if they had noticed the transformation, thought he knew they wouldn't. His head pulsed again and the pain intensified. If it weren't for Abe, he would have dropped himself on the floor, letting his body slowly waste away.

They reached another entryway, this one with a gate rather than a door. It was made with round, dark silver bars. Blinking lights ran around and down each one. Smith lifted his arm and pushed on it. It didn't budge. He gripped one of the rods and pulled. Again, nothing.

"Damn it!" He kicked the bottom of the gate.

Abe stepped next to his dad. Casually, he pressed a small button on the wall. The gate slid sideways into the wall with a squeak.

Smith glanced at Abe and Jonstin. Without a word, he walked through the opening.

The room was round with a vaulted dome ceiling. Stripes of shining gold lined the gun-metal walls, climbing to form a shining star at the pinnacle of the dome. The star shone dimly, casting a soft yellow light. In the center of the room was a square rug, a long white bench on each side. In the wall directly across from them was a gate identical to the one they had just walked through.

The three walked slowly to the center. Abe was the first to reach the rug. The moment his foot landed on it, the star above flickered then burst with glowing yellow light. The light traveled quickly down each of the gold lines, bathing the room in blinding light. As Smith's eyes adjusted, he was able to take in more of the room. There was what looked like a foreign letter engraved above the gate they had come through. A different one was above the gate in front of them. To either side of them stood solid white doors, each with their own symbol. It reminded Smith of a compass. Based on the map he had of the planet, that would mean the symbol above the gate in front of him meant east. *If* it were a compass. And *if* the native's logic of direction and maps was like that of the human race.

Smith sat down on one of the benches and ran his fingers through his hair. He had expected the bench to be hard, like metal. But it was soft, and it formed to his body as he leaned back. It was the most comfortable thing he had ever sat on. Exhaustion spread over him as his body began to relax. They'd been through hell, and that took a lot out of a man.

"Let's rest for a bit," he said.

Jonstin sat on the next bench over. Abe sat next to his dad.

Beetles flickered in and out of Smith's vision. He closed his eyes and thought of Evalee.

***

Evalee was always fascinated by the idea of meeting an alien race. She would tell Smith all her theories and dreams as they lay in bed at night. What might they look like? What would their cultures and customs be? Usually, Smith just listened. Closed his eyes and dreamed along with her words. Listening to her vocalize her dreams like that was one of his favorite memories.

Once, he interjected into her thoughts and mentioned how he would love to talk with an alien over a bottle of beer. Evalee shook her head at this.

"No, no, my love." She smiled. "That *could* happen. But it's far more likely that we'll never be able to fully communicate with an alien species the way we talk with each other."

Smith asked why.

"Any number of reasons, my love," she said, and rested her head on his chest. "There's no guarantee their idea of language will be the same as ours. They could have a vastly different biology that can produce different sounds than we are incapable of. Or their logic, their entire way of thinking, may not even be reconcilable with our own.

"Or, what if they don't have vocal cords? And to compensate, their minds have become telepathic? Our minds would not be wired to receive telepathic messages."

"Some form of sign language?"

"Perhaps. But suppose they have five limbs to sign with? Sure, we may learn to understand that. But how could we respond?"

"This is the closest to pessimistic you've ever been." He smiled and kissed her forehead.

"Oh, not at all. If both species were willing, we would come up with some way to communicate. It would just be different and more difficult than translating between, say, Japanese and English."

"But I could still have a drink with one?"

They both laughed.

"As long as she's not an alien whore, sure."

She pushed herself up on her arm, leaned in and kissed him tenderly. Deeply.

Soon, they were both asleep.

***

Before he opened his eyes, Smith stretched his hand out in search of Evalee's hair. It wasn't there. He opened his eyes and was looking up into the yellow star on the ceiling. Everything came rushing back and he closed his eyes again, trying to force himself back to that simpler time. When aliens and foreign planets were only the dreams of adventure. One thing they never tell you about adventure: it can be soul crushing. It's a thin line between adventure and tragedy.

He pushed himself to a sitting position. Abe and Jonstin sat at the bench across from him, taking turns sipping from a bottle of water.

"Welcome back," Abe said and handed the bottle to his dad.

Smith nodded a thanks and took a few sips. He hadn't realized how thirsty he was, but once he tasted it, he had to force himself not to guzzle all the water down. With a sigh, he stood and walked to the next door.

"Let the adventure continue," he mumbled.

Jonstin tried to speak more than once, but Smith told him to be quiet. He needed to think. To question. To wonder.

Where exactly were they? Maybe, somehow, they had ended up on the wrong planet? He dismissed the idea quickly, though, for the planet was mostly what had been expected. There was only more life, more chaos, than expected. More death and, somehow, more beauty, Smith realized.

"Damn," Smith whispered. "Evalee would've loved this place."

The other two didn't seem to hear him. The floor slowly angled downward, and they soon reached another door. It had one glowing vertical bar sticking out of it.

"Go for it," Smith said to Abe. "You've got more luck with doors than I do."

Abe laughed and grabbed the bar with his good hand. He twisted it inward until it clicked into a horizontal position. With a grunt, he pushed, and the door opened merely a few inches. Pushed again. Something outside cracked and the door broke free, revealing a yellow forest.

The sun filtered through the large leaves. A light mist hung over everything, making it look as though the trees were floating above the ground. They walked out and breathed in the fresh, cool air. It smelled like citrus and copper. Smith hoped they could find some fruit.

Something wet landed on his hand. He looked at it and saw what looked like a drop of... blood? Cautiously, he looked upward. A long, thick branch stretched out and down from the nearest tree. It was cracked from the opening of the door, and a thick red liquid slowly dripped from the wound. Smith carefully smelled the drop. A sweet citrus mixed with the metallic tang of blood. He considered licking it, but without testing it, he wouldn't take the risk. And he'd left all of that equipment with Sylvia's group. He crouched down and wiped it off in the soft earth.

With both hands, he scooped up the soil and let it slowly fall between his fingers. They had amazingly engineered soil on the ship, but nothing compared to the natural.

"Farmer." Jonstin broke the silence.

"Huh?" Smith said.

Jonstin motioned with his head to the door. A lone smokie sat just inside, its nose pointing directly at Smith. As if it were looking at him. The creature angled its head to point at the broken branch. Its head disconnected from its body and lazily floated up to the tree's broken limb. A thin stream of smoke stemmed from its nose to the branch. Smith, of course, knew the smoke was not smoke, but still could not think of them as nanites. The smoke formed a circle around the break and slowly twirled around it. As it did, the body of the smokie remained perfectly still and headless. The circle soon broke and returned to the head, which then returned to the body. Above, the branch looked as though nothing had been wrong. A perfect repair.

The smokie stood and walked past the three as if they were not there, making its way deeper into the woods. It went the same way Smith thought the ship would be. Smith and Abe quickly fell in line behind it. Jonstin attempted to question the decision, but was ignored. For some reason, the smokie was moving in the same direction they were. And there was nothing they could, or would, do to change that.

Chapter 26

Tashon, Doran and Rosa stood atop the ship, their eyes peeled for any sign of danger. Everyone else was sequestered inside the ship, as far away from an opening as possible. No one to become an addition to the horrifying creature.

The sun had just crested the mountains, the rays slowing thawing the nighttime chill that had crept into Tashon's bones. He had spent the last twelve hours standing guard. An hour earlier, Doran had come to relieve Tashon of his shift, but Tashon had stayed. Told the cook that he wasn't tired, though in truth he couldn't bring himself to leave. He had to know what Aleron was doing. What Aleron's new shadow was doing, what it might do with Aleron, *to* Aleron. What it might do to everyone. Had to know because, whatever happened, Tashon was at fault. And there was no convincing him otherwise.

"Something's coming," Doran whispered.

The three crouched and moved to the edge, then lay on their stomachs. They peered down to find a black creature slowing making its way through the trees. It had an airy, ethereal quality like the shadow but, thankfully, it was not. Whatever it was, it walked on all fours, its head held high as though it owned the forest. Slowly, it approached the tree that Doran's knife had hit. A few feet away it sat and stared at it for a moment and then, somehow, its head disconnected from its body. It flew to the tree and blew a thin line of black smoke into the slit from Doran's knife. For a few minutes, the body and head remained still. With a sound not unlike a sneeze, the tip of Doran's blade fell out and thudded onto the ground. The smoke emerged back out of the hole, hovered over it a few moments longer, and returned to the head. The hole now gone, the head returned to the body.

The creature looked back the way it had come. Footsteps and voices approached. Tashon tensed. He felt the others do the same. His heart pounded—no one should have been out there. Did more of those creatures from the Fourth latch onto dying passengers? Tashon had to shove the thought down. One was more than enough.

Then, he began to recognize the voices. But it couldn't be. They had searched everywhere and found no sign of Colony Six.

Smith, Abe and Jonstin came into view. Tashon jumped to his feet, screamed and ran down to greet them.

"Tash!" Smith yelled and squeezed him in a crushing hug.

"Smith." Tashon smiled, though he could barely breathe. "Damn, Smith. Let go!"

"Tashon, looks like you came back to help. But you didn't need to join us. What the hell happened?"

Everyone went silent. Eyes glanced around, all avoiding Smith's gaze.

Johann finally spoke. "Let's go up top," he said. "We need to hear what happened to you, too. Everyone else, return to whatever you were doing. Remember, *stay inside the ship*. We'll hold a meal at noon."

On top of the ship, the cool breeze brushing their faces, Johann and Tashon told of their journey. Tashon purposefully left out his feelings of guilt and regret. This was not the time, he told himself.

"Damn shame," Smith said. "But sounds like everyone did the best they could."

Johann agreed.

Tashon shrugged.

Smith, Abe and Jonstin began their story, leaving nothing out. At the end, Tashon gasped and stood.

"Wait, you left Sylvia and the others in the *open*? Out there, past the mountains?"

"Yeah."

"There was a massive storm there last night. Lightning, thunder. A downpour."

"No, no. That storm shouldn't have hit for at least a couple more days."

"He's right, Smith," Johann said. "Let's get a team together, send them out to help Sylvia and the others."

"We're going," Abe said, standing. "We've been through the mountains already. We'll get through quick."

Jonstin nodded his agreement. "Did any of the medic bikes survive the crash?"

"Maybe." Johann scratched his beard. "That's a good idea. I'll see what we can find. You all go get food and water, and whatever else you're going to need. Get back out there as soon as you can. I don't want to lose anyone else."

***

A group of six readied four tandem medic bikes outside the ship. Tashon and Smith ensured the medical kits were as full of supplies as possible. Jonstin and Rosa ran maintenance checks on each bike. Elric and Doran examined the blade that the tree had spit out. Everyone, including Smith, had decided Abe should stay at the ship. They'd taken off the bandaging on his arm, and the wound had grown. The skin below the wound was pale—it was not getting enough blood. If they didn't figure out what was causing it, and fix it, they would have to amputate. The young boy sat just inside the open airlock with Johann, watching the six make their preparations.

And off to the side, the lone smokie sat, silently observing. Tashon had heard Smith's explanation of what the creature was. But its presence still unnerved him. Its cloudy, air-like form reminded him too much of Aleron's fourth-dimensional shadow.

"I don't like that thing," Tashon told Smith yet again.

"Those things," Smith stuffed a handful of bandages into a medic kit. "Saved our lives."

"From bio-engineered beetles."

"Right."

"That tried to eat Abe's arm off. And blew out your ear drum."

"What?" Smith looked at Tashon, confused.

"I said, they ate...." Tashon stopped as Smith started laughing.

"You're funny, Smith."

"Thanks," Smith said as he buckled the last medic kit shut. "So, this thing that's happened to Aleron? Do we... I mean, you saw it. You think we need to be worried?"

Tashon looked at the ground.

"In the Fourth, when they surrounded me? I've never felt that cold. Those things, *that* thing." Tashon looked back up. "If it's anything like what I felt in the Fourth, all it wants is our souls."

"You really think that?"

"I... yeah, actually, I do."

Smith nodded. Tashon looked around and wondered whether he should tell Smith about seeing Evalee's face in the Fourth. Was the Fourth some sort of afterlife? A part of him hoped it was and, despite all that had happened while he was there, he hoped that he might get the chance to go back to that higher dimension.

"I think we're ready."

They flew between the trees, the bikes silently hovering inches above the ground. Smith and Tashon rode together, Smith in the front. Jonstin and Elric rode another, with Jonstin in the front. Doran and Rosa each rode their own. The smokie ran alongside them, dodging trees and roots with ease.

Tashon wanted to tell Smith everything he hadn't earlier that day. About his guilt and regret, but he knew it was not the time. The struggle that began on the ship was not over, and there was no telling what else Tashon might be required to do. What he might do and later regret. Was it a good thing to question each action based on how it will make you, and only you, feel after the act is done? When the time came, would he even have time to question? Did right and wrong have anything to do with it? And was it the ultimate good to do whatever necessary to save what was left of humanity? Tashon shoved the questions down and tried to replace them with less troubling thoughts.

Thankfully, the beauty of the forest was easy to get lost in. The yellow leaves seemed to sag more than they did the first day, their color faded. In contrast, the red lines that weaved and splintered up the bark shone more vibrantly. The more Tashon looked at them, the more he began to imagine that those lines were veins, pumping blood through each tree. But if that were the case, where were their hearts? Did they have minds of their own?

But lurking somewhere in all of that beauty was Aleron and his shadow. The shadow and his human puppets? Tashon still couldn't decide how to think of the creature. The thing. The monster, somewhere out there in that new world. Only a matter of time before it came back to steal more bodies.

The bike began to slow. Tashon turned his attention forward. In front of them was a door carved into the side of a towering red cliff. They came to a stop a few yards away. Smith hopped off, opened the door, and got back on the bike. The smokie sped off into the tunnel.

"I'll go in first," Smith said, which meant Tashon was going in first as well. Great. "Jonstin, you bring up the rear."

They sped into the narrow tunnel faster than Tashon would have liked. The walls blurred past him. Dozens of small white lights floated by, somehow moving out of the way just before being knocked off their path. Soon, they arrived at a gated door. Just on the other side of it sat two more smokies. The gate opened. They sped through the room, around four pristine white benches, and out another gate.

Down another hallway that felt no different than the last, then entered another large room. From the story Smith told, Tashon could tell it was where the "smokies" apparently recharged. All the spots on the table were full of rods from the smokies. Then another hallway, and another door. Tashon climbed off to open it. With a shove, it swung out and revealed a vast, gray desert. To Tashon, the forest had been an immense open space. But the desert was sheer nothingness. Gray, flat dirt underneath. And nothing above it until the sky.

"Let's go!" Smith called.

And off into the desert they went, hoping they wouldn't find more bodies.

Chapter 27

Smith's heart drummed in his chest, his throat. Sweat dripped down the sides of his head, despite the chill of the wind. The pain inside his head spread across his skull, stretching down into his neck. It was getting worse, but every time he rubbed his hand around his head, he felt nothing. If something were feeding and growing inside him, it wasn't causing any swelling. Which, he told himself, should mean that the headaches were only psychological, just like the large pair of beetles that hovered above his head.

He pulled the throttle harder, but the bike was already maxed out. Sure, it was faster than walking. But compared to the black ball of smoke that flew them to the mountains, the bikes were like snails. Smith had no idea how far Sylvia's group had walked before they got hit. How long it would take to get to her? Or if any of them would be breathing when they did.

He couldn't lose Sylvia. She couldn't die, not after all she'd been through. Not after all *he'd* been through.

Ahead, what looked like a pile of rocks. Smith knew it wasn't. Again, he yanked down on the throttle, as if through sheer will power he could make the machine exceed its limits. Instead, time seemed to slow the closer he got. What he first thought were people sitting up became people lying down. Some on their sides, some prone on their stomachs. He screamed as they got closer, trying to wake anyone who might only be sleeping. No one moved. He let go of the throttle and jumped off before it stopped moving. He tripped as his feet hit the ground and his knee slammed into the hard dirt. Warm blood dripped down his shin, but his mind barely registered it.

As they searched the bodies looking for survivors, he heard the soft whimpering of a child. He looked around, but saw nothing. With one shout, he silenced everyone and crouched, moving slowly around the motionless bodies. The sobbing came from a body that lay with its back to him. Smith recognized the hair and ran to her.

"Sylvia!" He dropped to his knees and rolled her over.

The side of her skull was caved in, a bloody crater from a chunk of hail that must've been bigger than Smith's fist. It was obvious with a glance that she was dead. But in her arms a young girl whimpered, the only survivor.

Jonstin walked over and sat down. With a gentleness Smith has never known the man to have, Jonstin pulled the girl into his lap and held her close. Smith looked at the sky and tried to breath. If Abe hadn't been waiting back at the ship, he would have forced himself to not breathe until he passed out.

Tashon sat down next to him.

"I'm sorry, Smith."

The old farmer shrugged and looked at the crowd of limp and crushed bodies. The two floating beetles flew to the dead, and helicoptered over them. They silently burst open, releasing hundreds of tiny beetles. The new insects rained down, landing on the bodies, plopping into the bloodied mud. They crawled over, around and through the corpses.

They sat for a while, no words between them. What words were there to say? Smith couldn't simply tell Tashon 'it's okay,' because it wasn't. Not really. It wasn't okay, wasn't right, that so many had died, and Smith was still breathing.

Tashon broke the silence. "I killed someone, Chief Farmer."

Smith looked at the young man. "What?"

Tashon looked away. "When we were trying to save the ship. Stabbed him. Right through the brain."

Smith took a deep breath, sighed. He didn't know what to make of it. He wasn't angry. Not upset. He just couldn't understand it. How could someone like Tashon, so smart and caring, do such a thing? Then again, if Smith had been there and someone was trying to destroy the ship, his home, he didn't know what he would have done. Then he thought, *How would someone like Tashon feel about himself after taking a life?* He looked closely at Tashon.

The young farmer's entire body was stiff. He kept trying to crack his knuckles, and repeatedly ran his hands through his hair. His eyes were dark. His face heavy, as if gravity were slowly pulling the skin away from his skull. Smith recognized it. Guilt. Shame. Self-hatred.

"Tash, I... It's okay. You did what you had to. It's better him than everyone on the ship."

"Do you really believe that?" Fresh tears pooled out of Tashon's eyes.

"I don't know, Tash. I don't know."

"I saw Evalee," Tashon whispered, almost to himself.

"You what...?"

"In the Fourth." Tashon rubbed his eyes and gently shook his head. "Saw her. Mom and Dad. Grace too."

"Tashon," was all Smith could say. It didn't make sense. Sure, theoretically fourth-dimensional beings existed. But dead people from the Third existing in the Fourth?

"It's crazy, yeah," Tashon said, agreeing with himself. "But I saw them. They're not gone. Not completely."

Smith nodded, knowing Tashon had seen what he said. But had it been real, or was it like Smith's ever-present beetles? Was there a difference?

Smith looked at his feet. "I've been seeing things that aren't there."

Tashon shook his head. "This wasn't a hallucination, Smith."

"No, I know. I mean that I have been having real hallucinations."

"Real hallucinations?"

Smith shrugged, nodded.

"Isn't a hallucination a hallucination because it's *not* real?"

"You're an ass." Smith smiled.

"Yeah."

They looked away from each other.

"What've you been seeing?"

"Those beetles I told you about? Those. Everywhere. One at a time. Or an army. Giant. Sometimes tiny."

"Is there" — Tashon choked on a cough — "one inside your head?"

"Maybe."

"Maybe we can find a working MRI back at the ship."

"And if there is a beetle laying down roots inside my skull?"

"Take it out."

"How? Without killing me, how?"

"Brain surgery isn't a new science, Smith. We would figure something out."

Smith didn't respond. If there was something living in his brain, it most likely already caused irreparable damage. Would continue to do so as long is it was there. It wasn't like a brain tumor, either. If what he was afraid was actually in there, it would be smarter than that. Right? It would be able to move to any part of his head, just like the headaches did. Wouldn't it just move away from the scalpel?

"Maybe," he said to Tashon.

"Do you see any now?" Tashon asked, a hint of pain in his voice.

Smith looked at the bodies in front of him. One beetle, the size of a child, slept on the face of a young man. A group of smaller beetles circled the air above, like vultures circling a dying animal. Another rolled like a pig in the bloody dirt.

"Yeah," he whispered. "A few."

"What do they do?"

"Taunt me."

Smith stood up and walked slowly toward his bike. Before he got on, he looked back at Sylvia's face. Gone. Dead. Like Evalee. Like so many others. *Would've been better to stay on Earth.* He stood up and looked around. *But then I never would've seen all this.* Were the losses worth all he had seen? His eyes watered and threatened to overflow. He looked around. The others stood by the bikes, as if ready to leave that place. And what else was there to do? They had no tools to bury the bodies. No way to get all, or any, of them back through the mountains. They would have to leave them to slowly blend with the earth underneath. Perhaps, Smith hoped, the smokies would protect the bodies. Or maybe the beetles would feed off them. Crawl through the ears and nest in their decomposing brains.

He choked down a scream and got on the bike. The others followed. They were on their way back. Across the gray desert. Into the mountains, past the charging room, and to the locked gate. Two smokies sat just inside, one facing them and one turned away. The gate opened as they approached.

A dozen smokies wandered about inside the room as they made their way inside. Smith stopped, unable to hold the tears and pain back any longer. A smokie walked to his side and sat down. Its head severed its connection with its body and floated to eye level with Smith. Its nose pressed to his forehead. A warmth spread from the point where it touched him. The warmth slowly spread across his forehead, started to heat the skin above his ears. As it came around to the back of his head, his skull pulsed. Pressed against his skin so hard he was sure it would explode. It was like something inside him was fighting against the heat the smokie was sending through him.

The smokie pulled away. The heat disappeared. The pulsing in his brain stopped. For the first time, Smith was completely convinced something was living inside his head.

PART FOUR

Chapter 28

Abe cried out in pain. His forearm was swollen to twice its normal size. A few hours earlier, the skin around the wound had peeled itself back, as if trying to get away from something inside the open sore. The round, pus-filled wound was now more than two inches across.

He lay on top of two crates, his feet dangling off the edge. Johann held his hand as an assistant medic frantically searched for antibiotics. It was the same one who had helped him after he was attacked. Winona scraped a portion of pus off for testing. She slipped and poked his arm.

"Ah, damn!" he said through clenched teeth.

She apologized and hurried off. Abe sighed and tried to catch his breath. He'd have to apologize to Winona later. She'd started her medic classes just weeks before they left the ship. She'd been thrust into the role during the most extreme of circumstances.

"Got it." The medic stood up and leaned over Abe's face. "It has a numbing agent, too."

Abe closed his eyes as the pain increased. He felt his skin split open another centimeter. Heard another bubble of pus push its way out. A scream leapt from his throat.

"I need to make sure the meds get all the way in. I'll have to inject it."

Abe opened his eyes. The medic held a syringe with a long needle. He tried to smile.

"Don't worry, Abe" Johann said. "It's not that big."

Every muscle in Abe's body tightened as he braced himself. The medic slid the needle in quickly and pushed down. A cool liquid filled the open wound and spread throughout his arm. The numbing agent took effect almost immediately and his heartbeat began to slow. His breathing calmed. He wanted to sleep.

The pain rushed back all at once, and Abe would have sworn his arm was on fire. He swore. Cried. His arm was going to explode. He knew it. The relieving cold of the medicine retreated from his arm, pushed out by more bubbles of pus.

"Holy shit," the medic whispered from some far-off place.

"Sed...." Abe forced the word out. "Sed... ative."

"All out." It sounded like the medic was singing.

It didn't matter. The pain grew worse. His skin split an entire inch more. He passed out.

***

Abe teetered in and out of consciousness. Voices spoke. Argued.

"... it off?"

"Can't... No."

"Skin... shoulder?"

"... time."

"Think...."

"No, look...."

In the depths of unconsciousness, Abe saw the wound that filled his arm. It floated on its own in a sea of black. It spun slowly. Sped up until it was a swirling nebula of deep red and vibrant green. It was captivating. Abe's mind could not pull away from it, no matter how he tried. From the black, a line of blue flames came in to outline the form. It spun faster, the flames spreading out as an invisible wind whipped them around the blackness.

For a moment, a face appeared in the center. His mom? It disappeared before he could be sure.

The form burst apart in a silent cascade of colors that lazily dissipated until he was left in darkness.

***

His eyes burst open. He looked at his arm, his eyes blurry with tears. Someone in a red medic shirt held a bone saw. It was nearly finished with its journey through his arm. Didn't know he had that much blood. It was everywhere. He felt the last layer of skin disconnect, and he was out half an arm. The medic turned on a soldering gun and quickly went to work cauterizing the wound. A sickening smell weaved into Abe's nostrils. He gagged and forced down a bubble of bile.

"Smells lovely." Johann's voice danced around Abe's head.

A form appeared behind the medic. A man and a deep, heavy shadow growing out of his back. Floating? No, his mind must be playing tricks. It approached the medic. Abe tried to shout a warning, but his voice wasn't working.

The man and his shadow moved closer.

No, wait, two men. Two shadows.

The medic, possibly sensing something, turned to this new visitor.

"Aleron! Aleron!" Johann called over and over.

The medic ran off. Johann grabbed Abe's good arm and pulled him to his feet. Abe took a step, stumbled, and collapsed to the ground, unconscious.

The next time Abe opened his eyes he was on the ground, Johann standing over him, facing away. It felt like his arm was still there, but when he looked down it was gone at the elbow. The remaining stump was covered in white bandages. He rubbed his eyes with his one hand and sat up. Johann turned around.

"You're awake," he said. "Can you stand?"

"Yeah, I think so." Abe held out his hand and Johann pulled him to his feet. "Where is everyone, Johann?"

Johann squeezed Abe's shoulder. "Aleron came back."

"That shadow monster?" Abe asked.

"Yes," Johann said. "That beast."

A terrified screeching echoed from inside the ship. The hairs on Abe's arms and his neck stiffened. He began to sweat. His mouth went dry. The scream was unearthly. Like nothing he'd ever heard.

Something was wrong.

Johann looked him in the eyes. "To it or away from it, Abe?"

"It sounds like someone needs help," Abe answered.

Johann nodded. "To it."

The two walked into the ship in search of the source of terror.

Chapter 29

Smith stood just outside the red mountains, the silver light of the moon filtering down through the leaves. A breeze swept through the air, shaking treehouse thick branches, sending the occasional leaf gently floating to the ground. Doran, Tashon and Rosa stood with him in silence. A calm night to rest in, to let the weight of all that had happened sink deep into his bones.

First contact. The most sought after and wondrous discovery in human history. And, somehow, it had not been one of fear or violence.

Yet more bodies had been added to the death toll. Even if the new species seemed to like humanity, the planet did not.

The planet had taken Sylvia, Evalee's sister—*his* sister—away, along with dozens of others. Stoned to death by a raging storm that had no awareness of her existence. Now that existence had ceased. Their existence blinked out in an instant.

Just like Evalee.

Gone.

Damn, Evalee. No more would he hold her. Never again would she pull his tired head onto her shoulder. Her kindness, her smile, her light, no more.

No more. Would the weight of her absence ever lighten?

How could such exhilarating discovery live alongside such devastating losses? Coincide with such horrors? Discoveries that the lost should have been there for. Discoveries that the dead deserved to see.

Smith's vision blurred and the trees around him spun. His head pounded, pulsed to a beat that did not match the rhythm of his heart. The skin on the back of his head stretched, pushed outward, as if a bubble were expanding inside of him. With a shout, he pressed his hands against it, trying to push it down. The skin writhed against the pressure, then stopped. He sat down in the dirt, pressed his back against a tree, and let his head fall forward. Tears streamed from his clenched eyelids.

Smith lifted his head and slammed it back into the tree, hoping that what he felt inside his skull was only psychological. He had wanted it to hurt, to shatter the memories of those he'd lost until they floated off like embers in the night. Wanted it to flatten his bulging skull, even if nothing was truly there.

The tree softened as his head hit it. The bark behind has back remained hard, supported him. But the skin of the tree behind his pounding head had changed somehow. It molded to his head, allowed it to gently nestle into the tree's flesh. Warmed Smith's entire body as it emanated a slow and calming pulse.

Smith's breaths began to slow. Eventually, his heart rate dropped until it matched the beat coming from within the tree. It was warm, comforting, as if the planet were welcoming him into its loving womb. He opened his eyes just enough to look at his companions. Each of them stood in front of him, staring down, their mouths moving. He could not hear them, and he didn't care. He felt safe, peaceful. He smiled at them and closed his eyes. The warmth and slow beating of the tree slowly lulled him into a sleep teeming with dreams of better days.

***

The warmth of morning sunlight gently pulled Smith from sleep to wakefulness. He found himself in a large bed, his wife sleeping by his side. Careful not to wake her, he rolled over and sat up, then stood. A large window let in a welcome breeze that carried the scent of fresh fruit. He walked to see the view, his bare feet sinking into a lush rug with each step.

Outside, two stories down, row after row of vegetation stretched before him. Trees and bushes so vibrantly green that they seemed to glow. He could make out each individual fruit on each plant. The apples shone a dark, bleeding red. Orange-peaches glistened a yellow orange, as if reflecting the brilliance of the sun.

Smith looked up. The sun vibrated in the dark blue expanse of the sky, sending out the brightest rays he'd ever seen, yet he did not cover his eyes. Towering white clouds swam lazily through the blue, casting large shadows on Smith's glorious farm. In the afternoon, perhaps there would be rain.

Evalee stood next to him. He interlaced his fingers with hers and they leapt out the window, gently gliding down amid the greenery. His feet touched down, and they walked. Past oranges, strawberries, bananas, peaches and so many more. They walked without stopping. Without talking. Enjoying that one endless moment of tranquility. The rustle of dirt and brush underneath their feet. The rays of light always beaming down just right to warm but not blind them.

He tried to stop walking but found that he could not. His legs, as if not his own, moved him forward at the same steady pace. As he passed each bush, each tree, the fruits came alive, if just for a moment. An apple spun a full circle, a strawberry swung back and forth. When he looked again, only to find them completely still.

He sighed and figured he must be tired.

But something crept just outside his conscious mind. Like a black dot that floats in the peripherals, only to disappear when attempting to look at it directly. It made no sound. It did not show itself. But the longer he walked, the more his conscious mind told him to relax, to enjoy the moment. The more he walked, the more something in the back of his head tried to raise an alarm.

Something was lurking, unseen, unknown, but anytime Smith tried to grab onto that thought, Evalee would squeeze his hand or rest her head on his shoulder, pulling him back into the beauty of their walk.

Out of mind, out of sight.

***

Tashon gripped Smith's shoulders and called his name, but he did not wake. Doran grabbed the farmer's hands and pulled, but the tree would not release him.

"He's breathing." Rosa placed an ear on his chest. "Heart's beating, too."

She stood and they quietly examined their trusted chief.

Tashon shrugged his shoulders. "He looks at peace."

"That doesn't mean anything, though." Doran furrowed his brow. "What if one of those beetle things is in his head? And, I don't know, laid eggs in his brain, and now the eggs are hatching, and they have to break out the back of his head and climb into the tree to survive?"

"That's ridiculous," Rosa said. "It doesn't even make sense."

Tashon scratched his head. "What he's saying makes sense. Something could be tearing his mind apart from the inside. Or, at least, whatever's going on isn't good."

"Shit, obviously," Rosa whispered. "Then what are we supposed to do?"

Silence.

"I need to get this little one back to the ship," Jonstin said.

Tashon nodded, keeping his attention on Smith as Jonstin's footsteps trailed off into the trees.

A smokie emerged from the trees behind Smith. It sat down, aimed its nose directly at his deaf ear. A thin stream of black floated away from the smokie's face, and slowly weaved its way into Smith's ear.

Chapter 30

Jonstin walked quickly through the trees, trying to remain calm for the girl he held in his arms. He could tell she was fine, and he had only left because he had to get away from the corpses.

He looked down at the girl he carried, wondering why he had picked her up. She had just been innocently lying on the ground, her face bloodied, the only survivor among dozens of dead. How could he have not?

The silence grew as he continued to walk.

He spoke to fill the void. "You know, I saw the way Smith looked at me when I picked you up. He was surprised. Like, 'Whoa, didn't see Jonstin being the one to do that.' And, you know, a few weeks ago I guess I wouldn't have. But, these last few days, it's been hell. Literal hell.

"I had a dream last night. Demons, red with blood, crawled out of the dirt and spread the blood over each of us as we slept. Drenched us in it. And somehow that was worse than death."

He stopped and looked at the girl. She looked at him as though he were insane.

"Probably shouldn't have said that. But I guess I figured that the best way to make this place not hell is to do things that people, or demons, in hell wouldn't do. Do the opposite of what hell people would do, right? So, I guess I'm just trying to not be a hell person."

The girl's eyes were closed. She was asleep, or pretending to be. But Jonstin couldn't take the silence, a part of him feeling that the demons from his nightmares might break through the walls and drag him away.

"Smith, though. He's not a hell person. He's... a saint. If I could live like he has, damn. The peace he must have in his soul. But me? No, no. Maybe someday."

The girl twitched and snored. Her body went limp as she drifted to sleep.

"So, I guess that's why I picked you up."

The door came into view and he went quiet.

He walked out to a setting sun, the trees casting long shadows. A swift breeze made him shiver.

The girl stirred and opened her eyes. "Trees?" she asked in amazement.

"Yeah. We found trees." He lifted her into a sitting position.

"Pretty," she whispered.

"They are." He smiled. "It's getting cold. Let's get back to the ship."

***

By the time they got to the ship, the sun had disappeared behind the horizon. Clouds hid the moon and stars. The breeze had become a steady wind howling around him. No one was out to welcome him back. No one guarding the open airlock. Barely enough light to see two steps in front of him.

His pace slowed. Worry filled his mind. A sense of dread pulled the hairs on end. His foot caught on something on the ground. He tripped, but did not fall. With a sigh, he crouched down to examine the culprit: an arm, severed from its owner at the elbow. The girl screamed as he jumped to his feet and turned around.

A voice echoed from inside the ship. Steps pounded toward Jonstin and the girl.

Two women burst out of the airlock, sweat dripping down their faces as they tried to catch their breath. It took them a few moments to realize Jonstin was there.

"It's chasing them!"

"Killed some," the other said, tears in her eyes.

"Okay. It'll be okay." Jonstin walked closer to them.

The crying woman saw the girl in his arms and screamed, reaching for her.

"Heather." She sobbed even louder.

"Aunt Londey?"

"Yeah, yeah."

The two held each other tightly. Jonstin felt a small flicker of satisfaction, knowing he'd at least gotten the girl to family.

The rest of him knew he was about to go into the ship, and he would be lying if he said he wasn't terrified.

Chapter 31

Abe stood at the end of a hall in the ship, Johann close behind. They peered around a corner, Abe trying to make sense of what he was seeing. Tashon and Johann had described the shadowy figure to him earlier, but seeing it firsthand pulled sweat from his pores, trickling down his arms and back. It was indeed two men floating slightly above the ground, a shadow growing out of each one's back. But they must not have seen the details.

Abe looked at the figure from the side. Aleron and the other man floated vertically, but slack. Each tentacle that connected their bodies to the shadows to was covered in what looked like thousands of thorns pointing in every direction possible. Like a living vine, sucking their life away. Each vine had physically punctured the skin, leaving bloody circles around each entry point. The pain it must have caused. The fear. Even if they had been terrorists, had been the cause of bringing the ship down, did they deserve that? Did anybody? Then again, Tashon had said the second man asked, even begged for it.

The four-bodied form floated in the middle of the next crossroads, as if lost in thought, wondering what life choices had brought a shadow to such a place. Or perhaps it was listening, hoping to hear another scream. A sneeze. A stumbling footstep. Abe dared only the tiny movement of sliding his head back behind the wall. He closed his eyes and focused on his breathing, trying to calm himself. Bring his thoughts to a more logical plane, as his mom had taught him to.

Running footsteps approached. Abe's head jerked to find the source of the sound. Two women were running toward him, about to cross the hall the shadows stood in. He snuck a look around the corner.

The soulless faces stared in his direction, the shadow slowly guiding it toward the sound. The women had no idea what they were about to stumble into. Abe centered his thoughts, knowing what his dad would do. Before the women could cross into the shadow's view, Abe, followed by Johann, ran right through the monster's view to the other side of the hall. Both yelled at the women to turn back.

They hesitated.

"Go, damn it!" Johann yelled.

They ran off the way they had come. Abe and Johann stepped back into the crossroads, directly in the shadow's line of sight. They stared at it for a few seconds until its pace increased. Dramatically.

"Run, Abe," Johann commanded.

His heart pounded as he ran next to Johann, down hallway after hallway. They crashed through a door, sped up a set of stairs. Slammed a door open a level up, running into the farming sector. The crash had destroyed the farm. Trees, bushes, fruits and vegetables were spread everywhere. The floor was covered in a thick layer of soil that had once been healthy. Abe wished for a moment that he could stay and clean it up, but that didn't slow him down.

Through another door, down two flights of stairs, and out onto the mechanical floor. Dozens and dozens of narrow hallways packed with computers, pipes and wires. The creature was behind them, its human puppets slamming against walls as it maneuvered the small halls. The only light to see by was a line of blinking red LEDs. Each time one flashed on, the hybrid monster was closer. There was no way they were going to outrun it. They hit an intersection and turned left. Abe slid into the opposite wall with his freshly amputated arm. The pain shot all the way to his neck. He swore and pushed himself harder.

The hallway ended at a closed door. Johann slammed into it at full speed. The door swung open and the two burst into a small room. Three faces stared at them. Two men in security uniforms and a girl in a hooded jacket, her face covered. The only door in the room was the one he had just fallen through.

"It's coming." The girl said it as a statement, as if she were accepting that the end was close.

Abe nodded a silent confirmation. The door burst open. Abe turned. The four bodies floated in a line, filling the doorway. Aleron hung in the front, his eyes focused on the girl. Behind him, his shadow. The tentacle protruding from his chest twisted back and into the other man's head. The last shadow was obscured by the darkness behind. Johann shouted at it to leave. As if he could control it.

One of the shadow's black tendrils burst out of Aleron's left eye, sending out a small spray of blood. It quickly snaked toward one of the security men, curved around him, and stuck into his brain stem with a loud spurt. He went limp, hanging vertically like a rag doll. Something moved, rippled inside of him. His skin vibrated, bubbled until, one by one, more tentacles exploded out the back of him. Each time one ripped out, a new spurt of blood sprayed the wall behind him. Soon, thousands of tiny black tendrils covered his back from his heels to the top of his head.

The room filled with a cold, soundless wind. The tendrils grew longer from the man's back, their ends slowly connecting, forming another shadow. When it was done, Aleron's shadow moved an arm up and down. In unison, all bodies and shadows did the same. The tentacle streaming from Aleron's eye shortened, pulling the new monster to Aleron's side.

All six heads turned to Abe, Johann and the other two in the room.

The other man stepped forward and futilely raised his fists. A new tentacle ripped through Aleron's other eye and attached to the new brain stem. The horrific process began again. Abe looked at the six heads. Each one seemed entirely focused on the creation of a new monster. If Abe was going to get out with Johann and the girl, now was the time.

Abe grabbed the girl's hand and looked at her, silently signaling they were running for it. He turned to Johann, who nodded his understanding. They ran. Abe rammed Aleron out of the way, shoved the girl out the door and dove after her.

They were both on their feet.

Johann ran past them. "Run! Faster," he called.

Abe moved his legs faster than he ever had. He refused to look back. Bile threatened to force its way up his throat as he ran down hall after hall. The girl ran next to him, sweat pouring down her face.

Eventually, they came to a stop. Abe's stump burned. Throbbed. Like nothing he'd ever experienced, but the cauterized wound was free from blood. He sat down, closed his eyes and tried to slow his breathing. Slow his heart rate.

It didn't work.

The girl sat next to him and smiled as Johann looked down the next hallway.

She smiled. "Thank you for helping me."

Abe nodded. "Yeah. I'm Abe."

She pulled her hood off. "Cosima," she said.

Johann whipped around and looked at the girl. "Cosima?"

Abe stood, seeing the anger in Johann's eyes.

"She's the one who attacked Tashon," Johann said.

Abe looked back at the girl.

She dropped her head onto her knees, and then shoved herself to her feet. Tears streamed down her cheeks, her entire face an image of grotesque shame.

"I didn't... I mean...." She choked on her words, the crying momentarily overtaking her. "Please let me come with you."

Abe looked at her. He could tell she was wracked with guilt.

"Johann, didn't Tashon say she seemed like she regretted attacking him?"

"Yes, she did."

"I do," she said, eyes wet.

There was no way Abe was going to leave her to become another puppet to the shadows. And when all of this was over, he knew she would have to answer for her actions. He would make sure the shadow didn't get her. But that didn't mean he had to like her.

"Let's go," he said, and walked across the room to a closed door.

He held it open and waited.

She looked at him, her cheeks wet. "What...?"

"We're going," Johann said. "Are you coming?"

A crashing echoed from behind her. "Thank you."

She pulled her hood back over her face and followed Abe and Johann through the door, up a flight of stairs.

By the time they reached the top, the door below them was flung open again, the bang of it bouncing up the walls. Abe tried to run faster. Yelled at Cosima to do the same. But he was running out of breath. He looked at Johann, a few steps ahead but quickly losing speed. They kept moving. One more flight of stairs. Then two. Three, four. A sign on the wall indicated they were at the housing district.

The three pushed through the door, walking side by side past dozens of disheveled housing units. Doors had been flung open. Clothes, dishes and chairs scattered across the floor. Again, the only light to guide them were blinking LEDs. Nearly everyone in the ship had taken pride in their units. Kept them tidy and pristine. Seeing it this way made Abe feel anxious. Unsettled.

On the other side of the door, Aleron pounded higher up the stairs.

Johann sighed. "We've lost it."

Abe coughed, pressed his hand against his throbbing forehead. "I need to sit."

They walked into the next unit and Abe sat on the couch. Cosima joined him.

Johann stood at the entrance. "I'll keep an eye out."

Abe closed his eyes and fell into a restless, twitching sleep.

Chapter 32

Keeping his breathing as quiet as possible, Jonstin crept through the dark and empty hallways of the ship, past the empty classrooms in the education sector. He had heard screams and footsteps but hadn't seen anyone or anything since he started searching an hour earlier. Had the women really seen what they claimed? Had Tashon? He decided it didn't matter — *something* was wrong in the ship. He could feel it seeping out of every dark corner, breathing out of every shadow, slowly creeping up his back.

The Ship of Nations, turned into its own version of hell.

He turned and saw that the hallway split in two directions. Up the stairs, toward the farming sector? Or maybe through a crushed door into what used to be the orphanage, where Tashon was raised? A series of shouts echoed down the stairwell. With a quick flick of his arm, he swung the door open and ran up, two steps at a time.

At the top of the first flight, he waited at the door. He heard voices, but he couldn't make out the words. He almost opened it, but remembered they could be terrorists, taking advantage of the horrors surrounding them. He pressed his ear to the door. Waited. Still, he could not understand the voices. He could either walk back or continue forward.

He chose to move forward. Cautiously. He held his breath and pushed the door open an inch. It swung silently. Inside was a line of a dozen men and women waiting for something out of his line of sight. They were covered in darkness, their faces and bodies concealed by shadow. He inched the door open. At the front of the line, a man stood, his arms lifted into the air. Another inch, and Jonstin told himself that was it.

In the center of the farm, eight figures floated a few inches above the ground. Each was tethered to a shadow. And each was connected to at least one other body by black snakes that stuck out through their chests or eyes or mouths or ears, or all of those and then some.

The man standing in front of the floating bodies began to shout, his arms still in the air.

"Great goddess, universe herself, please let me be joined with the tools of your—"

A new snake exploded out of a floating woman's ear and pierced the back of the man's neck. Thousands of snakes burst out of his back as his limp, floating body convulsed. The others in line, in complete control of themselves, raised their hands in the air and praised the universe.

Nine bodies. Nine shadows. Jonstin quietly closed the door. Had those people willingly thrown themselves at the mercy of that thing? Jonstin couldn't understand it. To him, it was obvious that the shadows had no deeper understanding of human life, no reason to choose willing participants over those who would flee in fear. Or did they? Were they systematically taking control of them? Or was it a raging, animal need that the first shadow had to feed?

Which was more dangerous?

Was there one consciousness controlling each body, every shadow? It had to be, Jonstin told himself. Otherwise, the original shadow was creating new consciousness out of human flesh. And he couldn't let himself believe that.

Whatever was happening, one fact would not leave his mind: this had to stop.

Eleven more people stood in line to become one with the monster, which gave Jonstin at least thirty minutes before the horde of bodies would leave the farm.

More than enough time to get to a munition locker and return, loaded and ready to face it head-on.

He didn't let himself wonder whether human weapons would have any effect on it.

**

Abe slowly opened his eyes and turned his head. Someone was making noise in the kitchen, probably his mom. He closed his eyes again, a small smile on his face. An itch crept onto his nose. He lifted his hand to scratch it.

His hand didn't touch his face.

He started to remember but, no, it had to have been a dream. A nightmare. The last thing he wanted to do was open his eyes. Blindly, he tried to scratch his nose again.

Nothing.

Eyes closed tightly, he moved his left arm across his chest to his right shoulder. He slowly ran his fingers down and stopped at his elbow. An image flashed in his mind: the beetle latching onto his forearm, getting ripped off, the gaping wound it left behind. He remembered seeing the medic sawing through his arm. Running. He remembered running. What had he been running from?

"Shit," he screamed as he sat up, the image of the soulless bodies rushing back to memory.

"Abe!" A girl ran over and knelt beside him. "Are you okay?"

He ran a hand through his hair. "We have to do something."

She put a hand on his shoulder.

He looked at her, trying to imagine her taking a knife to Tashon. He couldn't. Despite what he knew about her, he trusted her and hoped that trust wouldn't haunt him later.

"You okay, Abe?" Johann asked from the doorway.

Abe sighed and rose to his feet. "I'm all right." He looked at Cosima. "Why did you join them?"

"The Extinctionists?" She stood up. "I've been asking myself the same thing. But when I was in it, I told myself I didn't have a choice."

Abe shook his head and looked up at her. "Sorry, but that doesn't make sense."

"Aleron is—or was—my brother."

Abe locked eyes with her for a moment then turned away.

Johann blew out a loud breath and shook his head. "Damn," he whispered.

Cosima continued. "Our parents were killed during protests in Toronto. They weren't even a part of it. We were adopted by H for H. But he never got over what happened to them. He finally convinced himself that everyone was to blame for his pain. Our pain." Her eyelids filled with tears, but she held them back. She coughed. "Okay, what're we going to do?"

"I don't know." Abe paused to think. "Johann?"

"You think we can take on that four-dimensional beast?"

Cosima's eyes went wide. "We're fighting a multidimensional monster?"

Abe shook his head. "No. We've been *running* from a multidimensional monster. But, yeah, we need to figure out how to fight it."

"Would anything three-dimensional even hurt it?" she asked.

"I would think we could at least do damage to it," Johann said. "The bodies it has control over, at least."

Cosima nodded. "Yeah, yeah, when it first appeared, they knocked out the two bodies it was attached to. It flew off."

"But it didn't separate them?" Abe asked.

"No. I don't think we could break the bodies away," Johann said. "At least not without killing them."

Abe met Johann's eyes. "You think they're alive now? Like that?"

Johann sighed and rubbed his eyes. "Probably not, Abe. Probably not."

Cosima shrugged. "But...." She closed her mouth.

"You're still hoping to save your brother," Abe said.

"Yeah. I just wonder. Maybe in an earlier jump to the Fourth, something there latched onto his mind, somehow. And maybe that made him start this whole Extinctionists group?"

It was possible, Abe thought. But he didn't think it was likely. If those things from the Fourth could attach to a human mind, or come to the Third, anytime the ship jumped to the Fourth, why hadn't they before? No, he decided. They were only able to come over after the tesseract engine had been damaged. Otherwise, their journey out into the universe would have ended decades earlier.

"Maybe," was all he said.

They sat in silence for a few minutes, Abe relishing the calm. Allowed himself to believe for just a moment that they were safely floating out in the universe.

A loud crash shook the ceiling above them.

Chapter 33

The smell of fresh fruit enveloped Smith as he lay in on his back, Evalee's hand in his. The green grass stretched high above his head, brushing the side of his face. He watched towering white clouds lazily make their way across a deep blue sky, the sun beaming. He rolled onto his side and looked into his wife's eyes. She smiled and placed a hand on his cheek. The warmth of her touch spread through his entire body and he felt peace. Happiness.

But something still lingered in the back of his mind. What was it?

Evalee pulled him close and kissed his forehead.

"I love you," she whispered, and gently pressed her lips to his.

Smith smiled. "I love you, Ev."

Something rustled in the grass behind him. He whipped around and sat up, eyes darting around the grass in search of whatever had made the sound. He saw nothing.

"Smithy." Evalee put her hand on his shoulder and gently pushed him back down. "We're the only ones here."

"I just thought I heard...." He sighed. "Right, never mind. Maybe I'm just tired."

Evalee agreed and rested her head on his shoulder, her hand on his chest. For as long as he'd known her, her hair smelled so distinctly like her. It wasn't the shampoo or conditioner she used. It was a comforting mixture of vanilla and citrus that he had never smelled before. He pressed his nose into the soft curls and inhaled, the full sense of peaceful content returning.

He was overcome with the feeling that he was where he needed to be. He closed his eyes and slowed his breaths.

When he opened them again, they sat on a bench at the top of a towering cliff. Far below, an immense, unadulterated wilderness stretched out in all directions. Trees with leaves of every color imaginable. Rolling hills and piercing mountaintops. Birdsong rang up from the foliage. The sky above was clear blue, not a single puff of pollution to dampen the sun's rays. He smiled and kissed Evalee's head.

He looked to his right. A massive, rolling river silently poured off the cliff edge and into the wilderness below.

Something dark splashed under the surface. He stood to get a better view, but Ev's hand grabbed his shoulder and pulled his attention back to her. His smile returned and he gently pulled her up to stand next to him. They walked to the edge of the cliff. The wind whipped past them, fluttering Evalee's hair into his face. It would have been the perfect evening, except for a deep black shadow darting through the trees far below, heading toward the bottom of the cliff.

"You saw that, right?"

"Let's just enjoy being together while we can, Smithy."

He looked down and the shadow was gone. The wind suddenly stopped. He pulled away from his wife.

Smith turned his face to hers. "While we can? What are you—"

Something behind him shook the ground. He spun around, arms raised. Nothing. But he *knew* something was lurking, unseen. And he *almost* knew what it was, but Evalee kept pulling him away from fully grasping the thought.

"Hey, everything's okay, Smithy." She placed both hands on his face and forced him to meet her eyes. "All that matters right now is us."

"I hear you. But there's something going on, I just...." He stopped and put his hand to the back of his head. His skin bubbled outward. He rubbed his fingers firmly across it and felt, just underneath his skin, the distinct bumps of vertebrae. The thing twisted against his touch and poked against the skin of his head with what felt like pointed claws.

"Ev," he screamed and turned to where his wife had been. She was gone.

All at once, the memories came rushing back. Her limp body on the ashen dirt, her blank eyes staring at a new sky. The weight of her body as he carried it to the hole he had dug for her, refusing to let anyone help lighten the load. The even heavier weight that fell on his shoulders as he placed her in the ground. Abe, sitting to the side, watching.

Abe. His son was still alive. Where was he? *Where am I?*

The pointed claws burst through the back of his head, like four serrated needles ripping through his skin. He screamed as the legs moved back and forth, slicing its way out. Warm blood trickled down as something clawed at flesh. It slowly squirmed through the small hole it had opened, Smith's flesh and brain matter squishing as it did. His head pulsed as the pressure intensified, the thing's back legs pushing against his brain to leverage its way out. With one last push that sent Smith to his knees, it popped out and thumped onto the ground.

Smith fought the urge to vomit. Carefully, he lifted a finger to the back of his head. The blood dripping down his hair was warm. His heart rate increased as he slowly moved his finger toward the hole. But he stopped himself. He knew the hole was there, and touching it would only make it worse. Then it hit him: he was still alive. Something had crawled out of his head, but he was still breathing. Still aware. Alert. He stood and looked around.

The cliff, the river, the waterfall, all gone. He stood in the middle of rolling sand dunes, the sun casting rays of heat. His skin burned. Where had the cliff gone?

"This isn't real," he whispered.

Something moved behind him.

"Shit!" He jumped back.

It was half a biotech beetle, covered in blood and brain matter that could only belong to Smith. It was far larger than it should have been, almost reaching his knees. It was the front half, and it was definitely still alive. Its beady eyes blinked and looked straight at Smith. In those eyes, he saw the pain and loss he had suffered since crashing down on the planet.

The beetle pulsed and doubled in size. Pulsed again and its eyes were even with Smith's, its antennae poking higher than his head, the point of its mandibles a few short feet from his face. It blinked its eyes again, and a stream of sorrow and pain seemed to flow from them directly into Smith's mind. That complete loss shot through his entire body and he fell to his knees with a gut-wrenching scream. It was a pain the enveloped his entire being, inside and out. He flipped his eyes back and forth, looking for Evalee, until he remembered she had left him. *No,* he told himself. *She died.* And with that thought, the pain intensified, flattening him in the sand on his stomach.

"I'm glad you didn't die like Mom," a voice whispered from far away.

Abe?

"Abe?"

"Abe!"

His son was still out there. He screamed and forced himself to his knees, screamed again and rose to his feet. He stared the creature down and felt a portion of his pain flow out of him. A small portion, but he suddenly felt lighter as it returned to the giant insect.

In response, it made a clicking sound and charged at Smith. He jumped to the side and ran, kicking up sand behind him as the oversized beetle bared down on him.

***

Tashon knelt in the dirt next to Smith, on the opposite side of the unmoving smokie, tightly grasping his hand. A large lump had appeared on the side of Smith's head, above his ear, just after the smokie blew smoke into it. The lump was now moving rapidly beneath Smith's skin. It darted erratically, around his forehead, then underneath his hair. Twice now it had sped behind Smith's closed eyes, pushing them out so far his eyelids partially opened.

Other than the mobile lump and the up and down of his chest, Smith was completely still. Completely silent. Tashon looked disdainfully at the smokie. Yes, Smith, Abe and even Jonstin had seemed to think the things were safe. Abe had even grown fond of them. But why would it inject part of itself into Smith's ear? Tashon hoped it was trying to stop whatever was causing the lump, but he couldn't help but wonder.

He decided to try something. He let go of Smith's hand and stood up. Walking a wide circle around Smith, he slowly approached the smokie from the side. The smokie made no indication it was aware of him. He stretched out his hand to push the smokie away, but as soon his fingers touched black, it sent a visible electric shock into his fingertip. The vibrating electricity traveled up his arm, into his shoulder, then down his side all the way to his foot. He dropped to the ground, the air bursting from his lungs. For a few agonizing seconds, he couldn't breathe.

"Chief Tashon!" Rosa shouted.

With a gasp, he sat up and looked at his fingers, arm and leg. The shock had hurt like hell but he was completely fine.

"Are you okay?" Doran asked.

"Yeah." Tashon looked at the black form. "I don't think it was trying to hurt me."

Rosa and Doran exchanged a questioning look.

"I think it was just telling me to stop."

"It looked more like it was telling you to stay the hell away."

Tashon shrugged. "Maybe."

He returned to his spot next to Smith and grabbed his mentor's hand. He watched as the lump continued its unpredictable dance across Smith's head.

***

Smith felt like his lungs would burst. He ran across flat sand, looking for shelter but finding none. Sweat rained down his face, blurring his vision and coating his lips with salt. The exhaustion, the pain in his head and the beating of his heart were all so intense that he was convinced everything around was real. And who's to say that what happens only in the mind isn't real? Smith knew all too well that the worst pain was invisible to the naked eye. Even if his body wasn't exhausted, his soul was.

He risked a quick glance back. The beetle had grown closer, the sharp tips of its mandibles a yard or less behind him. The pain and sorrow in its eyes so deep, Smith felt if he so much as touched the creature, he would fall into a hole and be lost in it forever.

The thought of being lost in nothingness flooded into him with a terrifying comfort. Would being nothing not be better than being constantly filled with pain?

"I'm glad you didn't die like Mom."

No. He forced himself to remember that he had felt more than just pain since Evalee died. He had smiled with Abe. Sang with Fritz. Made first contact. Built a bond with Jonstin, something he would have thought less likely than first contact.

But he had also lost Fritz just days after they had mourned together over a decades-old song. Lost Sylvia a mere two days after that. And had gone through all of it with the front half of a biotech beetle living in his brain. Again, he looked behind him and took a quick glimpse of the beetle's eyes, filled with anguish.

It was as if, while it had been in his mind, the beetle had grown and fed on the hell Smith had been living through. And it was going to use that personal hell to devour him.

If it caught up with him.

As he turned his eyes back in front of him, the landscape shifted from the flat, sandy desert, to an environment of stone. He ran, his footsteps pounding onto a black stone floor. All around him, countless stalagmites jutted from the surface. Each was matte white and covered with knife-like edges that would impale him if he didn't step carefully.

A form darted from behind one of the white stones in front and to his left.

Another beetle? Smith swore and cut to the right just before running into a towering stalagmite. It shattered behind him as the beetle slid into it. A single shard flew across Smith's cheek, leaving behind a thin line of blood. Again, a shadow darted in and out of view. Smith darted opposite of it, but soon he was seeing so many shadows that he knew he wouldn't last long.

With a primal scream, he willed his legs to move faster. Smith wondered if he was in his mind, why he was bound by his physical limitations? The answer came immediately. He wasn't in control.

Everything exploded with noise. Each stalagmite shattered simultaneously, sending shards in every direction. Smith lifted his arms to cover his face as time slowed. Shards slowly floated outward from their stalagmites, a rain of snowlike crystal. The beetle stopped in its tracks. From behind one of the exploding stones, a shadow emerged. Smith lowered his arms and watched a battle unfold.

Half a dozen smokies charged the beetle, their legs pushing off the stone floor with such force that cracks spread out from every leap. Piercing crystals still hung in the air when the first smokie leaped at the beetle. Its trajectory sent it directly toward the insect's eye, but before it made contact, the beetle's mandibles rotated and flipped upward. The right one struck the smokie in the center of its torso and sliced it in half. The black smoke disappeared. Six rods of metal slowly fell from the air and clanked onto the ground.

Time returned in full force and the remaining smokies were in the air. White shards shattered on the ground, sprinkling the deep black with glittering white stone. One landed on the beetle's back and drove its nose into the exoskeleton with a loud *crack*. The beetle flung its front legs into the air in an attempt to shake it off. The smokie remained in place, a thick ooze dripping down the beetle's side. Another landed on the bug's head, piercing its nose between the sorrowing eyes. Instantly, the beetle's movements slowed. It still shook and thrashed, trying to toss its assailants. But it did so laboriously, as if gravity had grown too strong for it to stand.

The remaining four smokies circled the struggling insect, then sat. One in front, one in back, and two on either side. Their heads detached from their bodies and rose until they were a foot above the beetle. The creature that had seemed so terrifying to Smith minutes before now stood motionless, staring into the distance, the two smokies on its back holding their positions. Cautiously, and with a deep breath, Smith took a few steps to the side. He needed to look into those eyes again. Needed to see, to feel, if the pain was still there.

As soon as his eyes met the beetle's, the insect burst into a rage. It emitted a deep, gut-wrenching tone that made Smith's organs feel like they would be ripped from his body. He fell to his knees. Saliva ran from his mouth, poured down his chin. Mucus dribbled out of his nostril, tears streamed from his eyes, and the mix glopped onto the ground at his feet.

The beetle's body heaved, shook, clenched. Smith's body remained still; he was unable to move. He saw nothing but blackness and intermittent flashes of everything that had ever caused him pain.

Searching for his lost dog as a young boy, only to find it dead on the banks of a poisoned stream. His sixth grade teacher dying in a pilotless plane incident.

Evalee.

His dad leaving to fight in another Middle Eastern war, only to return an empty man.

His apartment building collapsing in the religion riot.

The colony ship crashing.

Evalee.

The Ship of Nations falling from the sky.

Sylvia's body pummeled by hailstones.

Evalee. Her body resting limply in a hole.

Abe. Sobbing for his dead mother.

But Abe, still alive.

Smith forced his eyes open and rose to his feet, then fell back to his knees. Bile burst up his throat and out of his mouth. But he refused to fall into that hole again. With a gurgled grunt, he stood and moved closer to the beetle. As he took one heavy step after another, the smokie heads began to spin around the beetle. Soon, a circle of thick black spun above the struggling insect, forcing it into the ground. Smith straightened and walked stiffly forward until he was a dozen feet from the insect. As soon as their gazes met, the beetle went still.

Visible waves of pain and sorrow flowed from its eyes. Slowly, at a steady pace, they moved up and down up and down. The closer they got to Smith's eyes, the more he wanted to sink into the ground, disappear into darkness, and never return. Image after image, death after death, pounded inside his skull.

But ever so faintly, a voice forced its way in.

"The runniest shits ever," Abe's voice echoed.

The smallest of laughs huffed from Smith, and the waves of darkness slowed.

But continued its path. And Smith knew that it would always be there, threatening to force its way into his soul. He inhaled as deeply as he could, sucking the air into his lungs, his soul, and let it out with a primal scream that shook the ground underneath his feet.

He took a step toward the waves, head held high, eyes fixed temporarily on the pain. The heartache and images of all he'd lost flooded his senses. Tears and snot poured down his face. Still, he stepped forward. He was a yard from the waves. The tears came harder.

A foot away, and all he could see was blurred lines of black.

Both Smith and the waves stopped. He wiped his eyes clear, breathing heavily. The waves hovered not more than an inch from his eyes. He stared at them, willed them to become tangible. They hardened into polished stone, shaped a bit like snakes, and hovered above the ground. Smith grabbed them with both hands and ripped them from the beetle's eyes and slammed them onto the ground. All but the few inches directly in his grasp shattered. The pieces rose back into the air and shot toward the beetle, impaling its body and imbedding into its exoskeleton. The smokie heads ceased circling, returned to their bodies and trotted off. The beetle silently burst into a cloud of ashen dust.

Smith sat on the ground and looked at his hands. In each palm lay a three-inch piece of round, shining, solidified darkness. He shook his hands to remove them, but to no avail. With a deep breath, he willed them away. They remained. He rested his forearms on his knees, palms facing up. He slowed his breaths, keeping his eyes fixed on the darkness in his palms.

As he did, the dark stone began to melt—no, dissolve—into his skin. Soon, they were gone, leaving behind jet-black palm lines, as if he had traced them with a tattoo pen.

And Smith knew that no matter how many times he cleaned his hands, the black lines would remain.

***

Tashon paced back and forth in front of Smith's still form. Rosa and Doran leaned against the red wall by the closed door. It had been thirty minutes since the bump underneath Smith's scalp had gone still, but Smith remained unconscious. He wanted to grab Smith by the shoulders and rip him free of the tree, but was too afraid it would tear the back of his skull off.

So Tashon paced, ten steps one way, then ten steps the other way. Over and over and over. To distract himself, he tried to figure out what kind of nanotech controlled the smokies. Each individual piece of "smoke" obviously worked together, but were they sentient in some way? Or did they serve some sort of purpose, based on complex and specific programming? Based on all he'd seen and heard, Tashon guessed the smokies even had some sort of biological element, though he could not discern one.

And, despite what Smith had said, he still wondered whether the smokies were truly safe. Was the smokie somehow helping Smith? Or had all the smokies somehow convinced Smith, Abe and Jonstin that they were not a threat?

Tashon shook his head in frustration; that was an answer that would only come with time. And, of course, Smith and Abe believed the positive possibility over the negative. It was what Evalee had taught them to do.

A sharp breath escaped Smith's mouth. Tashon ran and knelt by his side. A thin line of smoke slowly squiggled out of Smith's ear. Once it was a few inches out, it stopped as if stuck on something. It stretched until it was a taught line, and jumped from Smith's ear. Something popped, and Tashon saw a ripped insect hanging from the end of the line of smoke.

The small worm of smoke reattached to the smokie's head, the insect hanging from its nose. The smokie did not move from Smith's side.

"What in shit's sake?" Rosa stood straight and huffed.

"This is hell," Doran said. "We're in hell."

"No." Tashon placed a hand on Smith's shoulder. "Not hell. Just—"

Smith gasped and opened his eyes. Doran and Rosa joined Tashon as Smith pulled his head away from the tree with ease and looked down at his hands. He slowly turned them over, so his palms were facing up.

"Smith, what—" Tashon stopped, staring at Smith's black palm lines.

Smith shrugged and clenched his fists.

"Am I here?" He looked at Tashon.

"Yeah, you're here," Tashon said. "And I think that thing saved you."

Smith turned to see the smokie sitting at his side, half a dead beetle stuck to its nose. He carefully grabbed the insect off of the smokie and squeezed it in his fist until it crunched. A sigh of relief flowed from his chest as he dropped the shattered biotech form into the dirt.

"Thank you," he said to the smokie as he stood up.

The doglike form stood and trotted away.

He nodded a silent thanks to the three who stood next to him.

Rosa put a hand on his shoulder. "What happened to you, farmer?"

Smith rubbed the back of his head. "I don't remember."

Chapter 34

Abe, Cosima, Johann and Bodhi stood in the stairwell outside the farming district. On the other side of the door the shadow was still feeding off a small group of willing participants. The last time Abe had risked a look, there had been a dozen floating humans with matching shadows, all connected with the dark tethers.

Jonstin ran up the stairs toward them, carrying a pistol. "Think this will help?"

"What happens if we kill one of them?" Cosima asked. "Will the shadow connected to it go away?"

"No way to know," Johann said. "And it depends on whether they're alive."

Silently, Bodhi pulled out a small screen and swiped vigorously across the screen while the others kept talking.

"So they're... my brother... he's... they're...." Tears welled up in Cosima's eyes. "His dead body is just a puppet?"

"Maybe." Abe put his one hand on her shoulder. "Maybe not."

"But even if they are alive...." Jonstin began, but didn't finish his sentence.

Cosima nodded, sniffed and then wiped her cheeks.

"Dead or not, more are going to get attacked if we don't take it out," Johann said. "What are you doing, Bodhi?"

Bodhi looked up from his screen. "Running some sims." He looked back at his work, fingers dancing across the screen.

Jonstin cleared his throat loudly. "Bodhi, what kind of sims?"

"Fourth-dimensional sims."

The others waited for him to explain further, but he continued to quietly run his simulations.

"Why?" Abe asked.

No response.

"This is bullshit." Jonstin stepped to the door and pulled out a pistol.

"Jonstin, don't," Johann hissed as the door flung open.

With gun raised steadily in front of him, Jonstin took five strong paces toward the tangle of bodies and shadows. He stopped, inhaled, and then pulled the trigger five times.

The first two shots missed their targets. The third and fourth each hit a shadow, causing no visible damage. The last bullet went directly through a woman's skull. Her body went limp, blood dripping down the side of her face. But she remained attached to the mass of bodies and shadows. In unison, all twenty-four heads turned to Jonstin.

Jonstin backed into the stairwell, and the entire group charged down the stairs.

"Damn it, Jonstin!" Johann seethed.

Behind them, the interlaced horde broke through the doorway, sending a portion of wall crumbling to the ground.

Bodhi led the group down the stairs, past each doorway that led to other floors.

"Bodhi, where are we going?" Jonstin called, glancing behind him. Aleron was one flight of stairs above, dragging the mass behind him.

Bodhi did not respond. He still grasped the screen in his left hand.

"Bodhi!" Jonstin yelled again.

Again, silence. They continued down the stairs. The slamming of their feet on the steps echoed off the walls, Abe's heart pounding in syncopation. The stub of his severed arm throbbed, and he thought it felt warm with fresh blood. The exertion was pumping the blood too quickly through his veins, pushing it out of a wound that hadn't been properly closed. He hoped it was only a slow drip and not a steady leak, but it was not the time to check. A crash shook the stairwell. Aleron, still leading the horde, was a mere half a flight behind them.

"Here," Bodhi shouted, slamming his way through a door. "Don't stop!"

They burst into a maintenance hallway with a straight shot to a closed airlock two hundred yards away. Bodhi pocketed the screen and sprinted for the exit, shouting behind him as he pumped his legs. Abe was right behind, with Cosima and Jonstin close on his heels.

"The shadow," he said through heavy breaths, "came from... the Fourth. If we lead... it to the other... part of the ship... with the engine, I think...."

The door behind them exploded open, broke off the hinges, slid across the floor and stopped just shy of Jonstin. They were one hundred fifty yards from the airlock. The hellish mass of forms had broken a hole through the wall, and it was gaining on them.

Jonstin tripped, but caught himself. "Shit!"

Bodhi pulled the screen out again and flicked his fingers across it without looking. One hundred twenty-five yards ahead, the airlock slid open two feet, and then jammed. Thirty yards behind, their pursuer pressed on.

For every foot they moved forward, Aleron moved two. The bodies that followed behind slammed and bounced off the walls, seemingly oblivious to the multiple contusions their bodies must be suffering.

"We have to slow it down." Cosima spoke almost too quietly for Abe to hear.

Abe kept running and looked behind him. Cosima had stopped and turned to face her brother.

"Jonstin, get behind me," she said.

Jonstin grabbed her arm. "Hell no! Keep running!"

She threw a clenched fist at his face and pushed him behind her.

"Go!" She walked, head held high, straight toward her brother.

Aleron, or the shadow, slowed. Each connected head focused solely on Cosima. Aleron matched her pace, and the gap between them slowly shrunk.

"Cosima!" Abe shouted, but a part of him knew that she wouldn't stop. When they had talked earlier, he had seen the guilt in her eyes. Her brother had caused the destruction of the Ship of Nations, but she blamed herself. This was her way of saying sorry. Of taking responsibility for not just her actions, but her brother's as well.

But still he ran to her and grabbed her shoulder. She turned and shoved him to the ground with surprising force. She looked at him with a fiery determination that he knew was unstoppable. Johann pulled Abe to his feet. Cosima turned back to her brother just as a new tendril burst from the left side of his chest, blood splattering the walls and floor. It snaked toward her, twisted around her head and pierced her brain stem. Just like the others. No hesitation. Abe had hoped Aleron would hesitate. Hoped to see some sign that life—and love for his sister—was left in Aleron, but there was no semblance of either.

Johann pulled on his arm. They turned and ran before more tendrils began to grow from Cosima's back. The group ran for the airlock and broke out of the ship into the cold night. For a few moments, they could try to catch their breath.

***

Jonstin stood outside the ship, the cold wind swirling around him. Tears streamed down his face. He had always imagined himself to be the hero. The savior. But a girl a decade younger than him had just sacrificed her life, perhaps even her soul, to save them. A girl he had barely known. He had always believed he would be the one to give himself so completely to help someone else. But perhaps that was the arrogance Smith had always seen in him. He shook his head, unable to rid his mind of an image he knew would never leave him: Cosima, walking straight toward a dark and unknowable fate. Had she lost all awareness when that first appendage made its connection? Or had she felt each black snake force its way out of her back? Was she in that moment aware of what the shadow had done to her, of what it would make her do to others, but unable to do anything to stop it?

Jonstin hoped he would never find out.

"We need to keep moving," Abe said, his voice trembling.

"No." Bodhi shook his head once. "We need to make sure it follows us into the side of the ship with the engine."

"That's a risk." Abe tried to sound calm, but Jonstin could hear the fear in the boy's voice.

"It is," Bodhi agreed. "But we can't risk losing it in the trees."

Abe remained silent. Jonstin looked at Abe and his arm, the fear and sadness all too evident.

"Abe, you okay?" Jonstin asked.

"Yeah, Jonstin. Crisp." Abe forced a smile. "Pure O_2."

"Copy that," Jonstin said. "You can go around the other side of the ship. Let Bodhi, Johann and me lead it to the engine."

Abe shook his head firmly. "No way."

Something pounded from inside the ship.

"Okay." Bodhi stood in front of the airlock and yelled. "Come get us, you pieces of shit!"

The engineer ran to the side, waiting for Aleron to break into the night air. For a few quiet moments, Jonstin hoped Aleron's monster had given up. Then the glass shattered outward as the heap of bodies and shadows tumbled out. The heads moved back and forth, then settled on the three men, though Jonstin felt they were focused solely on him, pleading with him to join their silent choir.

"Run," Bodhi screamed.

And they sprinted toward the other half of the ship in the hope that the engine would start again, that it would send the terrors that chased them back to the Fourth.

Chapter 35

Smith, Tashon, Rosa and Doran sped through the forest on the med bikes. They could see the ship a few hundred yards off, but no one was in sight. No lookouts on top, no guards at the working airlocks.

"What the hell?" Rosa spoke quietly as the group brought the bikes to a stop.

Silence, save for the whistling of a chill wind.

"Pieces of shit!" a voice rang out.

Tashon jerked his head to the left. "That's Bodhi."

"Then let's go." Smith revved the bike into motion and flew toward the stand, hoping Abe was somewhere amid the quiet emptiness.

Trees blew past him as he neared the ship, eyes searching the darkness for any sign of people. A scream burst from an invisible source. Smith knew whose it was immediately. Abe. The last time Smith had heard his son scream like that had been when Abe had broken his leg playing in the low-grav playground on the ship. It had broken in two places and took three surgeries to reset it properly.

"I see them!" Tashon called.

Fourth forms ran through the clearing between the two halves of the ship, a massive horde chasing them, a tangle of bodies and dark ghosts that moved closer to their prey with every passing moment. Smith had heard Tashon talk of the shadow and its synthesis with Aleron, but somehow it had attracted dozens more appendages, dark forms that seemed to emanate a sort of visible cold.

Smith looked back at the runners. Johann and Bodhi were in front, and Abe trailed behind, someone supporting him as they ran. Something was wrong with the boy's arm, but Smith couldn't tell what.

Smith turned the bike and headed straight to his son. Something had happened to him, and Smith hadn't been there. He had been off in the forest, pulled down by the weight of those he'd lost, forgetting about what he had left. He pulled up to Abe's side and called his name.

"Dad!" Abe cried the name as if he were a child again. "Dad."

Smith looked at his son, then at his arm. Gone. Jonstin helped the boy onto the back of Smith's bike.

Smith gasped. "Jonstin? Johann?"

"Talk later, Smith." Jonstin slapped Smith's shoulder and jumped onto Rosa's bike.

"I'm okay, Dad," Abe said from behind Smith.

Johann rode behind Tashon. "Glad you're all right, farmer."

Behind them, the beast continued to close in.

"We need to lure it into the engine side of the ship," Bodhi yelled as he got behind Tashon. "Go!"

Tashon pulled the throttle and the others followed, increasing the distance between them and the shadows. Smith felt Abe's arm wrapped around him, the stump of the other bouncing against his side. All he wanted was to stop running, to lift his son in his arms, to tell him it was all going to be okay. To tell Abe how sorry he was for everything.

"Shit!" Doran swore from next to Smith.

He looked over. A dark tentacle hovered just behind the cook's head, as if relishing in the fear that seeped from the man's sweat glands. Doran pumped his hand back and forth in a vain effort to make the bike go faster than its small electric engine would allow. The tendril drew a circle around his head and stopped, pointing between his eyes. It hovered. And in one motion whipped back around and struck him through the base of his head and burst out of his throat in a splatter of blood. His body was ripped from the bike, which slammed into a tree and fell to the ground.

A smear of Doran's blood dripped down the side of Smith's face. A sob bubbled up inside of him but stuck in his throat. He took a quick glance back to see roots expanding out of Doran's floating bloody. The beast had ceased its chase as it converted another soul into a lifeless puppet.

They broke into the clearing between the two ships, increasing their distance from the now unmoving shadows. But Bodhi had said they needed to lure the bodies into the ship. Were they supposed to let that thing keep chasing them? Smith knew why. The engine was there, and if the shadow had come from the Fourth, Bodhi was going to try to send it back. With the engine damaged, it would likely be a one-way trip, if it worked at all. The shadows would not be able to come back, but neither would anyone who traveled there with them.

And Smith wasn't willing to make that sacrifice. After everything, he wanted to see his son grow up. See how the planet would grow and evolve. Learn more about the natives. Perhaps find some of them alive. For the first time since they had crashed on the planet, he was not okay with the idea of dying.

***

Tashon stood with the others just inside the ship, the angle of the floor and walls reminding him of the agonizing trip he had made down with Johann and Bodhi after the crash. Now they were going to have to make the same trek, only up. And from three stories farther down than where they had climbed out. He realized he hadn't seen Johann. But if he wasn't hooked up with the shadows, he should still be alive.

Back outside, Doran's shadow was complete. Aleron jerked forward and quickly accelerated, the black leashes pulling his crowd behind him. Tashon looked at Smith, his shirt off, using it to wrap Abe's arm. Abe's eyes flicked open and closed, his face pale and soaked with sweat. There was no way Abe would make it to the engine. And no way Smith would leave him.

"Bodhi, sir, you need to get to the engine room." Tashon looked him in the eye. "I'll go with you."

"Me, too," Johann said.

"I'll make sure it gets in the ship." Jonstin glared in the direction of the beast. "Smith, you and Abe should go now and lay low."

"I'm with you, Jonstin," Rosa said. "Let's send this thing back to hell."

Tashon thought for a moment to protest the statement. He had been to where the shadow came from. It was, of course, the Fourth. But, for Tashon, the Fourth had become something entirely different than what he'd imagined. It wasn't a heaven or a hell. It felt to Tashon like it was an after that encompassed good, evil and everything in between. All in a plane that was higher than the one he inhabited. Was it a purgatory? Or just the next stage of being? Perhaps life after this one is not a final state, Tashon thought, but just the next stage of being. Tashon found some comfort in that idea.

But he kept this all to himself, for the monster approached. Smith and Abe dashed through a door looking for a place to hide. Jonstin and Rosa stepped back into open air, awaiting Aleron. Tashon turned to Bodhi, and they went through a doorway and began their ascent.

It was steep, and Tashon had to lean forward and grip the handrails to stay on his feet. Outwardly, it was slow and monotonous, but Tashon kept looking behind him. Expecting to see Aleron and his shadows floating behind him, ready to claim their next victim. His heart jumping at the smallest noise.

But they moved silently, as if talking alone would bring the shadowy possession upon them. Tashon had to focus on what lay ahead, no matter what it might be. Just get to that door. Make it to the next hallway.

The turns provided a short time of physical rest, at least. Anytime they moved sideways across a hallway Tashon breathed a sigh of relief, the short reprieve giving him just a few moments of clarity to keep going.

Soon, they made it to the engine room. Nothing followed them. No sign that their plan would fail.

"Let's just hope Jonstin and Rosa keep those bastards in the ship." Bodhi grimaced as he got to work on the engine.

***

Jonstin sprinted down an angled hallway, Rosa a few feet in front of him. The shadows not far behind. Broken pipes and exposed wires stuck out of the walls and hung from the ceiling. A few emergency lights lit their way, casting soft light into the darkened ship. Just enough to see a few dozen feet in either direction. They ducked down a new hallway and stopped to catch their breath. Waited to feel the ship shiver and burst into the Fourth. But when it did, would the engine be able to make the jump back? Jonstin knew that he would probably be stuck in the Fourth for the rest of his life. If the engine could make the jump at all. But it had to. If it didn't, the shadows would continue slowly engulfing what remained of the survivors.

"Bodhi better get the engine to work," he whispered.

"Shut up," Rosa said. "He will."

The thudding of bodies on walls grew closer. Jonstin stepped from behind their corner and stood in front of the beast. He screamed, then ran down a horizontal hallway behind Rosa, glancing back until he was sure the shadows were following.

They were, and he was sure they would continue to follow him, Rosa, Tashon and any human or living creature until the end of everything. It would not stop. He could see it in the way it moved.

Steady. Not fast. Not slow. And the complete lack of emotion emanating from it. No love, of course. But there was no hate. No want. As Jonstin saw it, an apathetic journey slowly acquiring body after body.

What drove the shadow? Shadows? Had existing in the Third driven it insane? Or was there intent behind its actions?

Jonstin looked behind again, and caught a glimpse of Cosima's empty body bouncing off a wall, being dragged by the countless black snakes that surrounded her. He turned back, pumping his legs harder.

Cosima. In the short time he'd known her, she lived with intent. Died with intent. What had Jonstin ever done that wasn't for himself?

A mechanical voice buzzed above their heads. "Attention. Five minutes to next jump into the Fourth."

Jonstin smiled at Rosa, nodded and then jumped back into Aleron's view. The leading body and its dozens of appendages shook violently, sending a soundless vibration at Jonstin. It stunned him, and he felt an intense anger pierce into him. Did the shadows sense they were being sent back?

Aleron leapt forward, clearing nearly ten feet of space in an instant, yanking the bodies behind him. The body of the former terrorist stood a mere yard in front of Jonstin. The pilot grabbed Rosa's hand and ran as a new tendril slid out of Aleron's left nostril.

***

Tashon laughed and slapped Bodhi's shoulder. They had gotten the engine to work. Barely. But would it be enough for one last jump to the Fourth? Enough to get rid of the possessed Aleron and his followers? Enough, perhaps, to atone for the countless deaths Tashon had caused? No, Tashon realized, he could never atone for such devastation at his own hands. But he hoped this was one step toward forgiving himself.

"We need to get out, Tashon." Bodhi turned and threw himself down the steep hallway, sliding to a stop on the wall below.

Tashon quickly followed, glad that he didn't have to maneuver Bodhi's dead weight down and across the disorienting hallways. They continued at a steady pace, the speaker announcing each minute that they were closer to jumping to the Fourth.

Sometime between the three- and two-minute announcements, Tashon and Bodhi bolted around a corner to find Smith and Abe hobbling toward a partially opened airlock. Smith had an arm wrapped around Abe's shoulders, keeping the boy upright. Blood dropped from Abe's arm. His skin was pale, sweat pouring down his face. His legs trembled beneath him.

"Two minutes until next jump to the Fourth."

***

Smith ran beside Abe, doing his best to push aside the fear that he would lose his son to the beast. There was no reason to fear that. The airlock was right there, and the beast was nowhere to be seen. But what if the airlock didn't open? With two minutes left, Bodhi, Johann and Tashon ran from another hallway and joined them. Smith looked past to Tashon, making no effort to hide his fear. Less than an hour earlier, he had hoped with certainty that Abe would make it. The first time he'd felt any hope in days. Did he hope in vain? He tried to take one step, then another, then another. He kept his eyes focused on the airlock, telling himself it would open. Bodhi typed a code into the keypad on the wall. It swished open with a gentle squeak.

Footsteps, echoing off the slanted walls, pounded toward them from a hallway to their left. Smith turned around. Rosa, followed by Jonstin, followed by Aleron and his floating corpses.

"Shit!"

"Damn it!"

They pushed harder, moved faster. Abe's foot caught on a broken pipe, and he flew headfirst at the inclined floor. His temple cracked against the cool metal and his body went limp, unconscious. Their pursuer came at them from around the corner.

"One minute until next jump to the Fourth."

As if angered by the announcement, the shadows vibrated, pulsed. An invisible vibrating wave hit everyone, dropping them to the floor. Disoriented, Smith pushed himself up and looked for Abe. The boy lay on his stomach, his head closest to the shadows, which stopped. All heads focused directly on Smith's unconscious son.

A new snake burst from Aleron's abdomen and moved straight for Abe. Smith cursed and jumped to save him but slipped and smacked his head on the floor. His ears rang and his head spun. The tentacle swung up then down, pointing straight to the base of Abe's skull. Just before it made contact, his body was pulled away and the tendril hit the floor, leaving a dark hole.

Smith blinked and realized Jonstin had gotten hold of Abe's legs and ripped him from harm. Jonstin pulled Abe up and handed him to Tashon. Smith forced himself to stand and run to his son. The tentacle swung back into the air.

"Go!" Jonstin screamed.

He turned his back toward the tentacle.

"Jonstin!" Smith yelled.

"Just g—"

The tentacle stabbed into the pilot's brain stem. His body went limp. Smith, knowing they needed to take advantage of the time Jonstin had bought them, turned and moved as fast as possible to the airlock. With wet eyes, he looked through the open door into the blinding light of a rising sun.

They were three stories from the ground below.

***

Jonstin felt the dark finger—he knew now that it was a finger—penetrate his skin and latch onto his brain stem. A cold, yet burning, pain passed through every nerve in his body. He went limp. Watched the other five standing by the airlock. Why weren't they leaving the ship?

On his left shoulder blade, a hole opened up as his skin peeled outward, making room for a new finger to grow. All over his body, his skin peeled back. Finger after finger grew. He felt the frozen burn pierce outward each time, yet it didn't bother him. It was how it was meant to end for him, he realized. Knew, somehow. As the shadow formed behind him, his vision started to change. His perspective shifted.

In part, he still only saw the airlock, his friends standing inside of it, stupidly waiting to get out of the ship. But he saw the mind of the shadow, too. And it was only one. The one behind Aleron. Everything it had connected to, everything that had grown from it, was in its control. They had all become a part of it.

And Jonstin's last realization was that he would be no different. Now that it had hold of him, he could do nothing to stop it. The darkness weaved its way deeper, freezing him. Burning him. It grabbed hold of the very essence of his being. His soul. And burned it. Turned it cold again. Burned it. His insides screamed.

The shadow finished forming behind him.

The pain stopped.

His mind went blank.

Chapter 36

Smith cradled an unconscious Abe in his arms and peered out the airlock. Thirty feet to the ground. The beast behind them that would come after them once it was done transforming Jonstin.

Jonstin. Jonstin was gone. Nothing to be done but get the hell off the ship. They had less than a minute to get off before they were all stuck in the Fourth. Smith scanned the trees below and around them. The ones that were close enough were too short, the ones tall enough too far away. They all exchanged glances without a word.

Was it all going to end like this?

Shadows emerged from the forest below.

Smokies. Five of them. Each floated off the ground, heading straight for the airlock. The first one stopped and hovered in front of Smith. Its body stretched out, formed a cocoon around the boy and lifted him from Smith's arms. The other four wrapped around the torsos of Smith, Rosa, Johann and Bodhi. Smith let out a sigh as the creature tightened around his chest and lifted him into the air. It brought him quickly, yet gently, to the ground.

Abe lay at his father's feet. The black head of a smokie covered the severed stump of his arm. Trying to repair it, Smith hoped. *It'll be okay, Smithy*, Evalee whispered to him.

Rosa, Johann and Bodhi stood on the other side of Abe. Sweat dripped from Bodhi's forehead, his breaths heavy. Rosa stood calmly, her gaze turned up toward the ship.

"Tashon," Johann said.

Tashon wasn't on the ground.

Smith followed Rosa's gaze. Tashon was being lifted out by a smokie. A lone black tentacle stretched out of the ship, flying toward Tashon.

Smith tried to yell his name, but all that came out was a stifled shriek. The snake latched onto Tashon and his head went limp. The smokie pulled on him, fighting a losing battle against the tentacle that slowly pulled Tashon back into the ship.

But then the ship buzzed, vibrated. The minute was up. The ship flashed. A second before it disappeared, the tentacle ripped out of Tashon's head, holding onto a small, glowing sphere soaked in blood.

Tashon's head popped back up, the ship and any sign of the shadows gone.

***

As the smokie gently carried Tashon from the ship, he had thought it was over. That he was safe. That he had, in part, redeemed himself of the deaths he had caused. He could never fully be redeemed, he knew. He could not bring the dead back. But at least the monster he had brought to Colony Six was being sent back to where it came from. Now, all he wanted was sleep.

His brain burst into flames as something forced its way into the back of his skull. It froze. Burned. Spread through each of his nerves. Froze his body stiff. Burned his insides with flames. *This isn't how it's supposed to be.* The thought shot through his body, tried to loosen his muscles. But thought alone was not enough to free him.

It spread through his body, searching. Then it found it—his essence, his entire self. And it began to dismantle it. Piece by piece. It grabbed hold of his hope. His joy. His fear. His despair. Each memory that had made Tashon *Tashon* was slowly drained from him. He tried to scream. To cry. To twitch.

He could do nothing.

He waited.

The fire.

The cold.

The pain.

Started pulling away. Life. Hope. Fear. Despair. Everything that made him *alive* returned to his toes. His legs. His torso. His heart. But the darkness was taking a part of him with it. A part of his... soul? Did he have a soul? Whatever it was, it popped out the back of his skull and left him.

His vision went with it, but stayed with him as well. From his eyes, he saw Johann, Smith, Rosa, Abe and Bodhi on the ground below him. He saw smokies. Knew a smokie was carrying him to join them.

But he also saw himself from above, as if from a camera. That camera slowly panned out. A bright light blinded this second vision for a moment. When it returned, he saw himself. His companions, new and old. Saw it all as if from the Fourth. And next to him, in that second eyesight, his mom. His dad. Grace. Evalee. They may be gone from the Third, but Tashon realized they never truly died. No one did.

He smiled as the smokie placed him on the ground next to Smith. The two embraced.

"Smith." Tashon pulled away and looked his mentor in the eye. "Evalee... she's not gone. Not really."

The old farmer stared at the young farmer with wet eyes.

"I'd like to believe that, Tash. I really would."

Smith looked down at his son. The smokie has stopped the bleeding and lifted the boy into the air. They all walked toward the remaining section of the ship, hoping they weren't the only humans left.

The End

ACKNOWLEDGEMENTS

Thank you to my Heavenly Father and Jesus Christ. Thank you to my beautiful wife and best friend, Meaghan. Thanks to my parents, and all my wonderful family. Thanks to Luke Dylan Ramsey, this book would not be what it is without his aid and insight. Thank you to Carol Powell and Josh Allen, the two best writing teachers I could have ever asked for. Many thanks to Dave Lane (aka Lane Diamond) of Evolved Publishing for believing in this series as much as I do. Thank you to my editor, Becky Stephens, and to Sam Keiser for providing the phenomenal cover art. And lastly thank you, reader, for taking the time to read this book. I hope you join me again as the journey on Aethera continues.

ABOUT THE AUTHOR

Author J.S. Sherwood has a passion for stories that show the existence of peace and beauty even in the darkest of times. He spent many years teaching English at the junior high, high school, and college levels, and now brings that love of great writing to bear in his own books.

When he isn't reading or writing, he's spending time with his wife, five kids, and two dogs in Arizona. Most likely they're outside, soaking up the fresh air and sunshine.

For more, please visit J.S. Sherwood online at:
Website: www.WorldsByJSSherwood.com
Goodreads: J.S. Sherwood
Facebook: @js.sherwood.7
Twitter: @SciFiSherwood

WHAT'S NEXT?

J.S. Sherwood is hard at work on the rest of the "This Foreign Universe" series, through Book 4. Please stay tuned to developments and plans by subscribing to our newsletter at the link below.

www.EvolvedPub.com/Newsletter

MORE FROM EVOLVED PUBLISHING

We offer great books across multiple genres, featuring high-quality editing (which we believe is second-to-none) and fantastic covers.

As a hybrid small press, your support as loyal readers is so important to us, and we have strived, with tireless dedication and sheer determination, to deliver on the promise of our motto:
QUALITY IS PRIORITY #1!

Please check out all of our great books,
which you can find at this link:
www.EvolvedPub.com/Catalog/

Thank you!